Llyfrgell CEREDIGION Library

MARK ROBSON

THE DEVIL'S TRIANGLE

EYE OF THE STORM

SIMON AND SCHUSTER

First published in Great Britain in 2012 by Simon and Schuster UK Ltd
A CBS COMPANY

1 3 5 7 9 10 8 6 4 2

Simon & Schuster UK Ltd
1st Floor, 222 Gray's Inn Road
London
WC1X 8HB

Simon & Schuster Australia, Sydney

Simon & Schuster India, New Delhi

A CIP catalogue record for this book is available from the British Library.

ISBN 978-1-84738-980-0

Typeset by Hewer Text UK Ltd, Edinburgh
Printed and bound by CPI Group (UK) Ltd, Croydon CR0 4YY

www.simonandschuster.co.uk
www.simonandschuster.com.au

CHAPTER ONE

The target had seemed much bigger up close. Now, standing fifty metres away, Sam was surprised to see how tiny it looked. A warm knot of nervous excitement writhed in his belly. He was holding a gun – a real-life deadly weapon. How many of his friends back home could say they'd fired a gun in the open like this? A few might have fired one on a range with the army cadets, but not many.

He glanced across the valley towards the hulking skyline of the City of the Imperium and felt his shoulders tighten. It was impossible to ignore. There was an ominous and brooding atmosphere surrounding it that pervaded the countryside for miles around, filling the air with an almost palpable tension.

Sam couldn't help feeling that the great walls had hidden eyes that were watching his every move. Was he far enough away to be safe? The rifle was sure to be noisy. Would the sound draw the attention of the inhabitants of the gigantic geodesic structure? He scanned the open ground around the city walls. There were no immediate signs of danger, but staying alert was essential here.

It had only been two weeks since he and his friend Callum had fallen victim to the Devil's Triangle and crossed into this strange parallel world, but even in that short time, Sam had learned to keep a close eye on his surroundings. The Devil's Triangle – most people knew it as the Bermuda Triangle, but Sam's father, Matt, had been calling it the Devil's Triangle for as long as Sam could remember. Now it was hard to think of it by any other name.

Poor Dad, he thought, picturing for a moment how frantic with worry his father would be by now. *Will I ever see him or Niamh again? I know he won't give up looking for us, because he's not given up on Mum in nine years, but I don't fancy his chances of finding me here.*

'Borrowing' his dad's boat without permission to go fishing that day with Callum while at their holiday home in the Florida Keys had seemed a good idea at the time, but Sam could never have anticipated the danger his rebellious trip would land them in. There was little point in pinning his hopes on his father managing to come and rescue them. Given what he now knew of how the Bermuda Triangle phenomenon caused crossings into this parallel world, the odds of any rescue party finding them were minuscule. If he and Callum were ever going to return home, it would be down to them.

Everything Sam had learned since arriving in this odd world made the chances of finding a way home seem increasingly remote. There were many things here that seemed familiar: the sun, moon and stars still in their well-known patterns, the blue sky, green plants and even some of the animals – but there were plenty of things he'd seen that he'd never have been able to imagine in a million years. And even though this world appeared to exist in the same space as Earth, Sam knew that when it came to getting home, he was as good as a million light years away.

Here, velociraptors were the dominant species. Not the primeval, lizard-eat-lizard prehistoric dinosaurs that Sam had learned about in school, but highly evolved raptors that looked to Sam like super-large scaly men with over-muscled legs, a residual tail stump and strangely distorted faces. The sharp teeth of a carnivore and the curved, blade-like central digit on each hand seemed to be all that remained of the velociraptor shape Sam knew from films and TV shows.

Hunching his head behind the rear sight, Sam raised the rifle towards the target and tried to steady the barrel. After a few seconds, he realised that shooting was going to be much tougher than Hollywood films made it seem. No matter how hard he tried, he could not seem to settle the front blade sight in a steady aim.

Sam could feel his muscles tightening as the weight of the rifle began to test his strength. If he didn't fire soon, hitting the target would become impossible. He began to tremble with the strain and then, for an instant, the sights seemed to settle on the target. Sam didn't hesitate. He pulled the trigger, reeling backwards as the recoil hammered the butt of the rifle into his shoulder. The explosive CRACK of the bullet as it left the chamber was deafening and Sam's ears rang with the aftershock.

'Ow!' he complained, lowering the muzzle and rolling his shoulder to disperse the pain flowering there.

'No, no, no!' came a voice from behind him. 'You'll never hit anything like that! Remember – ammunition is precious, Sam. Our supplies are limited. We're not playing games here. You must make every shot count.'

Claire Cutler's eyebrows were drawn together in a reproving frown.

'Sorry, Mum,' Sam muttered. 'It's so heavy. I just can't hold it steady enough.'

'Don't depress me, big man,' Callum pleaded in an overdramatic voice. 'If you can't do it, what chance will I have? I mean, I'm hardly Mr Universe, am I?'

Callum Barnes pushed his Austin Powers looka-like glasses up his nose and struck a pose like a body-builder showing off his biceps. Sam burst out laughing and even Claire found she could not maintain her stern face. Callum looked ridiculous. Despite being a couple of months older than Sam, he was a full head shorter and looked all skin and bone by comparison.

Sam was relieved to see that Callum hadn't lost his sense of humour after all they had been through. He felt a momentary pang of guilt for having neglected his friend over the past couple of days, choosing instead to spend hour after hour talking with his mother. There had been so much to catch up with after nine years apart, and to begin with, it had been hard to reconcile his vague memories of the smiling, gentle mother he remembered with the tough, decisive woman standing in front of him now. Sam admired her immensely for what she had done, but couldn't help feeling secretly just a little disappointed that she did not appear to have made more of an effort to get home. She was his mother, but even though there had been several moments of tenderness in the past few days, for much of the time he found it difficult to see past the tough outer shell of the rebel leader to the gentleness of the caring mother underneath.

What would Dad and Niamh make of this new Claire Cutler? he had wondered. *And, perhaps more to the point – would they ever get a chance to meet her?*

Callum had been patient and understanding, spending his time nosing about the rebel underground HQ and getting to know some of the others living there. Sam gave his friend an appreciative grin and a pat on the back. It felt good to be out doing something together again.

'Shooting a rifle accurately doesn't require brute strength, Callum,' Claire pointed out, giving him an encouraging smile. 'It's much more about technique.'

'But wouldn't a pistol be better?' Sam insisted. 'That would be easier to hold.'

'Unless you're really skilled, a pistol is pretty useless beyond about ten metres,' Claire told him firmly. 'You don't want to let a hostile raptor get that close without having put several bullets into it. Don't be fooled by the ridiculous things you saw in cop shows on TV back home. A rifle is a far better weapon for this place. Trust me. I know.'

'If you say so, Mrs . . . Claire,' Callum said, looking as uncomfortable as ever about using her first name. 'But I've never been good at physical stuff.'

'Don't worry,' she assured him. 'I doubt that I'm much stronger than you, Callum, but I've learned to use the levers of my body to create a stable platform. Combined with proper breath control, aiming becomes much easier. Think of it like an applied maths problem. Here – watch.'

Claire took the rifle from Sam, put her left arm through the sling strap and neatly twisted it once round her wrist before curling her fingers round the stock. Turning her body sideways on to the target, she drew the butt of the rifle tightly into her right shoulder and held it pointing down at the ground for a moment. The boys watched as she took several deep breaths through her nose – not gasping great gulps of air, but slow, deliberate inhalations. Thrusting her left hip out slightly, she raised the rifle and propped her left elbow on the shelf of her hip. Head cocked behind the sights, she looked rock-steady as she took aim and . . . *BANG!*

Even at fifty metres there was no mistaking the impact of the bullet in the middle of the wooden target.

'Cool!' Callum exclaimed.

'Nice shot, Mum,' Sam added, reminded again of how Callum had compared her to Sarah Connor in the *Terminator* films. 'How did you learn to shoot like that?'

'I had a good teacher,' she said, expertly flicking on the safety catch. 'And I *listened* to what he said. Now, try it again, Sam. But this time I want you to do exactly as I tell you.'

'OK.'

For the next few minutes, Claire manhandled Sam into a position resembling the one she had used. To Sam's amazement, the rifle was far easier to hold steady this time and his second shot blasted a hole through the top right-hand corner of the target.

'Awesome. Nice shot!' Callum cheered.

Sam lowered the rifle and rolled his right shoulder again. The recoil this time had not felt so severe, but his shoulder still hurt from the first shot. He was pretty certain he would have an impressive bruise later.

'Better,' Claire said, acknowledging his hit with a slight nod of her head. 'But you snatched the shot. Remember, if you want to be accurate, don't pull at the trigger – squeeze it gently. The best riflemen are relaxed as they take their shots.'

'What about in the alley?' Sam asked thoughtfully. 'There was no time for all this preparation there. When you ambushed those raptors, the bullets were flying thick and fast.'

'That's true,' Claire agreed. 'But that was close-quarters shooting. It was hard to miss. Our targets were never more than five metres away. Even half full of lead, a raptor can be deadly unless you've managed a mortal shot. They're dangerous until the final gasp of life has left them, so we had to down them fast. There was no room to take chances.'

'That makes sense,' Sam said, pursing his lips as disturbing images of the bullet-riddled bodies of the raptors filled his mind. It was one thing to practise shooting, but the thought of actually aiming to kill something, even a raptor that would tear him apart without hesitation, was unsettling.

'Also, raptors move incredibly fast,' Claire continued. 'Learning to hit a static target like this is just the first step. Shooting a moving target that will kill you if you miss adds a whole new level of difficulty.'

9

'Shooting at raptors sounds like my experiences with girls at school,' Callum volunteered thoughtfully.

'Really?' Claire said, her lips twisting into a wry smile. She placed her hands on her hips and adopted a stance that seemed to say *I was a high school girl once. Continue, if you dare!* 'How so?'

'Well, for a start girls also hunt in packs,' he said, keeping his face deadpan. 'And if you fail to take out the right one at the first attempt, you're as good as dead to the rest of them forever after.'

'Brilliant!' Sam laughed, shaking his head. 'And *so* true!'

Claire didn't say a word. She just nodded, her smile widening a fraction.

'Your turn I think,' she said, pointing at Callum. 'Safety on, Sam, and pass Callum the rifle. Let's hope his shooting is as sharp as his wit.'

It was hard to credit the monstrous-looking raptors with creating the many strange and wonderful technological marvels that Sam had seen since arriving here. However, he could not deny that some of their inventions made human technology seem positively backward. Indirectly, it was raptor technology that had caused humans to begin crossing into this world centuries ago. In their quest for a clean, sustainable energy source, the raptors had caused unpredictable tears to form in the fabric of time and space that kept universes apart – rifts that had caused many to cross between the two worlds. Yet for all of the scientific and sociological advances the raptors had made over millennia of evolution, the primal urge they felt to hunt and kill their food remained deeply ingrained. For the stranded human population, especially those rebelling against the raptor hierarchy, this made proficiency with weapons an essential skill set.

Callum took the rifle and did his best to imitate the techniques that he had seen Claire teach Sam. The recoil of the rifle made him stagger slightly, but to his delight, Callum scored a good hit first time.

'Look at that!' he crowed. 'First shot and I deliberately killed a piece of wood. I doubt that I'm going to be able to hear anything for the next week, but who cares? That was *very* cool.' Suddenly, he pointed up and to the right. 'Hey! What's that up there?'

Something large and silver-coloured was flying towards them at speed and against the breeze. It looked like a cross between a small hang glider and a large box kite. Although it was still a good distance away, Sam could definitely make out a figure sandwiched between the wings. Someone was flying the strange contraption. It looked like a raptor.

'So it's true!' Claire exclaimed. 'There've been rumours for some time that the raptors have been experimenting with building flying machines, but I didn't realise they'd managed to take to the air.'

'How did it get that high?' Callum asked. 'Do you think he jumped from the top of the city, or is that thing powered somehow?'

'I don't know,' Claire replied. 'It seems to be moving too fast for it to be a pure glider, so there must be some kind of power behind it. But if the raptors have mastered flight, we need to find out as much about the machines as we can. Come on. We're too exposed here. If we can see him, he sure as hell can see us by now. Let's hope he's too busy concentrating to care who we are, and that he doesn't have any sort of remote communication with the city.'

Sam grabbed the heavy rifle from Callum and followed his mother in a sprint towards a nearby stand of trees. Seconds later, they were all crouched behind tree trunks, peering out to see where the flying machine would go. It passed almost overhead, the whispering *swoosh* of its passage through the air and the soft whine of the large fan-like propeller at the back of the machine clearly audible.

'I'd say it's about fifty metres up,' Sam observed. 'But it's not descending. Do you want the gun, Mum?'

He held the rifle out towards her, but she gave a

slight shake of her head. Her eyes were following the flying machine and its pilot intently.

'I don't kill unless it becomes necessary, Sam,' she said softly.

'Even if you wanted to, it would be a tough shot,' Callum observed. 'Look at it go! Wow! I'd love to try that. It looks like great fun.'

The contraption raced away, its pilot apparently not interested in their presence at all. Claire looked thoughtful as it disappeared into the distance.

'I think we'll keep any further shooting practice for another day,' she said eventually. 'And, Sam, you need to remember that a gun should only be used in extreme circumstances. Our rebel group are *not* murderers. We use weapons for self-defence, and if necessary, to achieve the bigger goal of stopping the raptors from destroying both their planet and ours . . . but only if there's no other way. If I can't trust you to follow that simple principle, then your lessons end right now. Understood?'

'Yes, Mum,' he mumbled, feeling deeply chastened. He hadn't really considered the consequences of killing or seriously hurting the raptor. For all their fierce appearance, raptors were highly intelligent creatures. Sam could not imagine deliberately shooting another human, so what made him think that shooting a raptor was any more ethically acceptable?

His mum was right: he needed to take things more seriously. This wasn't a game on his Xbox.

'Good. Come on. Let's get back to the others. I need to talk to some people about what we've seen.'

They moved out from under the trees and walked back to the city in silence, each lost in their own thoughts.

CHAPTER TWO

Three days earlier...

Niamh Cutler could not decide if she should feel guilty, relieved or frustrated. It appeared her immediate search for her brother Sam and his friend Callum was over, and she had failed to find them. The US coastguards were still out searching, but she knew they wouldn't find anything. Through the strange telepathic bond that she shared with her twin brother Sam, she had learned a couple of things for certain. First, wherever Sam was, he had found their mother. Second, given that nothing had been seen of Claire Cutler in the last nine years since she disappeared somewhere off the coastline of the Florida Keys, it was safe to assume that wherever the missing boys were, the location was both remote and difficult to find.

Closing her eyes, she concentrated on her brother again, searching for any hint or whisper of what he might be feeling or doing. Nothing. She could still feel that he was alive, but that was it. Earlier that day, she had sensed his thoughts and emotions clearly, but now there was only the faintest glimmer of a presence in her mind. Why did the strength of her perception of Sam vary so drastically? It didn't make any sense. With a sigh, she opened her eyes and tried to relax into the seat.

Sitting in the back of a police patrol car, cruising along the Overseas Highway towards the Sheriff's Office at Key West, Niamh had plenty of time to think. It should have been the perfect opportunity to organise what she knew into some semblance of order, but the throbbing pain in her left ankle and the burning sensation of the graze up her left side and across her back were clouding her thought processes. Jumping from a moving bus had not been the smartest thing she had ever done.

Their holiday had started so well, but Sam had not been content with sunbathing around the pool and snorkelling on the nearby beaches. Instead, he'd had to go and take their dad's boat out without permission and get himself lost, along with his friend Callum. It was just the sort of testosterone-fuelled stunt that boys seemed to thrive on. *No wonder there are more boys born every year than girls*, she mused. It must be nature's compensation factor for boys' tendencies towards courting danger and getting themselves killed while doing stupid things – Darwinism in action.

But Niamh knew Sam and Callum were not dead. Despite Sam's pig-headed refusal to listen to reason before taking the boat, somehow, somewhere, he was still alive. Niamh felt it with a surety that most found hard to understand. Ever since she could remember, she had experienced a special bond with her twin brother that had manifested in flashes of what she could only describe as telepathy. For Niamh this phenomenon was not something she could initiate at will, though with Sam missing she had done her utmost to trigger episodes and analysed every incident and image she had received, no matter how bizarre it seemed. Sadly, she could not converse with her brother through the strange mental bond. The link was too ephemeral and unpredictable. However, at times she could sense her brother, particularly if he was experiencing intense emotions. That was how she had come to discover that wherever he was, Sam had found their mother.

Her mother was alive! Niamh found it hard to believe that, after all this time, her mother was really out there somewhere. Her heart raced with

17

excitement at the thought. It had not been easy growing up without a mother, but now it appeared that if she found Sam, then she would also be reunited with the mum she had never thought to see again.

Dad had been a constant support as she had grown up, but there had been more and more times recently when Niamh had yearned for her mother. Her body was changing and the insecurities she felt were not something she wanted to share with her dad. She was sure he understood the *theory* of female puberty, but he'd never experienced it for himself, so how could he help her? A bitter, clenching pang of jealousy tightened her stomach as she imagined Sam spending time with their mother. *It's not fair! He took dad's boat and caused all this trouble. And what happens? He gets rewarded by being reunited with our mum.*

'Life's got a strange way of rewarding the wrong people sometimes,' she muttered softly.

'You OK back there?' the policeman in the front passenger seat asked, glancing over his shoulder at her.

'Oh yeah!' she replied, her voice thick with sarcasm. 'Never been better, thanks.'

'Not much further now,' he added, apparently oblivious to her tone. 'Don't worry. We'll soon have you fixed up.'

'Great!' she muttered. 'I can't wait.' *Patched up*

and packed off to England, she thought. *And what then? There would not be much she could do to find* anyone *if she was stuck on the other side of the Atlantic.*

Besides, there were still several weeks to go before the end of the summer holidays and with her dad still in police custody, where would they send her? The police were not going to let her live at home in England on her own any more than they would have done here in the Florida Keys, and she couldn't go back to school until September. There were relatives she could stay with. That seemed the most likely outcome, but what was going to happen to her dad? The police seemed to think he had murdered Sam and Callum, which was a ridiculous accusation. Her dad was a gentle man. Even the suggestion that he could have killed the boys was one that Niamh found deeply offensive, and she knew he had been nowhere near them when they had gone missing. But how could she prove it?

Niamh's thoughts ran in circles until the patrol car eased to a stop in a parking space outside the pink concrete block that was the Sheriff's Office. One of the patrol officers opened the door for her and she swung both legs round so that she could initially put her weight on her right foot before testing the left.

'Ow!' she exclaimed, limping a couple of paces

clear of the door and leaning against the patrol car in the adjacent bay. Her left ankle hurt like crazy when she put weight on it, but at least she could still walk. Could she run? Not fast enough, she concluded. The two officers would catch her before she had taken more than a few paces. And where would she run to anyway?

'Here, let me help you,' the nearest policeman offered. He held out his arm. Niamh hesitated, momentarily frozen by an impulse to prove to these two men that she was not some wilting flower of a girl. But as the pain in her ankle intensified, she relented and took the man's arm, allowing him to lead her up the steps and into the building.

From the reception foyer she was led into a passageway to the left, and then left again into an office where she was guided to a comfortable chair.

'You're gonna be fine, Niamh,' the officer told her in his lilting accent, giving her a broad smile. 'I'm just gonna go and fetch a female officer and a first-aid kit. Sit tight for a minute, OK? Jim'll be outside the door if you need anythin'.'

Niamh nodded and he left the room. No sooner had the officer gone than Niamh was on her feet. She assessed the room. It didn't look like it was ever intended as a cell, with no bars on the windows and not even a lock on the door. Even so, she was as good as a prisoner with the other policeman standing guard outside. Hoping for a miracle, Niamh hobbled across to the window and tried the handle. To her delight, she found that it opened. The police clearly didn't expect any further trouble from her.

She hesitated. Should she try to escape and continue her search for her brother and Callum? The old Niamh would have sat back down and waited meekly for the police to treat her injuries and ship her back to England. But the events of the past few days had changed her. She had already successfully run from the police once. Afterwards, she had stolen a boat, gone spear-fishing for food, paddled a kayak and changed her appearance to hide from the authorities. Niamh had always thought of herself as a 'sensible' type, so it made for a surprising list. The policeman who had caught her had seemed pretty chilled, but Niamh was under no illusion that if she ran now, the police would not be so forgiving this time. But even with her injured ankle, it was still a tempting prospect.

Her heart began to pound as she took a brief moment to consider. The window was on a tilting mechanism where the bottom opened outwards. It didn't open much, but she was slim. She felt sure the gap was wide enough for her to squeeze through, but if she was going to go, she needed to decide quickly. Every second was precious.

'You *so* owe me for this, Sam,' she muttered.

Carefully easing her left foot and ankle down first, she took a deep breath and lowered herself out of the window. *If someone comes back now, I'll be locked up for sure*, she thought.

Squeezing her lower half through was the hardest part, and her breath caught in her throat as the graze on her back scraped painfully against the window frame. For once she felt thankful she wasn't more 'developed' as her torso slipped through the window and she slithered down on to the flower bed beneath it. Once fully in the open, she silently closed the window behind her as best she could before stepping clear of the flower bed.

The car park stretched before her like an ocean of open tarmac. How far could she get before they noticed she wasn't in the room any more? Gritting her teeth, she decided to find out. Aside from a handful of patrol cars, there were very few vehicles to offer her cover as she did her best to limp as fast as she could.

The car park exit was to her left in the far corner. Beyond that was a boatyard where she could see patrol boats and what appeared to be a private boat club, with a slipway into the sea. Should she try to hide among the boats? Remembering her journey to the station with the policemen, she thought the driveway out to the nearest actual road must be at least a quarter of a mile long. The police were bound to discover she was missing before she got that far, but there had to be plenty of good hiding places in a boatyard where she could wait and think about her next move.

An SUV with tinted windows appeared from the driveway and entered the car park. Niamh turned to intercept it, a crazy plan forming in her mind. Hobbling as fast as she could, she waved like a mad thing at the driver. To her delight the SUV changed direction and drove towards her. As it pulled to a stop, the driver's window wound down. Niamh looked inside and was relieved to see a lady with a friendly round face.

'You OK?' the lady asked, looking concerned.

'Yes and no!' Niamh gasped. 'I fell off my bike about an hour ago and wrecked it. A policeman kindly gave me a lift here from town, but he had to go into the Sheriff's Office for a meeting. I should have been at the Arboretum to meet my dad about ten minutes ago. I couldn't be cheeky and beg a quick lift, could I? It's only about a mile from here, but I hurt my ankle when I fell off the bike and it'll take me ages to hobble round there.'

'Sure, honey,' the lady said, her expression full of sympathy. 'I know where you mean. That'll only take a couple of minutes. I'm meeting my friend for lunch at the boat club, but I'm a bit early. Hop in.'

Niamh didn't hesitate. She had the door open in a flash and scrambled up and into the passenger seat.

'Didn't you ring your pa to let him know you'd be late?' the lady asked as she pulled away and U-turned back towards the exit road.

'I would have done, but I broke my phone when I fell off the bike and I can't remember dad's mobile number by heart. He'll be going frantic if I don't get there soon.'

'That ain't no local accent, is it, honey? You from Australia?'

'No, I'm over here on holiday from England.'

'Really? Well, ain't that a coincidence! I've got friends in England – Dave and Philippa Benson. They live in London. Dave's in marketing and Philippa runs a hairdressing salon. I forget the name of it now.'

The lady glanced across the car expectantly and Niamh had to bite her lip to keep from laughing when she recognised the implied question.

'Sorry,' she replied politely. 'I'm afraid I don't know them. But London's quite a big place and I live out in the country about an hour's drive away.'

The lady looked disappointed, but then continued to talk about Dave and Philippa anyway. As they left the car park, Niamh glanced back towards the Sheriff's Office main building. There was no sign that anyone had noticed she was missing yet. It appeared that her luck had changed again, but she knew she was a long way off making a clean getaway.

A few minutes later, they approached the dusty dirt track entrance to the Arboretum and pulled off the road and into the car park. There were only a handful of cars there and not a person in sight.

'Dad must be waiting at the ticket office,' Niamh volunteered in case the lady questioned his whereabouts. 'There's a lovely little room over there with information leaflets and displays about all the trees they have here. Dad loves it here.'

'Really? I can't say I've ever been in and taken a look around.'

'Oh, you should,' Niamh said enthusiastically as they pulled to a stop. 'It's a lovely garden with lots of unusual trees and bushes.'

'Well, I might just do that when I've got some time.'

'Thanks so much again,' Niamh said, opening the passenger door and lowering herself gently down out of the car. 'I can't tell you how much I appreciate it.'

'You're welcome, honey. You have a nice day.'

'And you. Goodbye.'

Niamh watched and waved as the SUV turned and crossed the car park back to the road, leaving a cloud of dust rising in its wake. No sooner had the car gone than she began to question her choice of drop-off point. The lady was now going directly back to the Sheriff's Office car park. One word from her to the wrong person could have police officers here in no time. Perhaps it would have been better to be dropped somewhere that offered more options for hiding.

What Niamh needed to do now was try to scrounge another lift to muddy her trail before considering a longer-term plan. Luck, it seemed, was with her. Ten minutes later, having told a variation of her story about falling off her bike to one of the wardens in the Arboretum, she was in the passenger seat of a pick-up truck on her way into Key West.

Bill very much looked the part of a botanist. His unkempt curly hair, beard and bushy moustache, together with his slightly scruffy-looking shorts and T-shirt, gave her the impression that he would rather live rough with his trees than in a comfy house somewhere.

'Where was it you said you wanted to be dropped off?' he asked as they left the car park.

'The Old Lighthouse, please,' she lied, glad that she had thought through this part of her story. 'Dad and I are staying there.'

'Nice place,' Bill nodded. 'Bit of history about it. Some great trees in the gardens there too.'

'There are,' she agreed. 'The smell is amazing in the evening. Makes it easy to understand why writers like Ernest Hemingway wanted to live here. Have you visited his house? It's just opposite the hotel.'

Bill shook his head. 'Never been much of one for readin' an' books an' the like. I guess with it bein' on the doorstep an' all, I just ain't gotten round to it.'

'Oh, you should!' she enthused. 'It's fascinating. Some superb trees in the gardens there too,' she added with a chuckle.

He laughed. 'Usin' my weak spot, eh? Just like a woman to do that!' he told her.

The main route into the town was stop-start all the way. Niamh hadn't been into Key West for a while, but the street names were all familiar. As they turned into Duval Street, she gave a start and began to scan through the faces of the many people strolling along the pavements. Most looked like tourists, but Niamh was looking for one face in particular and he was no sightseer.

When she had run from the police the first time, she had befriended a brother and sister – Tony and

Carrie Dale, who lived locally. They had listened to her story and despite knowing they could get into trouble, they had helped her anyway. If she was going to successfully evade the police this time, she would need to enlist their help again. Tony had said he was coming here earlier; maybe luck would stay on Niamh's side and she'd spot him. Even the thought of seeing Tony again set her heart racing. She had only met him yesterday, but already he seemed to have got inside her head. Was it really just this morning that he had rescued her from Monkey Island in his kayak? That seemed an age ago now.

As if her thoughts had conjured him up, she saw Tony standing outside a corner shop, his blond hair tousled and his tan positively glowing in the afternoon sun. Niamh instinctively opened her mouth to ask Bill to stop and let her out, but the words froze on her lips as the shop door opened and a dark-haired girl emerged. Niamh felt a cold chill run through her and her eyes narrowed as she stared at the girl with feelings bordering on hatred. It was Tessa: the girl who had told the police where to find her.

CHAPTER THREE

'It seems the raptors had human help developing that kite flyer,' Claire announced as she swept into the communal area of the rebel HQ. 'I've just got word from our source in the Imperium labs. Flying must be one of those things that gets in the blood, because the young man who's been helping them had a grandmother who was renowned for it. Have either of you boys ever heard of Amelia Earhart?'

'I vaguely remember her from some of the books and articles Dad read for his research,' Sam said. 'She was the first lady to fly solo across the Atlantic, but she disappeared mysteriously while flying across the Pacific I think. . .'

'Wait a minute,' Callum interrupted. 'Does that mean her disappearance is linked to the Devil's Triangle too?'

'That's right,' Claire confirmed. 'Not all of the crossings happen in the Bermuda Triangle region, remember. They happen wherever there are particularly powerful storms in this world. It just happens that the majority of those occur in a couple of regions. There have been a few famous folk turn up in various parts of this world over the years. Amelia was one. Lord Lucan, Glenn Miller. . .'

'What, *the* Glenn Miller?' Callum exclaimed. '*Chattanooga Choo Choo, Little Brown Jug* Glenn Miller?'

'That's the one,' Claire said, clearly amused by his reaction. 'I'm surprised you've even heard of him. I'd have thought you'd be into more modern music, Callum.'

'I play trombone at school,' he explained. 'You can't play trombone and not know about Glenn Miller! I love his music! It's brilliant.'

'I suppose. If you like that sort of thing.'

'Don't tell me Elvis is here too!' Callum added, clearly at least halfway serious.

Claire laughed. 'I'm afraid not. As far as I know, the King is dead and buried in Memphis.'

'You were saying about Amelia Earhart's grandson, Mum?' Sam prompted.

'Yes,' she replied. 'After we saw the machine yesterday, I got word to our agent in the science labs. His preliminary report this morning was sketchy, but it appears young David Earhart takes after his grandmother. Aside from adopting her surname, he's something of a pioneer when it comes to flying. With the support of a team of raptor scientists, he's developed that flying machine we saw. We understand it uses a hybrid combination of gliding and raptor electromagnetic technology.'

'Wow! Sounds cool,' Callum said enthusiastically. 'I wonder how that works.'

'I'm hoping we're going to find out,' Claire said. 'I'm going to put together an extraction plan this afternoon.'

'Extraction plan?' Sam asked. 'What do you mean?'

'I mean we intend to get our hands on David Earhart whether he wants to join us or not.'

'A *kidnap*!' Callum breathed. 'But why? What's this got to do with the Imperium's energy production policies?'

'Nothing,' she admitted. 'Well, not directly as far as we know. But if this new breed of flying machines is robust enough, a realistic attempt might be made to penetrate a storm system and cross back to our world. And even if the machines are not ready yet, the potential is there. If we can get back to our world, then we have hope of enlisting help to stop the Imperium. And make no mistake about it – we need help. There are those back home who will take the growing environmental threat here and its potential long-term impact on our world very seriously. Being realistic, our chances of changing things here without some extra back-up are very small.'

At the mention of crossing back, Sam instantly felt a pang of guilt. During the past couple of days, he'd been so caught up with the reunion with his mother, and overawed by the strength of her personality and her driving passion to lead the rebels, that he had barely given more than a passing thought to getting home. What would Dad and Niamh be doing now? Were they still out searching the waters off the Keys? What about the danger he had sensed Niamh facing a few days before? Was she all right? All of a sudden, he felt selfish and inconsiderate. How could he have been so easily distracted from his primary goal?

Closing his eyes, he thought of his sister. For a moment it was as if he could feel the turmoil of her anxious thoughts, then the sensation passed. He got the distinct impression that she was confused by a welter of worries and emotions. He knew Niamh sometimes felt his pain and emotions, but it was rare for him to sense her.

'Can we help you find this David Earhart?' Callum asked.

Sam opened his eyes, his heart beating fast as he tried to regain his focus.

'Getting him out of the Imperium labs is likely to be dangerous,' Claire replied. 'I'm not going to put you boys in more danger than is necessary, but you can certainly help with the planning. At the brainstorming phase all ideas are welcome.'

'Great!' Sam replied enthusiastically. 'If it could lead to a way for us to get home, count me in! When do we start?'

'Right now,' Claire said, unable to hide her amusement at the boys' excitement. 'I'll gather the others and we'll make a start. Nathan!' she called. 'Get the team together. We've got work to do.'

'Will do,' replied a gruff voice from the next room.

Sam instinctively glanced towards the door. Although he knew that his mother trusted Nathan completely, the man made Sam nervous. When he and Callum had first seen Claire's right-hand man, Sam had taken one look at Nathan's dark beard and moustache flecked with grey, his crooked yellow teeth and his long hair tied back in a ponytail, and had decided instantly that he looked like a pirate and completely untrustworthy. Although Nathan had done nothing to warrant Sam's suspicions, Sam could not shake the feeling that there was something unsavoury about him.

Gathering the team into the HQ's small living room did not take long. It was a bit of a squeeze, but everyone found a place to sit, either on chairs or on the floor. Claire stood in the middle of the room next to a low table.

Apart from Claire and Nathan, there were two other humans present – Alex and Sherri – and the other seven were raptors. Sam was pleased to see that these included Nipper and Grunt, the two raptors who had accompanied them from the Reserve where the boys had first been marooned in this world. Did this mean they had agreed to join the rebel group?

Sam looked at each of the raptors in turn as they settled themselves for the meeting. He didn't know all of their names yet, and doubted that he would have been able to pronounce them even if he had been properly introduced. The raptors towered over the humans, the smallest of them being at least two and a half metres tall. They had massive chests and powerful legs with bulging muscles that, combined with the characteristic scythe-like central claw they had on each hand and wicked-looking rows of pointed teeth, made them look like monsters, but Sam had seen there was a lot more to them than their intimidating appearance.

Alex was an enormous African-American man,

whose barrel-like chest and huge upper arms made him appear almost as broad as he was tall, though even he was dwarfed by the raptors. Next to him, Sherri looked tiny and delicate. Of all the people present, she looked the most out of place. Sam had asked his mother about her earlier in the day. Apparently, she was highly valued as a team member because, apart from being a brilliant physicist, Sherri was also an accomplished gymnast, which had proved a useful skill during several of their raids on Imperium facilities.

'OK, everyone, listen up!' Claire stated, calling the meeting to order. 'To clarify the situation, one of our spies in the Imperium labs has confirmed that the human, David Earhart, has helped the Imperium develop a working, powered flying machine that can be piloted by a raptor. The boys and I saw it yesterday, flying around outside the city. Aside from offering a potential vehicle to get back to Earth, airborne raptors could cause our field operations all sorts of problems. The technology they use to produce their holographic version of television is now compact enough to be equipped to those machines. That capability alone makes it imperative that we move to disrupt their progress. I don't want to have the Imperium filming us and broadcasting our activities to the raptor world unless I control the content of those transmissions.'

Claire began to click and growl, repeating her opening statement in the raptor language for the benefit of those raptors who didn't understand English. Sam watched her with considerable pride, as she appeared to make easy work of speaking the strange raptor language.

'We need to get our hands on David Earhart and the design of this flying machine of his,' she concluded. 'So – ideas, everyone. How are we going to extract him from the Imperium labs?'

'Storming the place is out of the question,' Nathan muttered, frowning. 'There are hundreds of raptors in there and the place would be swarming with Imperium agents within seconds if we tried an open move.'

'I could go in through the ventilation system,' Sherri offered. 'I've done it before.'

'True,' Claire said thoughtfully. 'But the raptors working for the Imperium are clever. They won't get caught out that way a second time. Besides, unless young Earhart is particularly small and cooperative, you wouldn't be able to get him out by that route. No. I think we need to try something different. Something the Imperium hasn't seen before.'

One of the raptors spoke in a rapid stream of clicks, tocks and growls. Everyone listened intently until he had finished. Claire thought for a moment and then responded in raptor, shaking her head.

'We don't want to compromise our spies,' she told everyone in English. 'We have too few in place as it is, and we have neither the time nor the people to risk an infiltration so soon after Nipper and Grunt sprang the boys the other day.'

Claire looked uncomfortable using the nicknames that the boys had given their two raptor guardians, but none of the raptors so much as flickered an eyelid. Nipper and Grunt had made it clear to Claire that they were perfectly happy with the names the boys used for them.

'Do you have a building plan of the labs?' Callum asked. Sam looked at him, intrigued to see what his friend wanted with the plans. So did every other set of eyes in the room. Callum pushed his glasses up his nose in an instinctive nervous reaction to suddenly becoming the centre of attention.

'Yes, Callum.'

'Can I see them?'

'Of course.'

'What about the neighbouring buildings? Could you get blueprints of those too?'

'I'm not sure,' Claire replied, her voice tinged with curiosity. 'But none of the neighbouring buildings are directly attached to the labs, so we can't go in through the walls, if that's what you're thinking.'

'No,' Callum replied. 'That wasn't what I had in

mind at all. I know you have guns, but I'm guessing they came from our world. They're human technology, rather than raptor. What sort of capability do you have for *making* equipment?'

'That depends on what it is,' Claire replied. 'If you want electronic gadgetry, then forget it. We don't have the resources to. . .'

'No! No, nothing like that,' Callum interrupted quickly. 'As far as I know, this should only require basic mechanical engineering skills and some raw materials to work with.'

'OK. You've got my interest, Callum. What do you have in mind?'

He told her. At the end of his explanation, Sam laughed aloud, but Claire's eyes went first wide and then thoughtful. She glanced across at Sherri, who nodded.

'You know what?' she said. 'You might just be on to something.'

* * *

Later that evening, Sam and some of the others were gathered in the living area. Sam was moving through some martial arts practice patterns, trying to clear his mind and release the anticipation and energy that had formed a tight knot in his stomach. He always found practising moves at home helped him centre and relax and he hoped the same would prove true here.

'Martial arts! Pah! All that posing isn't going to be any use to you in this world!' Nathan mocked, watching with amusement as Sam moved through one of the traditional patterns in the space he had cleared.

'Against a raptor? You're right. It's probably not,' Sam admitted. 'They're too big and fast. But I like the discipline and in a fight with another human I think what I know would give me an edge.'

'You think? I've never been convinced by all this flashy kung fu nonsense. All those kicks and spins; it's rubbish if you ask me. But I'm prepared to be proved wrong. Come on. Convince me if you can.' Nathan got up and stepped into the middle of the room to face off against Sam.

'Nathan!' Claire protested. 'What do you think you're doing?'

'Don't worry, Mum. It's fine. I'm sure Nathan has no intention of really hurting me.'

As Nathan locked eyes with Sam, Nipper growled a warning that needed no translation. Nathan laughed. 'It's OK, big guy,' he said, without looking round. 'I just want to see what the kid's got, that's all.'

'We don't have enough room in here for free sparring, but we could do an approximation of one-step sparring,' Sam told him.

'Whatever that means,' Nathan jeered.

'It's quite simple,' Sam replied. 'Easy enough that even you should cope with it.'

'Oooh! The boy's got attitude. I like that.'

'The way it works is this,' Sam explained. 'You can take one step with either foot and throw your best punch at me. I'll do my best to counter it. OK?'

'Fair enough,' Nathan said, giving him an evil-looking grin. Without warning, he stepped forward and threw a hard right-handed punch at the middle of Sam's chest, but his fist had no chance to connect. Sam was ready. He swayed left and with a hooking motion, he grabbed Nathan's wrist with his right hand, and twisted it hard until Nathan's hand was palm up. Nathan found himself bent forward, his arm locked out straight, but Sam hadn't finished. In one fluid motion, Sam leapt upward and brought his elbow down over Nathan's in a counter-attack that would have snapped the restrained arm at the elbow had Sam not stopped short.

There was a moment of stunned silence.

'Cool!' Callum exclaimed. 'You've got to teach me how to do that!'

'Nice move, kid,' Nathan said grudgingly, standing up and rubbing his elbow. 'That was pretty impressive.'

Again without warning, Nathan stepped forward

and threw a left, but again Sam was ready. Stepping right this time, he brushed the punch aside with his left forearm, flashed a side kick up to brush Nathan's ribs and slid back out of reach, arms back up in a classic guard position before Nathan had a chance to move.

He tried to come at Sam again, but this time Sam caught the fist in the palm of his hand and folded Nathan's arm back on itself into a different lock before sweeping his legs out from under him with a hooking kick that dumped him on his back. Again, the counter-attack was vicious and Nathan found himself staring up at the point of Sam's elbow that was poised to drive down into his face.

Callum clapped enthusiastically. Everyone in the room looked suitably impressed by Sam's moves. Even Nipper, Grunt and the other raptors looked on with interest.

'That's enough! Both of you,' Claire said, her voice disapproving, although Sam thought he could also detect a certain sense of pride from his mother too. 'Let him up, Sam. You've made your point. It's good to know you can defend yourself, but let's not risk anyone getting hurt. Tomorrow is an important day. Save it for another time.'

Sam helped Nathan to his feet. The look that Nathan gave him was far from friendly, but he was pleased to see that it did now hold a measure of respect.

* * *

'How did you convince your mum that you should be a part of the extraction team?' Callum whispered.

Sam turned and winked at him. 'Mum couldn't do it,' he replied. 'She's terrified of heights and I think that after my tae kwon do demonstration last night, she realised I am as well able to look after myself as anyone else here. Apparently, Nathan's got a dodgy knee and Alex is renowned for being clumsy. Sherri will need someone to help her lift out the panel and the raptors don't have the dexterity. That left you or me.'

'But I'm the better climber,' Callum protested.

'Shhh!' Claire hissed, turning the red glow of her filtered torch back along the tunnel towards the two boys and glaring at them. She pulled an imaginary zip across her lips.

Sam nodded, mouthing the word 'sorry'. As soon as Claire turned away again, he grinned ruefully at Callum and shrugged. He couldn't tell if his friend could make out the gesture in the darkness, but there was nothing he could do about that now.

The streets never got truly dark in the City of the Imperium, but at four in the morning, it was as dark as it was going to get. The gigantic glow lamps that hung in the air far above the streets were routinely dimmed in the small hours to save power, leaving the pathways between buildings gloomy and thick with eerie shadows.

As he clambered out of the underground passage and into the ominous silence of the street, Sam marvelled once again at the vast structures around him. This was a city of improbable angles, with seemingly endless geodesic structures, all built within a gargantuan outer shell. In some ways it reminded Sam of how he had always imagined Atlantis. He found it quite easy to picture this city sitting on the seabed, hundreds of metres below the surface of the water.

Nipper, Grunt and two smaller raptors that Claire called Einstein and Newton were accompanying Claire, Sherri and the two boys. Because the two boys understood nothing of the raptor language, Claire had consulted with the rebel raptors and had given each of them a respectable name for the boys to use, before nicknames that she deemed unsuitable began to appear. As most of the raptors had been scientists before joining the rebels, she had named each of them after a famous human scientist. Sam had struggled not to laugh when she had introduced them as: Einstein, Newton, Edison, Crick and Watson. Callum, however, thought they were great names, and it had not taken long at all for the boys to associate them with the appropriate raptors.

The group had stayed underground for as long as possible as they travelled across the city, zigzagging through the underground labyrinth of tunnels like sewer rats until they were as close to the Imperium laboratories as they could get. The building they were aiming for was apparently the raptor equivalent of a secondary school. Newton had assured them there would be no one in the building at this time of night and, true to his word, getting inside did not prove difficult.

Sam and Callum crouched deep in the shadows as Einstein and Newton set to work on bypassing the magnetic locks on the doors and disabling the security systems. Nipper and Grunt positioned themselves on either side of the boys, each laden with heavy equipment. Despite the obvious weight of their burdens, neither showed any sign of fatigue. Claire and Sherri watched the street in both directions for any sign of trouble, but nothing moved.

There was a sudden *click* followed by a *swish* and the front doors to the building opened. They had done it. They were in. Without pause, Newton and Einstein slipped inside. Sam scrambled silently to his feet and raced to follow with the others hard on his heels. The other raptors sped past him and disappeared into the building. Seconds later, they were all inside.

'Good work, team!' Claire whispered. 'It looks like we made a clean entry. Now let's get up to the roof. This is where the fun starts.'

CHAPTER FOUR

'Thanks so much for the lift. I really appreciate it,' Niamh said.

'You're welcome. You sure you don't want me to see you inside?'

'No need,' she assured him, hoping he wouldn't insist. 'It's very kind of you, but I'll just head inside and get myself cleaned up. Thanks again.'

'Sure thing.'

Niamh stepped out on to the pavement outside the white wooden fence that surrounded the Lighthouse Court Hotel. She gave Bill a wave, hoping he would drive off, but he didn't. It appeared he was going to wait and see her enter safely. *Just my luck to meet a gentleman when I don't need one*, she thought. The entrance to the hotel's front garden was through a high rectangular wooden frame that looked almost as if it should have a door set into it. The hotel itself was set back from the road, so at least she didn't have to enter the reception lobby straight off the pavement.

Once inside the fence, Niamh set off round the side of the building that housed the hotel reception. Hiding out among the bushes, she waited a few minutes and listened. She thought she heard Bill's pick-up pull away, but she waited a little longer, just to be sure.

As soon as she was certain that he had gone, Niamh nipped back out through the front gate and across the road to walk along the pavement outside the Ernest Hemingway Museum. The two-metre high red brick wall that surrounded the writer's house seemed almost out of place among the wooden fences and wooden-built houses that dominated Key West. She passed by the museum gate and continued to the next junction.

A scruffy-looking artist, with his easel and a display of his work set out on the pavement, looked up and nodded as she passed. She returned the nod, instinctively picking up her pace a little as she walked by. He looked comfortable in his knee-length shorts and sandals; far more comfortable than Niamh felt in the heat of the afternoon. Despite only having left the air-conditioned environment of Bill's truck a few minutes ago, she could already feel the first beads of sweat trickling down the middle of her back.

On the far side of the street the bottom metre of a square-cut telegraph pole had been painted white, and the street names were painted vertically downwards in black paint over the top.

'Whitehead and Olivia,' she muttered aloud. She looked right along the narrow pavement on Olivia Street. Cars lined this side of the road and trees from Hemingway's garden overhung the pavement. It was not wide enough to park cars on both sides. She didn't know this area well, and for a moment she considered continuing along Whitehead Street until she found a larger street with more people; wandering around the backstreets of Key West could be dangerous. But the longer she delayed, the less chance she had of catching up with Tony and getting to somewhere the police were unlikely to find her. The shop next to Flamingo's Café where she had seen him about six or seven minutes earlier was only about two blocks from here, but there was no telling where he would be by now.

Don't be a wuss! she ordered herself. *You can't do this alone. You need Tony's help and you'll never get Sam and Callum back unless you take some risks. Get moving. Now!*

Crossing the road, she turned right and began to

trot towards Duval Street, her eyes darting around constantly for any sign of movement. Seconds later, she emerged from the narrow road into the bustle of the busy tourist area and turned left. As her fear of meeting strangers on the quiet backstreet subsided, some of Niamh's tension eased and she slowed back to a fast walk.

Now she was in the heart of Key West and, while it would not be at its liveliest until late evening, even in the heat of the late afternoon it was busy with people window-shopping. The pavements here were wide. On either side of the street very few of the buildings seemed to be the same shape or size. However, one design facet that did seem popular was the white, ranch-style gallery balconies above many of the shop fronts.

She scanned ahead for Tony and Tessa, barely needing to weave round people at all as she strode forward, but there was no sign of them. Niamh was still about a block and a half from where she had last seen them from the car. It would only take a couple of minutes to get there, but she didn't want to charge headlong into them. If possible, she needed to keep Tessa from seeing her. Niamh had few doubts that Tessa would betray her to the police again in an instant if given the chance.

Ahead she could see the next junction. As she

searched both sides of the street, something caught her attention that set her heart racing. At the next set of lights, just behind a white pick-up, was a police car.

Niamh did not hesitate. She turned left and entered through the door of the nearest shop. As she stepped inside, she realised it was an art gallery. Several tourists were browsing the long, narrow shop. Stepping straight past the nearest person, she positioned herself so that she could see back through the front windows.

'Can I help you?'

It took a moment for Niamh to realise that the woman was talking to her.

'No, thanks,' she replied, moving around so she could keep eye contact while watching the road with her peripheral vision. 'Just browsing. It's my dad's birthday in a few days. I'm just looking for ideas.'

The police car cruised past and Niamh could not help switching her focus and following it with her eyes as it went by. The car was in view just long enough for her to see that there were two officers inside. Was it just a regular patrol? Given the crawling speed they were doing as they passed, she felt sure they were looking for something, or someone – most probably her. Their HQ would have radioed out that she was missing again by now.

I've got to find a way to disguise myself – and fast, she thought.

She *had* to find Tony and get away from the centre of Key West; it was her best chance of evading the police. Darting out of the front door of the shop, Niamh turned left. Tony could be anywhere by now. As she walked, she felt a prickling sensation down her back. Something was not quite right. On instinct she glanced over her shoulder and a cold shock of horror ran through her. The patrol car had pulled to a halt a little way down the street. Its hazard lights were flashing and one of the officers was already out of the car and walking in her direction along the pavement on the other side of the road. He wasn't moving with any sense of urgency, so it seemed unlikely that he had spotted her.

Her body tensed, desperate to run, but the quiet voice of reason inside her mind said *Don't. Running will draw his attention.*

Barely able to breathe for the tension inside, she gritted her teeth against the pain and strode along the pavement, trying to disguise her limp. Determined not to look back a second time, she concentrated on searching ahead for Tony and Tessa.

'Please be easy to spot,' she muttered. 'Please.'

She looked across at the vertical street-name sign as she approached the next junction – Petronia. It was a narrow one-way street. She paused briefly to look to her right and then crossed the road at a brief trot before slowing again when she reached the other side. Her ankle was throbbing, fit to explode 'Don't look back,' she breathed. 'Just keep going.'

There he was! Tony was ahead. He was standing outside a clothing store on the far side of the street, leaning against one of the old-fashioned lamp posts that looked like they had been there a hundred years or more. Tessa was looking in the window of the shop, her attention drawn by something on display. Niamh glanced at the sign above the door. *Evan & Elle*, she read. After a moment, her brain registered the humour in the shop title and her eyes went back to it. She read it a second time and smiled. Given the state of her nerves, it felt good to smile. *I'll bet it was a Londoner who named that shop*, she thought.

Angling between some bikes that had been chained to stands and what looked like a newspaper dispenser, she stepped up to the kerb, looking both ways before making a quick dash across the road through a useful gap in the traffic. During her scan for traffic, she noted that the policeman had fallen back a little way, but he was still moving along the road in her direction. She had to keep moving.

Niamh walked right up to Tony and placed a hand on his shoulder. He hadn't seen her coming and jumped at her touch. As he registered who she was, his eyes widened with shock, but Niamh's warning look stopped him from speaking.

'Outside Sloppy Joe's – fifteen minutes. Alone,' she ordered softly, barely slowing as she continued past him.

She itched to look back to see what he would do next. Although she barely knew Tony, she felt certain he wouldn't disappoint her. Somehow he would meet her as she'd asked. In the meantime, she would have to keep from being picked up by the police again.

Sloppy Joe's was a fair walk. Was it five blocks or six? She should have given Tony more time. It was probably going to take her the full fifteen minutes just to walk there, but it was too late to worry about that now. She couldn't go back. Why on earth had she picked it? A famous tourist location, and a bar no less – they wouldn't even be able to go inside and talk! There were loads of places closer. Being a local, Tony would have known them all, but for some reason Sloppy Joe's was the first name that had sprung to mind.

In the heat of the afternoon sun, the stinging from the scrapes and bruises Niamh had sustained from her earlier leap out of the moving bus began to increase, as she forced herself to keep up her brisk pace. It seemed that the further she walked along Duval Street, the more her tension eased and the more painfully aware of her injuries she became. It was with no small amount of relief that she finally saw the black and white frontage of Sloppy Joe's ahead. On the central awning was written *Pina Coladas*. Just the thought of any drink made Niamh realise how thirsty she was; at this point she would have willingly killed for a tall glass of chilled orange juice.

Limping right up and underneath the awning, Niamh was relieved to stop. She leaned against the wall right at the corner of the street. The urge to sink down to the pavement to rest was strong, but the danger that this would draw attention kept her on her feet.

Her tongue felt swollen and her lips were dry.

'Hiya!'

It was Niamh's turn to jump.

'Tony! You scared me!'

'Sorry about that, but what're you doin' here? I thought you were headin' out of the Keys.'

'I was,' Niamh explained. 'But it's been a bit of a crazy afternoon.'

'Before I ditched Tessa, a cop passed us. From the way he was scannin' Duval Street, I'd say he was looking for someone. Was he after you by any chance?'

'I'm not sure,' she replied. 'But I was trying not to take any chances. How did you get ahead of me?' she asked as Tony stepped fully into the open from round the corner to her right.

'I left Tessa with a lame excuse, left Duval and paralleled along Simonton in case she tried to follow me,' he explained. 'You don't look so good . . . Jeez, what have you been doin'? Those are some scrapes! Have you been fightin'? Are you OK?'

'I've felt better.'

'Let's get inside. You need to clean those cuts and grazes up, and I'm bettin' you could do with a drink.'

'We can't,' she protested, looking towards the entrance to the bar. 'I'll never pass as old enough.'

'Not in here,' Tony laughed. 'My aunt Jo-Ann lives about two blocks from here on Eaton. She's friendly and she always has plenty of cool juice in the fridge. Come on. I don't know what you're doin' in Key West, especially as Carrie sent me a text sayin' you were on a bus to Miami, but from the look of them scrapes I'm guessin' you've got another good story to tell.'

Niamh pushed away from the wall and took a sharp intake of breath as her ankle threatened to buckle under her weight. Tony was there instantly. He put an arm round her waist, his body positioned to prop her up.

'Thanks,' she gasped, her face hot with embarrassment at the intimacy she felt in his touch.

'You're welcome,' he grinned. 'Or perhaps I should say "My pleasure". That is what you Brits say, isn't it?'

'Yeah,' she said weakly.

They crossed the road and had begun to head back along Duval Street when Tony stopped suddenly and dragged Niamh around to look at the adjacent shop window.

'That policeman is comin'.'

'The same one?'

He glanced across her. 'Yep,' he confirmed, sounding nervous.

'He could be on a regular patrol, I guess, but something tells me that's unlikely. Quick! Let's get off Duval. Which is the quickest way to your aunt's place?'

'The quickest way is back past the cop. Come this way. It's a little further, but we'll be out of his sight more quickly. If we don't move quick, he'll see us.'

'Don't worry,' Niamh said softly. 'If he's looking for me, then he'll be looking for a girl on her own. I doubt he'll look twice at a couple.'

'Where did you learn to be so devious?'

'I read a lot.' She grinned.

Trying to relax and act casually, Niamh let Tony lead the way along Duval and off into a side street.

Even though her ankle was throbbing with pain and her shoulder felt like it was on fire, she felt lighter than air as he guided and supported her. Reunited with Tony, her confidence soared and suddenly she felt more positive about making progress with her search for Callum and Sam. If anyone could help her, it would be Tony and his sister.

CHAPTER FIVE

The roof of the school was neither flat nor sloping, but almost like a scaled-down landscape with rolling hills and an occasional steeper mountain peak. As Sam emerged out through the forced panel and on to the roof, he noted that the shapes of the geodesic panelling here were every bit as irregular as they were on the walls. There was a strange sense of strength about the irregularity. All of the panels seemed to fit together in an elaborate three-dimensional jigsaw that, while strange to the eye, gave an impression of solidity.

Einstein and Newton had taken the lead again and were bounding over the lumps and bumps of the roof surface, their claws clicking against the panels with every leap. Sam followed as closely behind as he could, but with more care and stealth. When he caught up with the raptors, he held back from the edge, as there was no safety rail. Raptors, it seemed, had no use for such features. Nor, apparently, did they fear heights. Einstein prowled along the very edge of the roof with no regard to the deadly drop. His concentration appeared set on the gulf between this rooftop and that of their target. Turning, he beckoned to Nipper and Grunt, who were approaching with the heavy bags of equipment. They wasted no time. Within a matter of seconds, an impressive frame was slotting together, each pole sliding into place with a reassuring clunk.

'Blimey!' Callum gasped. 'Look at them go!'

Einstein lifted out the special, heavy-duty cross-bow contraption and slotted the bolt in place. Laying out a coil of lightweight rope, he passed the end to Claire, who tied it off on one of the crossbars of the frame that was still under construction with a self-tightening knot. Sam watched her work and noted that she kept her eyes averted from the edge of the building throughout.

Einstein hefted the crossbow up to his shoulder and took aim. Angling the bolt high above the target roof, he fired. There was a loud *thunk* and a *whizzzzzzz* as rope fizzed out of the coil in a high arcing snake towards the roof of the Imperium laboratories.

Sam held his breath as it went. The bolt would have to penetrate the surface of one of the panels on the opposite roof, to give the grapples a suitable hold, as the smooth surface of the tightly interlocking plates offered no suitable grip. But what if it didn't break through as the raptors said it would? He needn't have worried. Einstein knew exactly what he was doing. He and Newton had done their calculations perfectly. The metallic torpedo punched downwards and smacked through the neighbouring rooftop, puncturing a panel with a clean entry hole. Whether by luck, or by exceptionally good shooting, Sam didn't know, but the grapple pierced one of the highest points of the roof.

Einstein turned and fired a quick sequence of clicks and growls at Newton, who replied with a short grumbling answer.

Claire placed a hand over her mouth to stifle a laugh.

'What did they say?' Sam asked.

'Einstein asked Newton if it mattered that the entry hole was close to the edge of a panel,' his mother said, looking thoughtful. 'And the nearest translation I can give to Newton's response is: *Who knows? Ask me one on apples*.'

'A raptor with a human sense of humour!' Callum sniggered. 'I think I'm going to like him.'

'Way to fill me with confidence!' Sam complained. 'Are you sure these raptors know what they're doing?'

'Don't worry, son,' Claire soothed. 'You won't be going first and the raptors are heavier than you. You'll be fine. I wouldn't be letting you go if I didn't believe that.'

He looked at her and saw the truth of what she was saying. He could see there was worry in her eyes, but belief was there in greater measure. She trusted her team implicitly.

'Thanks,' he said, and drew her into a hug.

'I wish I was going with you,' she sighed. 'Sherri and the raptors will keep you as safe as I could, but I'm not saying you won't be in any danger, Sam. Just make sure you do as you're told, or there'll be hell to pay when you get back to base. Now I've found you again, I'm not planning on losing you any time soon.' She smiled at him, her tough exterior breaking for a moment.

'Don't worry, Mum,' he assured her. 'You're not going to get rid of me that easily. I won't do anything silly, I promise.'

'Time to go,' Sherri interrupted.

The frame was finished and secured. The cable had been routed over the top and Grunt was tensioning the cable-like rope with a ratchet mechanism that he had mounted within the structure of the frame. Nipper clipped his runner over the rope, twisted his hands through the safety loops and gripped the runner bar. With a flash of his impressive rows of teeth, he lifted his legs from the rooftop and began the long slide to the neighbouring roof.

The cable sagged quite dramatically under his weight to begin with, but Grunt continued to ratchet up the tension even as he went. By the time he reached the roof of the Imperium labs, Nipper was sliding at a terrific speed, but it was nothing the raptor couldn't handle. Deliberately dropping from the runner, he hit the rooftop and rolled to his feet like an acrobat.

'Impressive!' Callum whispered to Sam. 'You sure you want to do that?'

'He won't have to,' Sherri told him. 'Watch and learn, boys.' She reached up and clipped her runner over the cable, wound her hands through the safety loops and she was off. The dip in the rope this time was much less and Sherri raced across the gulf between the buildings at breathtaking speed. The *zizzzzzzz* of the runner on the cable sent a thrill up Sam's spine as he watched her race across the gulf. At the far side, Nipper was waiting, braced for her arrival. Having attached a short piece of rope to his runner, the raptor had drawn it back up the rope as far as he could reach. As Sherri's runner collided with his, Nipper hung on to the short piece of rope, absorbing as much of the energy of her slide as he could. Sherri was so light that he managed to slow her almost to a stop before she touched down on the roof.

Newton went next. He was the strongest and fittest of the scientist raptors. In a fight, Sam doubted he would be anywhere near as effective as Nipper or Grunt, but Newton was still far bigger and stronger than any of the humans. He crossed on the zip wire with less grace and athleticism than either Nipper or Sherri, but he landed safely on the far roof.

All remaining eyes turned to Sam. He got to his feet, heart beating fast. Reaching up, he clipped his runner over the cable and twisted his hands through the safety loops, as he had seen the others do.

'Good luck,' Callum whispered to his friend.

'Stay safe,' Claire added.

Sam nodded, unable to speak for the fear rising in his chest. Although he did not suffer from vertigo, he was painfully aware that there was no safety net here. If he fell, he would die. Tensing his stomach muscles and gripping the handholds as tightly as he could, he raised his knees to his chest and gravity began to bite as he started to accelerate down the wire. He felt a thrill rush through his body as he passed over the edge of the building and zipped out, high above the ground. His whole body clenched tightly as the pitch of the *zzzzzizzzz* of the runner against the cable increased to a whining scream.

The other building was approaching fast. Too fast, it seemed. If he hit the rooftop at this speed, he was sure to break something. But Nipper and Newton were there, braced and ready to absorb much of Sam's momentum. As his runner struck Nipper's, Sam's knees swung up so high with the deceleration that they almost touched the wire above. His arms threatened to wrench from his shoulder sockets with the force of it. Even as he slowed, Newton caught him round the waist, taking his weight and allowing him to let go of the runner.

'Ow!' he muttered, rubbing at his shoulders.

'You OK?' Sherri asked.

'Fine,' he replied through gritted teeth. 'But I think I'm going to feel that tomorrow.'

She gave him an encouraging grin and a wink. 'Look out,' she warned. 'Equipment inbound.'

The final runner was zipping towards them with a heavy bag attached. It made the transit safely and no sooner had Nipper detached it from the runner than he and Newton were moving across the roof and away towards the opposite side of the building. Sherri beckoned Sam to follow. Before he did, Sam took one final look back up at the rooftop that he had just come from. He could just make out his mum and friend waving. Raising a hand in brief salute, he turned to follow the others.

This is it, he thought. *It gets serious from here on in.*

Trying to step lightly, Sam followed Sherri's lead across the rooftop. The two raptors had already reached the far edge and Newton was directing Nipper with a series of low clicks, grunts and lots of gestures. Although Sam was far from being an expert on raptor body language, it was clear that Nipper had a good deal of respect for the raptor scientist, doing everything Newton directed without so much as a shadow of a question. As Sam had come to trust Nipper's judgement, his estimation of Newton began to rise rapidly.

From the heavy bag of equipment, Newton pulled out four harnesses and tossed them to Sherri. She quickly sorted them into size order and showed Sam how to buckle himself into his. Meanwhile, Newton attached a rubbing strip to the edge of the building and then, with a device that looked like an oversized drill, he made easy work of slicing four small holes into the rooftop in a precise line, each about a metre apart. The machine made a barely audible hiss as it cut through the dense surface material of the building, leaving Sam wondering how on earth it worked.

Next out of the bag came what looked like four small plastic wheel cases. Newton studied each one before placing it next to one of the holes he had made. Then, using his curved claw, he hooked something from inside the first case and forced it down into the hole he'd made for it. There was a soft, satisfying *clunk* as it locked into place. One by one, he did the same with the others before beckoning Sherri forward. She checked his work and nodded to him.

Newton pointed at Sherri and then at the first case. Again, she nodded. Bending down, she picked it up and attached it to her harness with what looked like a classic carabiner clip – a metal loop with a sprung gate that rock climbers and abseilers used. She signalled Sam forward to the second case.

'Now remember what I said earlier,' she warned softly, connecting Sam to his case. 'This first switch setting on the casing will allow the inertia reel to lower you down to the right height. If you mess with it and click it too far, you'll simply descend all the way to the ground and you'll be of no use to us at all. It won't pull you back up if you go past. Only click it to the second setting as you swing through the open panel into his room.'

'Got it.'

'OK, here goes. Good luck, Sam.'

66

'You too.'

Sam watched as she twisted the lever on the side of the casing until it clicked once. Nipper and Newton were still getting into their harnesses as Sherri took two paces and leapt off the top of the building. There was a fizzing noise not unlike the sound of the runner across the zip wire earlier and Sherri dropped from view.

If Sherri can do it, so can I, Sam thought. *I've got to have faith in myself.*

Stomach churning, he stepped to the edge and looked down. He could just make out Sherri some distance below. She seemed stable against the side of the building. It was a long way to the ground. *Don't think about it, just do it!* he told himself. Taking a deep breath, he stepped out into space, and his entire body tensed as he began to fall. The fizzing whizz of the cable escaping its encased drum peaked for no more than a couple of seconds before he felt the deceleration effect of the drum.

Sam's eyes snapped open as his right shoulder thumped into the side of the building. He pushed away awkwardly and his body spun a full 360 degrees before he impacted the surface again. This time he was ready. Hands and feet spread and poised, he cushioned the second touch, bouncing lightly away and down. Another touch and he was stable to the right of Sherri. She grinned at him, eyes sparkling with excitement.

There was another whine, followed rapidly by yet another. Sam looked up to see the two raptors descending towards them, Newton on the far left and Nipper to his right. Both dropped fast, looking awkward and unbalanced as they came. Nipper, who was clutching the drill-like tool that Newton had used to slice holes into the roof, stabilised about two metres below Sam and Sherri. Newton bared his teeth as he came to rest parallel to Sherri and gave several angry-sounding clicks. He pointed at a panel to his right, but Nipper was too low to reach it.

'I think Newton forgot to account for the weight of the equipment when he set the tensioners,' Sherri whispered. 'He's not happy.'

'So what happens now?'

Before Sherri had a chance to reply, Nipper provided the answer. Transferring the full weight of the heavy cutting tool to his right hand, he grabbed the rope with his left and hauled himself up. The tension in the rope had not been far wrong, so Nipper did not have to bear much weight. However, while the manoeuvring didn't tax the raptor's prodigious strength, the result of Newton's slight miscalculation made the next few moments difficult. Wielding the cutter with one arm looked all but impossible, but Sherri sidestepped and helped stabilise it from Nipper's right, while Newton directed where to cut from his left and between the three of them, making no more than a barely audible hiss, they made short work of cutting the entire door-sized panel away from the side of the building.

As the panel came fully loose, Sam and Sherri were waiting. They lifted it away from the surface without a sound and held it steady while Newton repositioned himself to take it from them. As he took the weight, Sherri leaned across and clicked his inertia reel through to the second setting. He dropped away, holding the panel, inertia reel fizzing as he went. Nipper let go of his rope and dipped below the level of the hole, while Sherri kicked away from the wall and swung on her rope in an arc that took her in through the opening. As she crossed the threshold, Sam heard the click as she switched the lever on her drum to its second setting. He watched as she landed lightly and vanished inside.

Sam did his best to copy Sherri's example, but it was not as easy as she made it look. Fingers ready on the inertia reel switch, he pushed away from the wall and swung in an arc towards the opening. However, rather than swinging in cleanly as Sherri had, his left shoulder brushed the side as he entered and he spun through 180 degrees. In a panic, he clicked the switch through to the second setting, but he did so a second later than was ideal. He had already started to swing back outwards as he dropped, meaning he was right on the lip of the freshly cut hole. Arms windmilling in an effort to regain his balance, he teetered on the brink of the dizzying drop outside.

Just as he was convinced he was going to fall, Sherri's hand grabbed the back of his shirt and dragged him back into the room. Regaining his balance, he turned, scanning the dark room for David Earhart. The bed was empty. His heart sank as he completed the visual sweep. This was definitely a human's living space, but there was no sign of anyone.

'Where is he?' he whispered.

'Good question,' Sherri muttered back. 'According to our information, this should be his room, but it looks like acquiring David is going to be a bit tougher than we bargained for.'

CHAPTER SIX

As soon as she saw the flashing lights of the police checkpoint ahead, Niamh felt dark, overwhelming panic rise inside. She would be caught again.

Tony's aunt, Jo-Ann, was a petite woman in her thirties with an eye for clothes that made her look younger and Niamh had been able to borrow a fresh set of clothing. She had also tied up her hair into a high ponytail, but the realisation that this was not going to be enough of a disguise had come too late. A policeman was flagging down the car. What could she do? Tony took hold of her hand and squeezed it. She flicked a glance at him and then it struck her. She knew what she had to do.

'Just go with me here,' she whispered.

His aunt slowed the car and wound down her window as they approached the checkpoint. As she did, Niamh put a hand behind Tony's head and pulled him towards her. For an instant, he stiffened with shock, but he got the idea pretty quickly as she pressed her lips against his in a long, passionate kiss, drawing his head round in front of hers. Tony's arms found their way round her torso and he leaned right across her, settling into a comfortable position and blocking any view the policeman might get of her. To her delight, Tony was a good kisser and she realised that as deceptions went, this was by far the most pleasurable one she had ever tried. Relaxing, she began to move her lips against his.

'Evenin',' Officer. What's up?' Jo-Ann asked.

'We're lookin' for a runaway English girl,' he replied. 'You may have heard about her on the news.'

Jo-Ann paused for just an instant before answering. Niamh's heart was beating like crazy. Would Jo-Ann say anything about her being English? If she did, the game would certainly be up.

'Can't say I've heard anythin' and I can't help you, I'm afraid,' Niamh heard her say. 'Just runnin' these two kids back to my sister's in Big Pine. Not seen any strangers today.'

The policeman played the light from his torch over them through the window. It didn't stay on them for more than a second or two. 'Sorry to keep you then,' he announced suddenly. 'Have a good evenin'.'

The car began to move, but they continued the kiss until they were well beyond the roadblock. Niamh's heart was pounding – partly from the excitement of her narrow escape, but more as a result of the intimacy with Tony. Finally, he pulled away.

'That was unexpected,' he whispered.

'Hmm. Sorry about that,' she replied.

'Don't be. It was a good idea.'

'And it was nice,' she added softly, glad that the darkness in the back of the car was hiding the heat burning in her cheeks.

'It was, wasn't it?' He sounded pleased.

'So what's the game, you two?' Jo-Ann asked over her shoulder. 'You got cosy rather suddenly back there. And don't think I can't hear you whispering. Do you know anythin' about this missing girl?'

'Us?' Tony exclaimed, sounding for all the world as if he was shocked that she could ask such a thing. 'We're just gettin' to know one another, that's all. Why would we know anythin' about a missing girl?'

'I don't know,' she said, a note of suspicion still clear in her voice. 'It's just that . . . oh, never mind.'

Niamh wanted to tell Tony not to get too cocky, or to go thinking that her kissing him meant that he could now kiss her whenever he felt like it, but neither comment found its way from her mouth. Her left arm was still behind his back and his right was still draped round her shoulders. Both felt more than good. She leaned her head against his shoulder and looked through the gap between the front seats at the road ahead. It was quiet, rush hour having finished some time ago. They had passed one check-point, but there would be others if she was to try to leave the Keys again, and she could hardly take Tony with her all the way to Miami and kiss him at every road block.

As nice as that might be, she mused, half consider-ing the idea. The chance of it working was minimal. They had been lucky this evening. The fact that Jo-Ann had been driving them had probably swung it. If they had been on a bus, the policeman would almost certainly have questioned them and there was no disguising Niamh's English accent. The moment the police heard her speak, she would be detained for sure.

Jo-Ann had been lovely from the moment Tony led Niamh into her house and introduced her as his foreign exchange friend, Tamsyn Rodgers. Sticking with her story about falling off her bike, which was consistent with her injuries, had seemed best. Jo-Ann didn't question it, and had been most sympa-thetic and gentle when cleaning up her cuts and scrapes, applying suitable dressings with a practised hand. They had sat chatting for over an hour before

Jo-Ann had suggested they stay for a meal and offered to drive them back afterwards to save walking to the bus stop. Niamh was grateful for Jo-Ann's kindness, but knew she could ask no more of her. If she was going to get away from the Keys altogether, she would need to find a more convincing disguise and possibly another mode of transport.

There had been no chance to do more than give Tony the barest account of her adventures since leaving on the bus early that afternoon. As they pulled into the Dales' driveway, Niamh wondered what she would do now. There was another car in the drive, which meant one of Tony and Carrie's parents was home.

'Don't worry,' Tony whispered, as if reading her mind. 'It's all sorted. You'll see.'

Niamh climbed out of the car and clasped her hands together, uncertain of what to do next. Tony was quick to walk round to her, arriving just as the front door opened. There was no mistaking the lady there for anyone other than Carrie and Tony's mother. She looked just like a mature version of Carrie.

'Jo-Ann! How lovely to see you! Thanks for bringin' Tony home,' she enthused.

'You're welcome, Lara. It gave me an excuse to stop by.'

'Come in then, come in. And you must be Tamsyn

– welcome. Carrie was just tellin' me about you and asking if you could stay over for a few days while your parents are away. There's no problem with that at all. We'd be delighted to have you stay.'

'See?' Tony's hand in the small of Niamh's back propelled her gently forward.

'Thanks, Mrs Dale,' she replied. 'That's very kind.'

'Please call me Lara, Tamsyn. Mrs Dale makes me sound like my mother-in-law!'

Niamh was ushered inside where Carrie was waiting to give her a welcoming hug. While Lara and Jo-Ann headed for the kitchen area to make coffee, Carrie, Niamh and Tony slipped away into Carrie's room and closed the door behind them.

'So what happened?' Carrie asked in a rush. 'I was amazed when Tony texted me to say that he was bringin' you home. I watched you get on the bus to Miami this afternoon. How did you end up in Key West?'

Niamh sighed and sat down on the edge of the bed. 'It's been an interesting day . . .' she began.

Both Carrie and Tony, who had not yet heard the full story, barely interrupted at all as she explained what had happened. It was through gritted teeth that she recalled the silly mistake that triggered the chain of events. Borrowing a mobile from a fellow passenger to ring her dad had been a bad idea. Jumping from the moving bus in a bid to escape the police had not been much better. It hadn't prevented her from getting caught and taken to the Sheriff's Office.

'You're amazin'!' Carrie breathed when Niamh finished her story.

'I agree,' Tony said, his blue eyes twinkling.

Niamh shook her head. 'Not amazing,' she disagreed. 'Foolish, lucky and scared is more like it. After everything that's happened today, where am I? Almost back where I started! I did learn one thing though. When the police caught me on the bus, I had a really clear feeling from Sam that he has found Mum. Wherever he is, Mum's there too. My problem now is trying to decide if that's a good thing or not.'

'Of course it's good,' Carrie said immediately. 'If nothin' else, you know they're both alive. You know that they're together.'

'I'm beginning to wonder about that,' Niamh said hesitantly. 'What if it turns out I'm some kind of medium and what I'm sensing is Sam's ghost?'

The room fell silent for a moment and Niamh shivered as a sudden chill ran through her body.

'That's nonsense and you know it,' Carrie said eventually. 'You told me earlier that you were sure Sam was alive. Didn't you say you felt he'd been in danger? What sort of danger could frighten a ghost?'

Carrie was right. Of course Sam was alive, and perhaps more amazingly, so was her mum. The sudden ache in Niamh's chest as she considered this made her realise just how much she missed her mother. Wouldn't it be fantastic if she could find them both and restore their family after all this time? The ache became twisted with a sensation of guilt as she realised just how little credence she had given her dad's search for her mother all these years. He had never given up, but Niamh and Sam had never tried to help. How had he kept his hopes alive all this time when no one around him had shared his belief?

'Yes, but I'm no closer to finding out where they are,' Niamh grumbled, clenching her right fist and hammering the side of it repeatedly into her left palm. The feeling of helpless frustration was overwhelming. 'When I was waiting for the bus earlier, I got a strong sense of where Sam might be. I think he and Mum are a good distance north of here, but how am I going to get out of the Keys?'

'You might not be able to physically search for them right now with the cops all out lookin' for you, but there's no reason not to do a virtual one,' Tony offered, looking thoughtful.

'A virtual search? What, you mean on the internet?'

'Well, maybe in part online,' he said. 'You told me this mornin' that your dad is an expert on the Bermuda Triangle, right?'

'Yes.'

'Well, do you think there was anythin' in what he was investigating? Is there somethin' weird going on out there?'

'Before now I didn't really believe there was, but since the boys' disappearance it's impossible not to think about that. I keep getting these images and feelings from Sam that make little sense.' She paused, trying to find the right words. 'On the day he disappeared, I felt *something* happen to Sam. And now I feel a definite sense that he's found Mum. I don't understand how they can be together again, yet I *know* they are.'

'So what if your dad *was* on the right track? Couldn't we follow up on his research? Maybe we could find somethin' he missed. Did he have notes or anythin'?'

'Dad's spent years researching and he was incredibly thorough,' Niamh said, giving a shrug. 'It's hard to imagine we'd find anything that he hadn't gone over a hundred times already, but it's worth a try. He had loads of notes on his laptop, but the police are bound to have taken his computer from the house by now.'

'Back-ups?' Carrie asked.

'There are back-ups,' Niamh answered, her voice suddenly thoughtful. 'He had back-ups on disks, pen drives and on the PC back home in England. Getting them shouldn't be too big a problem. I know Dad's password and there's someone I could ask to try and get into my house. If the police there have seized the home computer, then we may be sunk, but. . .'

'You never know, Niamh, a fresh perspective on his notes might cough somethin' up,' Tony suggested enthusiastically.

'Nice image, thanks for that! But you're right. I'll try anything that might help me work out what's happened to Sam. It's well past midnight in England, but if I can borrow your phone to send a text, Carrie, I'll see if I can get a friend of mine to help us out in the morning.'

'Sure.'

Writing the text to Beth was not as easy as Niamh imagined. There was no end of stuff that she wanted to write, but after several false starts, she settled on sending a brief message asking her to log on to Facebook in the morning, which would be early afternoon in England; that way they could chat online and Niamh could explain properly. She started and ended the message with **URGENT**.

That should get her attention, she thought.

The idea of being able to find something that her dad had missed seemed ridiculous and yet the prospect of trying excited her. What if between the three of them they could see something he had overlooked? Given how many mystery buffs around the world had studied the Bermuda Triangle looking for clues to all the missing ships, planes and people, the idea that three teenagers could do any better at finding a reason for the disappearances seemed ludicrous. However, it did give Niamh something positive to focus on while she waited for the police to lose interest in looking for her and she could head out and continue her search for the boys.

'Done?' Carrie asked.

'Yes,' Niamh replied, as she handed back the phone. 'We can't do anything tonight, but with any luck, I should be able to get Dad's notes sent through to us tomorrow.'

They chatted for a while, but it was not long before Niamh was yawning so frequently that Carrie suggested she go to bed.

'Sorry,' she apologised. 'It's not the company, I promise.'

'It's not your fault,' Carrie told her. 'It's Tony's. He has the same effect on all girls. Come on. I'll show you to the guest room before he puts you completely to sleep.'

'Ha ha! Very funny, sis,' Tony drawled, pulling a face at his sister. 'Night, Nia— Tamsyn.' The correction was a timely reminder to all of them that they would have to be careful.

Carrie led Niamh out of her bedroom and left to the neighbouring room. Niamh glanced over her shoulder just in time to see Tony blow her a kiss. She raised her eyebrows momentarily and then rewarded him with the best smile she could.

The guest room was relatively small, but very tidy. The lilac and cream linen on the bed looked fresh and inviting and Niamh sank down on top of it with a big sigh.

'Heavenly,' she said, laying back and closing her eyes.

'You know where the bathroom is,' Carrie said. 'And you can wear more of my clothes tomorrow until we can get across to one of the local stores and buy you a few supplies.'

'Thanks, Carrie. You're the best,' Niamh said sleepily. 'What time do you normally get up?'

'Between eight and nine usually, but Mom and Dad are normally up and out by eight.'

'If I'm not up by eight-thirty, could you wake me, please? I'll need to get on the computer and speak to Beth at about nine.'

'Sure thing. Sleep well.'

Niamh thought there would be little danger of her doing anything other than sleeping well, but after wearily removing her clothes down to her underwear and slipping under the covers, she found it remarkably hard to relax enough to slide into sleep. The events of the day kept playing over and over in her mind. So many things had happened, but one thing her mind persistently returned to was the kiss with Tony. She replayed the memory time and again until it was etched in her mind so brightly that it was hard to think of anything else.

Eventually, she got so annoyed with her preoccupation that she berated herself. *Oh, get over it, Niamh! It was just a kiss. There are far more important things to worry about than a boy!* And holding that thought in mind, she finally relaxed enough to cross the barrier into sleep.

CHAPTER SEVEN

Sherri unclipped the rope from her harness and used the carabiner to clip her inertia reel on to a nearby cupboard door handle. 'Come on, Sam. We've come this far. I'm not leaving without David.'

'Wait for Nipper,' Sam urged.

Sherri didn't listen. She was already at the door and cracking it open. With her tight-fitting black outfit and her furtive movements, she looked like a cat burglar. Her hair was scraped back and tied in a neat ponytail and her eyes were constantly on the move. Nipper, on the other hand, could never look anything like a cat burglar. He was making quite a bit of noise as he attempted to scramble up and through the freshly created window without dropping the cutter.

Sherri threw him a sharp frown. 'Keep it down!'

she hissed. 'We don't want to wake the entire science lab staff. Come on, Sam. The corridor's clear. Follow me.' And she was gone, slipping through the door and out of sight.

Sam grabbed the cutter from Nipper, struggling with its weight as he dragged it into the room and marvelling that the raptor had held it with one arm. With both hands free, Nipper all but leapt into the room after it. The raptor glanced at the door through which Sherri had disappeared and then at Sam. Baring his teeth, Nipper gave a short burst of quiet clicking noises. Sam did not need to understand the raptor language to guess that Nipper was saying something about Sherri, and he doubted it was complimentary.

There was no time to waste. Sam detached his inertia reel and secured it next to Sherri's. Nipper followed his lead and they both went to the door. Sam peered out. The corridor was empty in both directions. Which way had Sherri gone? There was no obvious way of telling. With a gesture to Nipper to go left, Sam turned right and ran lightly along to the next door. It was slightly ajar. Inside he could see a dim light and hear the sound of low voices.

Sam peered in through the narrow opening. Sherri was inside, being held at knifepoint by a young man who was wearing nothing but a pair of sleeping shorts. She had her hands in the air and was whispering urgently at him, but the man did not look impressed. Sam backed away from the door for a moment and waved frantic gestures at Nipper who was already some distance down the corridor checking doors. It took a few seconds to catch his attention, but as soon as the raptor saw Sam's signal, he raced swiftly and silently back.

Sam didn't wait for Nipper to arrive. He stepped in through the door.

'Another one!' the man said. 'And this one barely more than a boy! How many of you are there?'

'Enough,' Sam said, keeping his voice much lower. 'Is this David?'

'Yes. I'm sorry. He surprised me,' Sherri replied. She began to lower her right hand. Sam could see the pistol holstered at her lower back. 'I didn't expect him to be sleeping with a big knife under his pillow.'

'Keep your hands up,' David ordered, waving his knife menacingly.

Sherri complied.

'Seems pretty paranoid,' Sam observed, walking forward slowly. 'I wonder why someone would keep such a big knife in their bed.'

'Stop right there!' David ordered, turning the knife towards Sam. 'I don't want to hurt anyone.'

Sam stopped. Nipper appeared at the door, but Sam raised his hand in a gesture that kept him at the threshold. Strangely, this felt like a situation he could handle. His four and a half years of tae kwon do training might not be much use against raptors, but from the way David was holding the knife, Sam could tell he was no fighter.

'David, we're not here to hurt you,' Sam said softly. 'I'm sure Sherri will have told you that.'

'Stay back, Sam,' Sherri ordered. 'I promised your mother I'd keep you out of trouble.'

Sam ignored her and took another slow step closer, keeping his hands up where David could see them.

'I know who you are and I want nothing to do with the anti-Imperium group,' David said, turning his knife towards Sam. 'You're all traitors. Get away from me. Leave me alone.'

'Traitors to what, David?' Sam asked.

'To the Imperium of course!' he replied, waving the knife first at Sherri and then at Sam. 'You're saboteurs who create chaos, trying to destroy all the good work that we're doing.'

'That's not true,' Sam said, keeping his voice unflustered and moving another slow step closer. 'It's what the Imperium want you to think. Yes, we want to stop some of what they're doing, but only the stuff that's doing more harm than good. The Imperium know that their energy programme is causing a global catastrophe, but they're shutting their eyes to the facts and working hard to keep everyone else in the dark. Worse, their actions are causing problems in my home world – the world your grandmother came from. Don't get me wrong – much of what the Imperium scientists are doing is wonderful. Your flight technology, for example, is fascinating. We'd love to understand it and help you develop it further.'

'You would?' David asked, his frown deepening. 'Why? What's your interest in flight?'

'Personally, I'd like to use it to find a way home,' Sam replied. 'We saw your flying machine outside the city. It looked very impressive.'

'Did you cross in an aircraft?' David asked eagerly, his eyes lighting up at the prospect.

'No, we were on a boat.'

'Shame,' he said, clearly disappointed. 'I'd love to get my hands on a flying machine from your world. My work is a starting point, but it's nothing like the machines that my grandmother flew and I know from the other human scientists here that aviation has progressed a lot in your world since then.'

'From what I saw, it's more than just a start. You're a pioneer, just like she was. If you come with us, we can help you develop it and take you with us into a world where flying machines have developed far beyond anything even your grandmother dreamed of.'

'Jet aircraft,' David said, his eyes going distant. 'I've heard about them of course – planes that can travel several times faster than the monorail trains. It doesn't seem possible.'

'But it is. Imagine flying through the air, as you do in your machine, but so fast that not even a bullet fired from a gun could catch up with you.'

'I don't fly in my machine,' David spat, his eyes still flicking between Sam and Sherri, trying to determine who was the greater threat.

'What?' Sam asked, genuinely surprised. 'Why not? Don't you want to fly the machine you created?'

'I do,' he said instantly, his eyes suddenly burning with an inner fire as his passion came to the fore. 'But the raptors won't let me. They say I'm too fragile and too important to risk.'

'Come with us then,' Sam urged. 'Help us replicate your machine and you'll get to fly your creation, I promise.'

Nipper barked a low warning from the doorway.

'We're out of time, Sam,' Sherri gasped. 'We've got to get out of here. Someone's coming.'

In a flash, Sam whipped his left leg up into a

crescent kick that swept the knife from David's hand and sent it clattering across the room. Without pause, he stepped in, grabbed David's wrist with a hooking motion and twisted his arm behind his back.

'Please don't try to fight,' Sam urged. 'I don't want to hurt you, but if you make this difficult for us, then I will. Now, let's go!'

'Nice move,' Sherri observed. 'You'll have to show me how you did that sometime.'

She pulled her pistol from the holster at the small of her back and ran to the door.

Sam steered David after her, pushing him forward as fast as he could without losing control. Nipper took over from there, picking David up and tucking him under his arm, much as he had done with Sam on the day they had first met. Raptors were approaching at speed along the corridor behind them. Nipper was too encumbered by David to fight, so running was the only option.

Sherri aimed and fired a quick volley of shots down the corridor at the approaching raptors. One went down, but the rest barely hesitated in their charge.

Nipper led the way, sprinting the few steps along the corridor to the room they had entered through. Sam ducked inside after him with Sherri close behind. Sam slammed the door behind her and wedged it shut with a nearby stool. It wouldn't hold for more than a second or two, but he hoped that would be enough to allow a clean getaway. Sherri grabbed Nipper's inertia reel and clipped it on to his harness.

'Put me down!' David protested. 'I don't want to go with you. Leave me alone!'

'If I were you, I'd pray that Nipper doesn't drop you,' Sam said, grabbing his own reel. 'It's a long way down.'

'What the? What are you doing? Arghhhhh!'

David's cry faded as Nipper leapt out through the window and dropped from sight. There was a loud bang and the door shuddered as someone tried to open it.

'Go!' Sherri ordered Sam. 'Get out now!'

With a last check to ensure his rope was properly connected, Sam ran to the opening in the wall and jumped into space after Nipper. This time he actually enjoyed the falling sensation. The wind rush and the heart-stopping rate of descent lasted no more than a second or two before the retarding action of the arresting gear kicked in and he swung back towards the wall of the building. The high-pitched screaming protest of the rope through the inertia reel gradually died as his plummeting descent slowed. He kicked off from the wall once . . . twice, slowing each time. The ground rose up to meet him, but to his surprise, it did not stop rising as he expected. He impacted the pavement, still travelling faster than he would have liked.

Legs buckling under the impact, the shock of hitting the ground took Sam's breath away. Lying flat on his back, he watched Sherri's descent. She was slowing faster than he had and Sam suddenly realised what had happened. In their rush to escape, he and Sherri had grabbed the wrong reels. The one he had clipped to his harness had been set for Sherri's diminutive form, so it hadn't slowed him as much as he expected. Sherri had the opposite problem. The one she was now attached to was set for his heavier weight and she had slowed to a stop some five metres above the pavement. There was nothing he could do to help. She was stuck.

Sherri twisted and turned in the air, trying to disconnect from her harness for several seconds. Then, without warning, she dropped and the rope dropped with her. Sherri twisted in the air like a cat and landed on all fours, rolling to her right on impact. The rope continued to drop, snaking down into a pile all around her. It was then Sam realised it had been cut. Raptor faces were looking out through the hole they had sliced in the side of the building, but they were far too high up for even a raptor to consider jumping to follow.

Sherri was on her feet in a flash.

'Come on!' she urged. 'Let's get out of here.'

Sam groaned as he forced himself to his feet and unclipped his carabiner. He could already feel where he was going to have some impressive bruises later. Even as he stumbled away, his rope began to fall into a pile behind him. They had cut that, too.

Nipper and Newton were already aboard one of the high-speed unmanned cabs that served as the city's primary transportation system. From previous experience, Sam knew to expect a hair-raising ride through the city in the box-like contraption. Nipper was holding David, who was protesting and struggling in vain to escape Nipper's iron grip. Sherri leapt on board, with Sam hard on her heels. No sooner was he in through the door than Newton slammed it shut and the car accelerated away so quickly that Sam had no time to find any sort of balance. He stumbled and fell, landing in a crumpled heap on the floor at the back, adding more bruises to his rapidly growing collection.

'Owwww!' he groaned, struggling to find his feet.

Sherri had been more prepared. As she had entered, she had grabbed for a handhold and managed to retain her balance. Even as the car zoomed away from the science labs, she pulled a cloth from an inner pocket and clamped it over David's mouth and nose. He struggled for a few more seconds and then slumped, unconscious.

'I should have done that to begin with,' she muttered. 'Are you OK?'

'Nothing broken,' Sam groaned, rubbing at his back where it had smacked into the rear seating. He recovered his balance enough to climb into a seat and gain a solid handhold for balance. The car seemed even more manic in its headlong race through the city than the last one Sam had ridden and he rocked as the cab flung them through the streets and on to the madcap racetrack that was the main thoroughfare through the city.

'So why didn't you use your knockout stuff earlier?' he asked. 'Or your gun? David would have been a lot easier to handle if he'd been out cold, or looking down the barrel of your pistol.'

'I hoped he might join us willingly,' she replied. 'My mistake – sorry. He'll be out for a while and he'll probably have a nasty headache when he wakes up.'

Sam nodded and looked out through the back window of the cab. 'Do you think we'll be followed?'

'It's possible, but unlikely,' said Sherri. 'I think we took them so much by surprise that they'll have problems tracing us. While we were looking for

David, Newton made some quick modifications to this car to make sure it's not easy to follow. We'll ditch it in a minute and send it on around the city. When they finally do work out how to follow it, the car should lead them on a merry wild goose chase while we take to the under-city tunnels.'

Sam nodded. Despite a few unforeseen glitches, the operation had worked almost exactly as they had planned. He felt like a secret agent, or a member of an elite squad like the SAS. All he was lacking was a gun and if he could convince his mum he was responsible enough, he might be allowed to have one of those soon. Although he was hurting in several places, he felt a rush of elation unlike anything he had ever felt before.

If I'd known being an eco-warrior could be this much fun, I'd have signed up to Miss Turner's Go Green Club years ago, he thought, clinging on to his handhold as the cab swerved right without warning. *But somehow I can't see Miss Turner organising the school's Go Green Club to leap off buildings and kidnap scientists. It's a shame – she would probably get a lot more members if she did.*

CHAPTER EIGHT

The approaching wail of a siren woke Niamh from deep sleep with a start. Hurling off the duvet, she began scrambling into her clothes, eyes searching for her footwear and the nearest escape route. Why hadn't she thought to plan for this before she went to sleep? Fumbling with the button on her shorts, she barged through the bedroom door and all but fell into the hallway even as the sound of the siren passed the house and began to recede into the distance.

Heart pounding and breath rasping, she leaned against the wall for a moment and slowly sucked in a shuddering, chest-filling breath of air as she fought to regain some composure.

'Mornin', Niamh. You OK? You look like you just saw a ghost or somethin'.'

As far as Niamh could tell, Carrie had not even noticed the siren. She did her best to give Carrie a smile, but she could feel that her face wasn't responding.

'Just feeling a bit jumpy,' she admitted.

'Come on through to the kitchen and I'll get you a cup of tea. That's what you Brits like to drink in the mornin', isn't it?'

'Tea would be lovely,' Niamh agreed.

A few minutes and half a cup of tea later, Niamh was sitting at the breakfast bar eagerly tapping at the keys on Carrie's laptop and feeling worlds better.

'She's online,' Niamh announced excitedly. She clicked on Beth's name and a chat window opened at the bottom of the screen. With quick finger strokes, she typed a greeting.

Morning, Beth. You OK?

There was a slight pause and an answer appeared with a gentle popping sound.

Afternoon! Great thanks. You?

Then underneath appeared:

What's so urgent? Boy news?!

Niamh thought for a moment. Beth lived just across the road from her and the girls spent all their free time together. In other circumstances, after not having spoken to Beth for so long, Niamh would have been dying to fill her in on her kiss

97

with Tony, but sitting next to Carrie, on her bed and using her laptop, it didn't seem appropriate to chat openly with Beth on Facebook about her brother. Besides, now wasn't really the time for boy talk; she needed to get Beth to get the notes from her dad's computer.

'Tell her you need her to get your Dad's notes,' Carrie urged.

As it happens, there might be . . . ☺ But before I tell you about that, I need a favour. You busy today?

Tease! Go on. What do you need?

Can you go to my house and log in to Facebook from the computer in my dad's office? You know where the spare key is. Dad's password is Cla1re01.

Oooh! I suppose so. Are you sure you're dad won't mind though?

No, it's fine, honest.

OK. But come on as I'm doing you a favour you have to spill some boy goss! Who is he?

Niamh felt her face begin to heat up. What could she say about Tony with Carrie sitting beside her? There was no reason to think that Tony had told his sister about their kiss in the back of the car yesterday. How much should she say?

His name is Tony. No juicy details till you get to Dad's computer. I'll wait online.

Pictures?

Niamh glanced at Carrie, her cheeks burning.

Carrie laughed. 'I'm sure I can find somethin' for you,' she said.

Yes.

Cool! I'm on my way! ☺ Give me 5 mins.

The green dot disappeared from next to Beth's name, signifying that she had gone offline.

'So, you and Tony are an item then?' Carrie stated more than asked as she leaned back against the headboard. 'That was fast work for him. He's not normally so quick when it comes to girls.'

'I wouldn't say "item". We got to spend some time together yesterday afternoon, and we like each other, yeah,' Niamh mumbled.

'See? I told you he was into you, didn't I?' Carrie put her arm round Niamh and gave her waist a gentle squeeze. 'I'm glad you two are hookin' up. You'll be great together.'

'I hope so.'

'I know so.' Carrie swung her legs off the bed and got up. 'Do you want some breakfast? I'll go make it while we wait for your friend to get to your house.'

'That would be nice. Thanks.'

'What would you like? Pancakes? Waffles?'

'Just some toast, thanks. I'll come with you. We can take the laptop through to the kitchen.'

Tony was in the kitchen. He'd laid the breakfast

bar with place settings, bowls and plates, and had poured three glasses of fruit juice.

'Mornin', bro'. This all looks very organised. Should I ask what the occasion is?' Carrie teased.

'No occasion,' he replied, trying to look nonchalant. 'Just looking after our guest.'

'Guest? That's a bit formal, isn't it?' she said, giving him a cheeky wink.

'Oh, leave him alone, Carrie,' Niamh said, giving her a friendly push on the shoulder. 'He's being very sweet. Thanks, Tony. Where should I sit?' She put the laptop down on the breakfast bar where they would all be able to see the screen and gave him a warm smile.

'The middle will be fine,' he said.

'So that you get to sit next to Niamh wherever I sit,' Carrie observed. 'Sharp move, bro'. I like it.'

'Carrie!' Niamh warned, taking the middle seat. 'It's fine if he wants to sit next to me, because I happen to want to sit next to him.'

Niamh could feel her face burning again at her declaration, but the smile Tony gave her made the feeling of embarrassment worthwhile. She took her place and began sipping at her orange juice, hoping that the chilled drink would help to cool her flushed cheeks.

'OK, I'll stop my teasing. I assume that was Mom I heard leavin' a little while back.'

'Yeah, and Dad went to work just after seven.'

'Thought so. Well, as you're playin' host, Tony, Niamh would like some toast, and I'll have pancakes with maple syrup, please.'

Tony's eyebrows rose as his sister sat down to Niamh's right, placed her hands on the breakfast bar and smiled at him.

The computer gave out a popping sound that announced someone was sending a message on chat. Niamh ran her finger over the mouse mat and the screensaver disappeared, leaving the familiar format of Niamh's Facebook home page.

'Wow! That was quick,' she said, looking at the screen. 'Beth must have sprinted.'

In your dad's office. You were saying about Tony...?! Need I ask if he's hot?

Niamh looked across the breakfast bar at Tony who was loading the toaster with bread.

Yes, I think you would say so. I'm looking at him now.

He's there! ☺ Could be awkward.

You've no idea! His sister Carrie is sitting next to me. She says she'll find me a photo to send you later, but can you do something for me first?

Sure.

Open Word. Then click on Open Document.

Done.

There should be a folder called Devil's Triangle or something similar.

Got it.

I need you to email me a copy of the folder to my hotmail address.

Hasn't your Dad got this with him on his laptop? I didn't think he went anywhere without it.

Dad's not here right now and there's something we need to find out.

OK. Just a mo . . .

There was a long pause, then another pop.

Can't attach it. There's loads of sub-files and dozens of documents in each.

Niamh groaned.

'What's the matter?' Tony asked, moving around the breakfast bar so that he could see the screen. Niamh was glad that the earlier dialogue about him had scrolled off the top of the window.

'Beth can't email the whole folder because it's too big and it would probably take ages to attach each document individually.'

'Use online storage then.'

'What? How do I do that?'

'There's loads of websites who offer online storage that can be accessed from anywhere with an internet connection,' he explained. 'It's simple: upload the file to a site, access it from here, copy it on to our computer and delete the online copy. Job done.'

'Why does technology have to be so . . . technical? It would have been so much easier if she could have just emailed it.'

'I can do it for you,' Tony offered. 'How about I talk to your friend and you girls finish making breakfast?'

Niamh nodded and dashed off a quick explanation to Beth.

Handing over to Tony. He's going to talk you through some online thingy that should mean you can send me the file.

Cool!

For the next few minutes the girls chatted and laughed as they heated Carrie's pancakes, and Carrie tried to convince Niamh to try spreading both peanut butter and 'jelly' on her toast. The girls bantered about the different cultural food clichés they associated with either side of the Atlantic, with Tony throwing in the occasional comment. All the while, Tony's fingers tapped away on the keyboard.

'Got it!' he announced suddenly.

'Really?' Niamh asked. 'Brilliant! Thanks, Tony. Can I just have a quick chat with Beth before she goes.'

'Sure.'

Hi Beth – Niamh here again. Thanks for that.

No probs. Tony made it easy. Don't forget that you owe me a photo.

I won't. Will email a photo in a minute. Should be waiting for you by the time you get home.

Great. Hey, it sounds as though someone's opening the front door. Have you got a cleaner coming in, or something?

'Damn!' Niamh cursed. Her mind began to race and her fingers darted all over the keyboard, sending a string of short messages in rapid succession.

No

Might be the police

No time to explain

Shut down and get out. Quick!

Beth's status went from green to grey. She was gone.

'What's the matter?' Tony asked.

'I may have just dropped Beth into a whole load of trouble,' Niamh sighed, logging out of Facebook. 'I hope not, but she is not likely to be very pleased with me if the police find her in the house and decide to question her.' She minimised the internet window and double-clicked on the Devil's Triangle folder that now sat on the desktop.

She knew her dad had been collecting information about the Bermuda Triangle for a long time, but just how big was his master folder of information? A window opened with a choice of three sub-folders labelled *Sea*, *Air* and *Theories*. She clicked on *Sea*. Within *Sea* was a further selection of sub-folders labelled *Derelicts*, *Debris Found* and *Disappeared Without Trace*. She clicked on *Derelicts*. A long list of documents appeared, organised by date order. Top of the list was *The Mary Celeste – Dec 1872*.

'Wow!' Carrie breathed, her head appearing over Niamh's shoulder. 'Your dad really did his homework, didn't he?'

'Yep. He always has been thorough,' she said, opening the top file.

'So how do you want to do this?' Carrie asked. 'Should we all look at the files together, or should we copy the lot to other computers and each take a section separately?'

'Perhaps we could start by looking at them together and see how we get on,' Niamh suggested. 'I think we're far more likely to find fresh answers if we throw ideas around as we go.'

'Together it is,' Tony said, looking very happy with her answer. He climbed on to the stool to her left and sipped his orange juice. 'So, the *Mary Celeste*, then. Funny, I always thought it was the *Marie Celeste*.'

'Lots of people make that mistake,' Niamh told

him. 'But Dad told me that the *Marie Celeste* was actually the ship in a fictional story written by Arthur Conan Doyle some time after the events of the real mystery. I'm sure the similarity of the names was deliberate, but lots of people now confuse the fictional ship with the actual one.'

'Conan Doyle – the guy who wrote *Sherlock Holmes*?' Tony asked.

'Oh, yeah, that's right! The cool detective dude with the hat. Loved the film. Robert Downey Jr! Yum!' Carrie said.

'Really? You're jokin', right?' Tony looked shocked. 'He's ancient!'

'Fit though,' Niamh observed, giving Carrie a wink.

'Girls, girls!' Tony protested. 'Boy present! Can we keep our minds on the problem, please?'

'Oh, OK. If we must,' Carrie sighed. 'But we could do with thinkin' like a detective if we're going to solve this mystery.'

'Thinkin' *like* a detective, yes,' Tony agreed. 'Thinkin' *about* an actor who *plays* a detective . . . I don't think so.'

'You're no fun,' she replied, sticking her tongue out at him.

'Oh, look!' Niamh said, pointing at the screen. 'Dad's put a relevance note at the bottom. *Relevance – Low*. I wonder if he's done that with all of them.

That would make it a lot easier to sort through everything.'

He had. Niamh opened several of the files in the folder on derelicts and they were all noted as: *Relevance – Low*.

'I guess he must have decided that none of the derelict mysteries have much in common with your mum's disappearance.'

'Well, some of these derelicts were found a long way from the Triangle,' Niamh pointed out. 'The *Mary Celeste* was found near the Azores which is not even close to the Bermuda Triangle. Given that it was a long way away, a long time ago and that it was just the people who vanished, you have to admit that there's not much in common between that and my mum's disappearance.'

'Fair enough,' Tony said. 'But let's try not to rely on your dad's system, or we're not gonna reach any conclusions of our own.'

'Good point. So let's start by trying to think about the big picture. Boats, aircraft and people in the Triangle either disappear without trace, disappear leaving some evidence of disaster, which is often as baffling as the disappearance itself, or experience weird phenomena. But what does that tell us?'

'Maybe there's more than one phenomenon at work?' Carrie suggested.

'Or whatever is causing the mysteries deliberately varies its tactics to muddy the waters,' Tony added.

'Both good ideas,' Niamh said, grabbing a sheet of paper and a pen. Drawing two bubbles, she wrote *Multiple phenomena?* in one and *Deliberate variation?* in another. She stared at them for a moment and then added another bubble in which she wrote *Transported to somewhere remote?* 'Dad used the name the Devil's Triangle rather than the Bermuda Triangle because he felt it implied intent behind what was happening. If you were going to arrange for all these ships, planes and people to disappear, why would you do it?'

'Money,' Tony suggested.

'Power?' Carrie added, her voice uncertain. 'Not "take over the world" type power, but "do it because I can" type power. Some people get a real kick out of that sort of thing.'

Niamh noted both down and then shook her head and crossed out *Money*. 'It can't be driven by money,' she said. 'Or if it is, then it's not in any way I can make sense of. Look – this one says cargo untouched . . . same with this one. Cargo intact . . . cargo intact . . . and on this one a wallet with quite a lot of money in it was found in a jacket left in plain view on the deck. Some of the people who have gone missing have been wealthy, but there are never

any demands for ransom money. I can't see a
cial motive.'

She stared at the paper and drew another bubble.
In it she wrote *To hide something*. Staring at the
words, a shiver ran down her spine. What sort of
secret would justify making thousands of people
disappear? And who, or what, would be powerful
enough to make that sort of thing happen? Could it
be a government cover up? Was Tony right? Was
there something of such financial significance out
there that it was worth making so many things and
people vanish?

Drawing another bubble next to the one she had
crossed through, Niamh wrote the word *Money*
again and drew a linking line to the one marked *To
hide something*. Taking another piece of paper she
wrote a vertical list:

Why?

How?

Where?

When?

What?

Who?

'OK,' she said. 'Time to really start thinking like
investigators . . .'

▽
CHAPTER NINE

'Boys, we've got trouble inbound. Grab anything you don't want to lose. It looks like we're gonna need to leave in a hurry.'

Claire's expression was grim and determined as she swept through the common room and straight on through to the planning room, where the boys heard her repeating the message. Sam jumped to his feet, his chest instantly tightening with apprehension.

'That sounds serious,' Callum muttered, adjusting his glasses and staring after Claire.

'If the Imperium know where we are, then yeah, serious sums it up,' Sam said, moving to the door that his mother had disappeared through. 'I guess we stirred the hornets' nest last night. The Imperium big bosses can't be happy about losing David. I wonder what he's making of all this.'

'He spent quite a while talking with your mum last night. She's a persuasive lady, Sam. I imagine he's more onside than he was to begin with.'

'I hope so. If we've got to run, it'll be a lot easier to take him with us if he comes willingly,' Sam observed. 'I doubt Nipper will want to carry him again.'

Almost as if the mention of his name summoned him, Nipper appeared with Grunt at his side. Sam looked at the raptor's face, trying once again to read it for emotion. If there was anything there to read, Sam couldn't see it, but he could sense the tautness in the two raptors. They were ready for action.

'Let's grab a small backpack or two if you can find them,' Callum suggested. 'We'll fill them with as much food and drink as we can carry easily. We don't want to have to run with a heavy load if we're being chased.'

'Good idea,' Sam agreed. 'What about weapons? Do you think Mum will let us have guns?'

'I don't know. Do you really want one?'

'Are you kidding? If Scar and those other Imperium raptors are going to be chasing me, personally I'd like a tank, or a rocket launcher maybe. But I'll take anything I can get. I don't know about you, but I'd like to get home in one piece.'

111

'You in a *tank*!' Callum laughed. 'Now that *would* be dangerous. You can barely ride a bike in a straight line!'

'Ha, ha! Very funny. Come on. Let's see what we can do to help.'

The two boys followed Claire through to the planning room and found it was already a hive of activity. Nipper and Grunt entered behind them. Claire was barking out orders both in English and in the raptor language. Alex was distributing weapons and ammunition from the big metal cabinet where they were stored. Sherri already had a semi-automatic rifle slung across her back and was busy strapping boot holsters to her ankles for a pair of blocky handguns that she'd laid on the table next to where she crouched.

Bemused, David was sitting by a table at the far side of the room with his hands tied behind his back. He was staring with a dazed expression at the whirlwind of preparations going on round him. Sam tapped Callum on the arm.

'Why don't you go and talk to David?' he suggested. 'I'll see if Alex will let us have some firepower.'

Callum was happy to comply. He had been itching to talk with David all morning, but the opportunity had not arisen. The inventor looked to be in his early twenties, of medium build, with dark wavy hair and chiselled features. Callum could imagine girls flocking to him if it wasn't for the startled rabbit expression on his face. The sustained mixture of surprise and fear was almost comical. His eyes were darting around the room from person to person, as if he expected one of them to attack him at any moment.

'Hi,' Callum began. 'I'm Cal. I saw your flying machine the other day and I've been dying to ask you about it. It looked wicked.'

'It's not wicked at all,' David replied, flinching away from Callum's hand. 'There is nothing evil about flying.'

'By wicked I meant it looked cool . . . erm, great, fantastic, brilliant. Sorry.'

'Oh! Well, in that case, thanks.' He looked around the room. 'Do you know what's going on? This all looks a bit desperate.'

'I don't know for sure, but from what I can tell, your friends from the Imperium are getting a bit too close for comfort,' Callum explained. 'We're just preparing in case we have to relocate in a hurry.'

'You realise they'll kill you all if they find you?' David asked. 'They'll kill me too, if they think I've joined you.'

'They have to find us first,' Callum said, grinning.

'We're pretty well hidden here. Besides, if they do find us, Claire is a clever woman. I imagine she has an escape plan worked out.'

'You imagine? You don't know?'

'I trust her.'

'Rather you than me,' David said, shaking his head. His eyes flicked around the room nervously. 'I don't trust anyone any more. Trusting people will land you in trouble. Mark my words.'

Callum laughed aloud. 'It already has,' he said, raising his hands. 'How do you think I ended up here? My friend Sam over there told me it would be fine for us to take his dad's boat out for a quick fishing trip, and here I am in a strange world being hunted by highly evolved dinosaurs. There are times when I think I shouldn't have listened to him.'

'You trusted him and he let you down.'

'No. I trusted him and things didn't work out the way either of us could have anticipated,' Callum corrected. 'I don't blame him for what happened. Sam's a good guy. He kept us both alive through a monster storm. He's a good friend and I still trust him, even though I know he sometimes makes mistakes.'

'You're a fool then,' David said, his voice dismissive. 'I try not to make the same mistake twice.'

'Nice attitude! Have a lot of friends, do you?'

'No,' David replied, still not looking at Callum. 'I avoid social relationships of any kind. They only bring trouble.'

'So you're a self-styled Billy-no-mates. That's pretty sad, you know. Don't you ever get lonely?'

'Sometimes,' David admitted, glancing up at Callum. The fierce intensity in his brown eyes sent a shiver down Callum's spine. 'But I'm alive and I have purpose. That's enough for me.'

A distant, muffled sound of gunfire made Callum look round at Sam, who paused momentarily midway through stuffing a backpack with food. Out of the corner of his eye, Callum noted that David jumped with every report. The man was terrified. But more than that, Callum suspected that he was so paranoid that he was bordering on losing his mind entirely.

'Time to leave, people,' Claire ordered from the doorway. 'Nathan's engaged the searchers in the tunnels. We don't have long. Come on. This way. Follow me. Stay close.'

Sam tossed Callum the backpack and slung a rifle over his shoulder. Callum inwardly sighed and hoped Sam would not try to do anything heroic. His friend was impulsive and brave, but his luck could not last forever. Watching him fly between buildings on the zip wire last night had been bad enough. As he had watched Sam race out over the deadly drop, selfish thoughts had run through Callum's head. What if Sam got himself killed? Where would that leave him? Callum desperately wanted to get home, but he didn't want to go alone. He and Sam had got into this together. They should go home together.

Maybe David has it more right than I know, he thought as he ushered the reluctant young man ahead of him. *Sam has his mum now. His motivation to get home isn't as strong as it was. Perhaps I should be thinking more about what I can do without him.*

* * *

Sam felt breathless with excitement and fear. The weight and feel of the rifle against his back added to both. He was under strict instructions not to use the rifle except as an absolute last resort, but that did not take away from the fact that he had been entrusted with carrying a deadly weapon.

He was near the back of the group with Callum and David. Nipper and Grunt formed the rearguard as they dropped down through the trapdoor and into the tunnels. Nipper had been left deliberately unencumbered, but Grunt was carrying two heavy ammunition boxes. Claire and Alex led the way using filtered red torches to minimise the chances of drawing enemy attention with their lights. The whispered order was clear. No one else was to use lights of any sort. They were trying to evade the Imperium agents, not engage them.

The smell of damp, stale water in the tunnels added to the oppressive, claustrophobic feel of being underground. Unlike caves, these tunnels were all neatly squared and often the walls, flooring and ceiling appeared to be made of the same dense plastic-type material that the raptors used for the walls of their buildings, but unlike the clean structures above ground, the surfaces here were covered in slimy mould.

The sudden sound of gunfire made Sam's breath catch in his throat. It seemed much louder and closer than it had up in the planning room. Sam had learned from the rapid exchanges between Claire, Sherri and Alex that one of the remote alarms the rebels had set up in the underground passageways had been triggered. Given their activities of the previous night, Nathan had offered to investigate and had taken Watson, Crick and Edison with him.

From the sounds of fighting that were echoing through the subterranean passageways, it was not hard to figure out what had triggered the alarm.

'This way,' Claire whispered, and they were off, moving silently and rapidly through the labyrinth. The way the sounds of gunfire echoed around them it was hard for Sam to tell if they were heading away from trouble or towards it. All he could do was follow and trust those ahead of him. His foot caught on something and he stumbled forward, bumping into the back of a raptor, though it was too dark to tell which one. His instinct was to apologise, but he clamped down the impulse. No one would thank him for making unnecessary noise.

They wove through the tunnels, almost running along the wider sections, taking turn after turn until Sam began to wonder if they were lost. With an abruptness that took him totally by surprise, the raptor ahead of him stopped and like a caterpillar bunching its body, the group gathered together. A variety of whispered curses, growls and clicks were overridden by one louder one.

'Damn!' Claire swore.

Her expletive was followed by a deafening burst of gunfire as first one and then another weapon fired multiple shots. The tunnel around Sam came alive with the strobe effect of the flashing discharges of the weapons. The hulking silhouetted shapes of Newton and Einstein filled the passageway ahead of him. Initially, Sam couldn't see past them, but he could not resist manoeuvring for a better view. No sooner could he see than he wished he couldn't. Raptors were charging towards them from ahead. Their vicious teeth and savage expressions were captured in a fragmented sequence of flash images that jerked like a stuttering film, each frame appearing in time with the spitting discharges from the weapons of Claire and Alex.

A loud *thump, thump* from behind caused Sam to twist and look over his shoulder. Grunt had dropped the ammunition boxes and was crouched ready to spring forward. Nipper was also poised. What had they heard? Were there more enemies approaching from behind? Had they walked into a trap?

'Your gun!' Callum urged. 'Get ready, Sam.'

Sam hesitated a moment before acting. The rifle suddenly seemed clumsy and awkward in his hands and he fumbled with the cocking lever as he hooked his left arm through the sling and pulled the butt into his shoulder as he had been taught. His heart was pounding like crazy and his thumb hovered over the safety catch as he tried to decide which way to point the weapon. He had no clear shot forward as his line of sight was blocked by Einstein and Newton. Nipper and Grunt filled the passageway behind him. His mother had drilled him on the importance of only ever pointing a gun in a safe direction, so he kept the muzzle of the weapon pointing down at the floor. The thought that in the dark and confusion he might accidentally shoot a friend terrified him.

'Back up! Back up!' Claire ordered, her strong

voice carrying over the sound of the weapons fire.

Nipper growled a warning. Was something moving behind them?

'I don't think we can!' Sam yelled back. 'It looks like there are more coming up behind us. We're trapped!'

'We're going to die,' David groaned.

Sam felt a surge of anger at the dark pessimism in the man's voice. There was something about people who moaned at every turn that set his teeth on edge. He was tempted to snap at him, but as he opened his mouth to speak, something caught his eye. Was that movement Sam could see in the dark passageway behind them or was his imagination playing tricks on him? A muffled growl was answered by a sequence of clicks. Raptors were definitely approaching, but it was impossible to tell how close they were.

'Sherri! Cover the rear,' Claire ordered, firing another burst. 'We need space. Get us moving back. There's too many of them ahead.'

'Got it.'

Sam felt the raptors shift aside to let Sherri through and she pushed past him without apology as she moved to support Nipper and Grunt. Holding her rifle with her right hand, she raised her filtered torch in her left and played it along the passageway behind them. Initially, there was nothing to see.

The passageway looked empty. With cautious speed, Sherri, Nipper and Grunt began to move back the way they had come. Suddenly, they stopped again. Caught, reflected in the red light of Sherri's beam, Sam could see raptors' eyes coming towards him at speed.

CHAPTER TEN

'There's some seriously weird stuff in here,' Tony commented. 'Have either of you read the section on UFOs and USOs yet?'

Niamh looked over the top of her screen at him. The three of them were now working on separate computers – Tony on his laptop, Niamh on Carrie's laptop and Carrie on an old laptop of her dad's that she'd found tucked away in a cupboard. Pieces of paper were spread all over the kitchen table, covered in notes.

'No,' she answered, glancing across at Carrie, who also shook her head.

'I've heard of UFOs, but what are USOs?' Carrie asked.

'Unidentified Submarine Objects,' Niamh explained. 'What have you found, Tony?'

'It's hard to believe some of these reports, but there are so many! I got shivers running up and down my spine just readin' 'em.'

'What sort of reports?' Carrie asked, getting up and moving round to look over her brother's shoulder.

'Navy ships trackin' underwater objects movin' at speeds of 150 miles per hour. Military and civilian pilots reportin' flying objects that seem to stalk them in the sky. Weird clouds and fogs that don't follow the laws of nature. Here, let me read you this one. I love this! It's a direct quote made by the Director of Civil Air Defense at Lajas, Puerto Rico, who says he saw an object being chased by a military jet in April 1992. He said:

' "The saucer was metallic, silvery and highly polished, and it seemed to be playing with the jet. It would continually stop in the air suddenly, then just as the jet was about to catch up it would move away quickly."

'There's more, but you get the gist. Apparently, he was one of several witnesses. It's hard to imagine someone in that sort of job puttin' his reputation and career on the line unless he was pretty certain of what he saw.'

'Flying saucers!' Carrie scoffed. 'So you think Niamh's brother and his friend have been abducted by aliens? I don't get it. How would a UFO steal the boat? And if it did, then why for Pete's sake? I mean, some of the aircraft and ships that have disappeared have been massive. It would take a damned big UFO to pick up somethin' like the USS *Cyclops*. I've just been readin' about it. That thing was over 500 feet long and weighed about 20,000 tons before you start adding cargo!'

'I didn't say I thought that was what had happened. . .'

Niamh closed her eyes and concentrated, remembering again what it had felt like at the moment she had first experienced the strange tearing separation from her twin brother. Carrie and Tony continued to bicker, but their voices faded as once again she relived the moment in the pool.

Her memory of that instant was vivid. She remembered no sense of weird objects in the sky in Sam's thoughts at the time of his disappearance. There was shock and confusion, but there was no question of anything alien . . . then, unbidden, an impossible face, scaled, with sharp teeth and a cold intelligence behind its dark eyes reconstructed in her mind and she shuddered. It was a face she had pictured clearly just the previous day. Could it be that this creature had somehow taken Sam and Callum? She scrunched her eyes shut even tighter as she focused on trying to feel a link between the face and the moment the boys vanished. Nothing came. Although the image of the creature had come from Sam, it had come long after she had sensed he was on land.

'No,' she sighed, causing the other two to pause in their argument. She could feel their eyes on her. It was hard to know how much she could tell them about what she had seen without sounding crazy. 'Sam's in a strange place, but I don't think he was abducted.'

'What about a sort of space-time warp?' Carrie suggested. 'I was just readin' about this freaky thing that happened to a passenger aircraft where they apparently vanished off the radar screen for ten minutes and then suddenly reappeared again in the same place, carried on flyin' and landed safely. Once they were on the ground, air traffic control asked the pilots where they went during that ten-minute blank period and the pilots denied having ever been off course, or having experienced anythin' strange during their approach. The really spooky thing was that after landin', the pilots discovered all the watches and clocks on the plane were ten minutes slow, yet they had only done a time check about twenty minutes before the incident.'

'That *is* weird!' Tony agreed. 'You know, I never believed there was anythin' in this whole Bermuda Triangle thing until I started readin' these notes,

Niamh. Now, I'm not so sure. There's just so much stuff here. The thing that's scary ain't just the number of incidents, but the sort of people involved. It would be easy to laugh off a bunch of flaky wannabes lookin' for a bit of publicity, but a load of the people in these reports are solid, respectable types.'

'I don't think Sam's in a time warp either,' Niamh said, shaking her head. 'At least not one that just makes you lose track of time. I've sensed his fear at times. Wherever he is there are dangers. He's not in some sort of stasis.'

'OK, so we scratch UFOs and time warps,' Tony said. 'What about USOs?'

'I think we can cross those off as well,' Niamh answered. 'At least for the moment. I suppose there's a possibility that a USO could have done something without being seen by the boys. There was a sort of pulling sensation when I first felt something was wrong. It was almost as if he was being torn away from me. I don't know how else to describe it.'

'There's an awful lot of stuff about magnetic and electromagnetic effects in these notes,' Carrie pointed out. 'Maybe the boys are still here, but sort of invisible.'

'Have you been catchin' sneaky *Star Trek* time again, sis?'

'No!' she replied vehemently. 'You're the trekkie, not me. It was somethin' I read here in the notes.'

'Strange!' Tony said, his eyes going distant for a moment. 'It's just I saw an episode of *The Next Gen* a couple of weeks ago when somethin' like that happened. Two of the main characters suffered a sort of phase shift. They could see the rest of the crew, but no one could see them. It was as if they were ghosts, except they were alive.'

Niamh began to shake her head, but Carrie nodded.

'Yes!' she said excitedly, pushing her brother aside and keying back up through the file levels before opening a different chain of folders. 'Look at this. I read somethin' similar just a few minutes ago. Let me find it. It's here somewhere. I think it was called the Philadelphia Experiment. Yes. Look!'

Carrie sat back as the others scanned through the notes.

'This was back in 1943, Carrie,' Niamh said, shaking her head and pursing her lips. 'And Dad's noted the sources as questionable.'

'Yeah, but look at the claim!' Tony said, giving a whistle. 'It says they were usin' some sort of a strong electromagnetic field to make the ship undetectable to radar and instead, they inadvertently made the ship and crew vanish entirely!'

'*Riggghhhht!*' Niamh said. 'Invisible. Like the invisible man invisible.'

'And there were reports of it having teleported. There's a cross-reference here to something called the Hutchison Effect,' he noted. 'Anyone seen that yet?'

The girls shook their heads.

'Do we have to look at that now?' Carrie asked. 'My head's spinnin' with all this stuff. Who's up for a swim?'

'I don't know,' Niamh replied. 'I think we might be getting somewhere here.'

'It doesn't have to be a long swim,' Carrie said, stretching and arching her back like a cat. 'I'm just gettin' stiff from all this sittin' and starin' at the screen. I'm strugglin' to concentrate and I think I'd be more alert after a quick dip.'

'OK, you go, but I'd better stay inside. It's probably better if I don't risk being seen.'

'Our pool's pretty private,' Carrie assured her. 'There's no houses overlookin' us out back. It should be fine. Come on. I've got plenty of spare bikinis. What about you, bro'? You comin'?'

'In a minute,' he said, his eyes still glued to the screen. 'I just wanna check out this Hutchison Effect. I'll be right behind you.'

'I should stay too. This electromagnetic thing looks promising.'

'Oh no you don't!' Carrie chuckled. 'If you stay, the two of you won't come at all. Come on, Niamh! Take a quick break. The information will still be there when we get back.'

Carrie took her by the hand and led the way through to her bedroom where they pulled out Carrie's extensive collection of swimwear. Her bikinis were rather more daring than Niamh was used to wearing, but she found one that covered enough for her to feel comfortable. She looked at herself in the mirror.

'Dad would have a fit if he saw me in this! Especially if he knew I was going to be swimming with a boy I fancied.'

Carrie gave her a cheeky wink. 'Less is more around here. You've got a great body. What's to hide?'

Niamh put on an obviously fake posh accent and pointed at Carrie's bikini, which barely covered anything at all. 'One doesn't flaunt one's assets with such blatant exhibitionism in England.'

They both laughed.

'Well, it's a good job we're not in England then,' Carrie said. 'Come on. Let's go through the living area to the deck and do a bit of flauntin'. I'm bettin' Tony will change pretty quick when he sees you go by.'

Niamh felt her cheeks flush with embarrassment, but she couldn't think of a suitably quick reply. Tony was still glued to his computer screen and Niamh could hear a distorted voice coming from it. Niamh started towards him, eager to see what he was looking at, but Carrie immediately took her by the arm and steered her towards the patio door. Tony glanced round briefly and Niamh was sure she saw his eyes widen as he saw her. She felt her chest tighten. He was quick to look back at the screen. Was he worried that she might think he was staring?

'You not comin', then?' Carrie teased.

'Yeah. I'll be right there,' he replied, glancing round at Niamh again and flashing a smile at her. 'I just googled the Hutchison Effect and found some videos of his experiments on YouTube. You need to take a look at this later. Experiments aside, this dude has serious mad scientist hair that's bound to give you a laugh!'

'So what sort of things does he do on these videos?' Niamh asked, pausing by the door. She was tempted to shake off Carrie and temporarily abandon swimming to check it out.

'He keeps on about somethin' called zero point energy and by puttin' different stuff into a strong magnetic field, he makes it do weird stuff. It's freaky, but hey – the clips ain't goin' nowhere.'

'So what's the connection with the Philadelphia Project?'

Tony clicked the pause icon and got to his feet. 'I'll tell you in the pool,' he said. 'Be right there.' And he left the living area at a run.

'Told you,' Carrie whispered.

'I reckon he just needed the toilet,' Niamh suggested, playing down his speedy exit.

Carrie gave her a knowing smile and although Niamh tried to remain outwardly indifferent, secretly she hoped Carrie was right.

'Perhaps I should just take a look at the video,' she added, taking half a step back towards the computer.

'No! Swim! Now! Come on. The sooner we get in, the sooner I'll let you come back and look at the freaky scientist!'

Stepping out from the air-conditioned living room, the heat hit like a sledgehammer. Niamh wasted no time in heading for the water. The Dales' pool was a similar size to the one at her father's house in Summerland. Without knowing how deep it was, Niamh did not want to risk diving in. Instead, she walked to the edge and stepped straight off the side to drop into the water. Allowing her legs to fold as her feet found the bottom of the pool, she stayed under the water for a few seconds before drifting back to the surface.

The temperature of the water was perfect. Cool enough to be refreshing, yet warm enough not to take her breath away. As she broke the surface, she stroked her hair back out of her eyes. It felt a guilty pleasure. Leaping high and curling into a ball, Carrie bombed into the water beside her with a tremendous splash for her size.

'You're a maniac!' Niamh gasped as Carrie surfaced. 'You couldn't have got much closer.'

Carrie just grinned and pushed off into an easy crawl stroke to the deep end of the pool where she paused, holding on to the edge. 'Race?' she asked.

It felt frivolous and wrong to even contemplate having fun while the boys were lost and her dad was being held by the police for a crime Niamh knew he hadn't committed, but it did not look as if Carrie was going to let her get back to the search without letting off some steam. Niamh paused a moment before answering. Perhaps if she raced, that would be enough.

'You're on,' she agreed. 'How far?'

'Four lengths OK?'

'Sounds good to me.'

Niamh swam to the deep end using a gentle breaststroke. No sooner had her hands touched the end than Carrie said, 'Ready set go!' as fast as she could, and pushed off.

Taken by surprise, Niamh took a split second to react and follow. *Cheat!* she thought instinctively. Then she mentally laughed at her reaction, realising that she would probably have tried something similar if she'd known Carrie a little better.

Concentrating, Niamh powered forward, digging hard with her cupped hands and kicking as fast as she could. Without goggles, it was hard to see much. She squinted, trying to assess if the water was going to be deep enough at the shallow end for a tumble turn. It was and she flipped, pushing away hard from the wall and giving several strong dolphin kicks before breaking the surface again.

She could feel that she had pulled alongside Carrie, but it was hard to tell if the American girl was aware of her yet. The pool was not long. She barely took a handful more strokes before she flipped again. Although Carrie wasn't using tumble turns, she was knifing through the water at an impressive pace. As Niamh flipped through the final turn, she could tell she had the edge, but without her superior turning technique, it would have been much tighter.

Touching first, Niamh looked up to see Carrie make her final stroke and touch. The sound of clapping made her look round. Tony was standing on the side with a broad smile on his face. He was wearing a pair of Bermuda shorts with a tropical beach pattern. They suited his golden skin and bleach-blond hair perfectly.

'Nice win!' he said. 'There's not many girls around here that can beat Carrie in the water. You swim well.'

'I like swimming. It's one of the few sports that I get on with.'

'It shows,' Carrie panted, placing a friendly hand on Niamh's shoulder. 'Great swim! You'd give Tony a good race. I never beat him, but I think you'd have a chance.'

'If you think I'm good, you should see my brother,' Niamh replied. 'He's far better than me. In fact, he's irritatingly good at most sports.'

'Good-looking?' Carrie asked, tilting her head slightly to one side and giving a suggestive smile.

'He's my brother! How do I answer that? If I say he's drop-dead gorgeous, will it help you stay focused on looking for him?'

Carrie laughed. 'Of course!' she said.

'In that case he's drop-dead gorgeous and a sucker for a blonde with an American accent.'

'Now you've got her attention!' Tony laughed.

He jumped into the pool to join them, and for the next twenty minutes the three of them played a variety of games that involved either chasing a ball, or each other, around the pool. All were noisy.

Despite Niamh's strong initial desire to get straight back to the search, she found the laughter and enthusiasm of the Dales infectious. It was not long before she was drawn fully into the games and laughing along with them, especially whenever she and Carrie ganged up on Tony to beat him. He pretended to look hurt at times, but he was clearly play-acting. Indeed, it was such fun that she stayed in the pool far longer than she intended and with all the noise they were making, none of them noticed the front doorbell ring.

Tessa could hear squeals of laughter and splashing noises coming from the Dales' pool. She rang the bell again, but knew she was wasting her time. Tony and Carrie would never hear it above the racket. Was it just the two of them making all that noise? She couldn't tell. Still angry with Tony for abandoning her in Key West yesterday, she turned to leave.

'Damn you, Tony!' she muttered. 'Why do I keep chasing you? You're not that much of a catch. I can do better than you.'

Tessa strode away from the front door determined to leave, but she only got halfway down the driveway when she paused. Where else would she go today? Annoyed as she was with Tony, she itched to join him and Carrie in the pool. She was wearing a bikini under her clothes. Surely it wouldn't hurt to slip around the house and join them? Hesitating a moment longer, she made her decision.

Doing her best to paste a friendly smile on her lips, she turned and marched back up the driveway and round the side of the house.

CHAPTER ELEVEN

The eyes were racing towards them through the darkness. Sam raised his rifle, gritting his teeth and feeling for the safety catch.

'Don't shoot!'

The voice in the darkness was Nathan's and the two raptors speeding along the passageway towards the beleaguered party were Edison and Crick. A red-filtered torch rounded a corner and danced along behind them. Sam heaved a sigh of relief and lowered his rifle, his heart pounding.

'Nathan?' Claire shouted between firing controlled bursts down the passageway ahead. 'Give me some good news. We can't go this way.'

A sudden flash of bright orange light flared along the subterranean corridor behind them and a deafening BOOM echoed in its wake. A sudden blast of dust and small debris driven by the shock wave blew through the party. Sam barely managed to keep his feet under him. Others were not so fortunate. Sherri tumbled backward, colliding with David and Callum and taking all three of them down to form a shadowy heap. As he reeled, Sam shook his head to try to clear the ringing in his ears from the shock of the explosion, while a glowing after-image of the flash moved wherever he looked. With their extra bulk and low centres of gravity, all of the raptors held their balance.

'I'm sorry, Claire, but I lost Watson,' Nathan gasped, staggering to a halt about ten paces away. 'There was nothing we could do to save him. There were too many of them. That blast should've slowed 'em. With any luck, the charge will have collapsed the passage and trapped them on the other side.'

'Damn it, Nathan!' Claire cursed. She fired a longer burst that spoke volumes about her frustration. 'You should have been more careful! You were supposed to be investigating the alarms, not engaging in firefights. Not only that, but you've just sealed our only way out of here.'

'No,' he replied. 'The ancillary southern loop should still be open. I blew the tunnel beyond the entrance. Follow me, but be ready in case any of them were quick enough to make it through.'

'OK. In that case, you take the lead. Me 'n' Alex'll hold this lot off,' she ordered.

Everyone was back on their feet again and they began to move. But even with Sherri and Nathan shining their filtered torches, it was hard to see more than a few metres through the dust that now filled the passageway in the direction of the blast. Sam held his arm across his mouth and nose, using the sleeve of his shirt as a filter. Although it made a difference, there was no avoiding the dust. His eyes streamed tears and he blinked and squinted in an effort to see what was happening.

Within seconds, everyone was coughing, including the raptors. The sound they made was short and sharp, sounding more like a bark than a human cough. Between the noisy, sporadic gunfire, all the coughing and the oppressive, dust-filled darkness, Sam began to imagine the walls of the tunnel squeezing in on him.

It was horrible. The more he coughed, the more he wanted to cough. He heard someone retch, though he couldn't tell who it was. Following the dim light of Nathan's torch through the murk, he stumbled forward. They moved slowly. Cautiously. And it was well that they did.

Without warning, a dark shadow leapt towards Nathan's torch. It was unclear how Nipper anticipated the attack, but somehow he did. Exploding forward in an astonishing dive past Nathan, the raptor intercepted the attacker in mid-flight, deflecting its charge into the wall. The impact was brutal and both went down in a dark, rolling mass of teeth and claws. Sam did not see how Nipper dispatched his opponent, but whatever he did was quick and effective.

With the Imperium raptor dead, Nipper got to his feet slowly and raised his hands in case one of the humans with guns mistook him for the attacker in the poor light.

Nathan gave a grunt that Sam guessed was 'Thanks' in raptor language, and he took the lead again. This time, Nipper took up position next to Nathan and they moved forward a little faster.

They pressed on into the dusty darkness to the previous bend. At the corner, Nathan stopped and Sam could just see the red glow of his torch playing across the tunnel wall. There was a scraping sound and a whispered order to follow on.

The branch passage that Nathan led them into was so narrow that it forced the party to switch to moving in single file. Sam had never been afraid of the dark, or of enclosed spaces, but he could feel the tension building in his body and mind. He wanted to get out of the tunnels soon. It seemed likely that if they were forced to keep fighting running battles in these dark underground walkways, Watson would not be their last casualty. He didn't want to think about who might be next.

'Where are we going, Sherri?' he whispered. 'Or are we running blind?'

'We've got a secondary HQ hidden a good distance away from the city,' she answered, keeping her voice equally as quiet. 'The facilities there are basic, but it's well concealed. Don't panic, Sam. Claire and Nathan know what they're doing. The Imperium have been trying to catch them for years and never come close. They'll get us out of here. You'll see.'

'I'm not panicking.'

It was true. He wasn't panicking. But he knew it would not take much to tip him over the edge. He felt coiled tight, as if he was ready to explode at any second. Sam could not imagine the Imperium raptors taking kindly to the losses they had sustained today. If by kidnapping David last night they had stirred the hornets' nest, today's events would make the Imperium hierarchy more determined than ever to catch the rebels.

He heard the scraping sound again. It came from behind him this time. Had the entrance to this passage been concealed? He wasn't sure. However, the sound of Claire's shooting had ceased and by unspoken agreement, everyone was now trying to move as silently as possible. It seemed likely that they were in a section of the underground labyrinth that the Imperium raptors might not know how to access. Surely it would not take them long to find the entrance? It could not have been far from where Nathan had set his charges. The raptors that Claire had been holding at bay with her gunfire would soon realise that their quarry was gone and that there had to be another exit from the tunnel.

Nathan led the way at speed. No one spoke again for a long time, though there were still some stifled and muffled coughs. Minutes stretched as they pressed into the silent darkness and Sam lost all sense of how far they had travelled and how long it had taken them. The urgency of their pace did not let up, but the longer they pushed on into the darkness, the more Sam felt as if they weren't going anywhere. It was as if they were on a gigantic treadmill in the dark. The only thing that gave any sense of progress was an occasional bend, most of which seemed to be to the right. There did not seem to be any interconnecting passageways.

'Pick it up, Nathan,' Claire called suddenly from the back of the group. 'I think we've got company inbound again.'

'I'll do my best,' he replied.

The next thing Sam knew, he was jogging . . . and then running to keep up. The passageway kinked to the right again, but this time he was going so fast that he didn't see the bend coming. Grazing his left arm on the wall, Sam spun round, barely keeping his feet as he did so. He cursed. The skin burned where he had scraped it.

'This is fun!' Callum panted from behind. 'Remind me . . . to write . . . a suggestion . . . email . . . to Disney . . . when I get home. Something . . . like this . . . would make . . . a great . . . ride . . . at Disneyworld.'

Despite the fear that gnawed in his belly and the pain emanating from his upper arm, Sam found himself smiling as he ran. Callum could find humour in any situation.

'They're closing!' Claire's warning was followed by a short burst of deafening weapons fire. The shocking staccato stabs of sound set Sam's heart pounding again. In the confined space of the narrow passageway, the noise assaulted his ears.

The hulking shadow of Grunt ahead of him momentarily gained definition, illuminated by the flashes from behind. The raptor was pulling away, so Sam accelerated still further. He could feel more than hear the footfalls of David and Callum immediately behind him. They were flying along at a dangerous speed now. If there was a sudden bend in the passage, then hitting the wall at this speed was going to do a lot of damage. Sam pushed the thought from his mind and concentrated on following the moving shadows in the dim red glow ahead.

A sudden widening of the passageway took Sam by surprise. The air felt different in the wider tunnel. There was a fork ahead. Nathan raced into the left passage and Sam followed. There was another burst of gunfire from behind. The sound did not pound at Sam's ears with quite such shocking intensity this time.

Probably due to the wider space between the walls, he thought. They had covered soundwave theory in physics last year, but he couldn't remember much. *I bet Callum could give a precise explanation and somehow manage to make it funny!*

His throat was beginning to burn with the heat of his panting breath and he had the familiar dry, metallic taste of blood at the back of his tongue.

Callum might know his physics, but I bet he's hurting more than me right now.

He slowed, sensing the group ahead bunching up. They had reached a T-junction. Nathan led them to the left again. They could not have run more than a hundred metres before there was a sharp turn to the right. As Sam rounded the turn, he nearly ran into the back of Grunt, who was slowing to a stop. They had reached a dead end.

What now? he wondered. *Had Nathan taken a wrong turn? Were they trapped?*

'Hold this for me,' Nathan ordered someone ahead.

Sam craned his neck to see what was going on. Nathan was climbing up the side wall. Suddenly, a shaft of daylight stabbed down, causing Sam to squint and look away. It was blindingly bright. There was a slight pause and then Nathan called out again.

'It's all clear. Everyone up. Fast as you can!'

They surged forward. Grunt passed up first one, then the other ammunition box, and began to climb. As he shot up the wall like a spider, Sam realised there was a set of what looked like half-hoops driven into the wall to form a ladder. Eyes watering in the glare of daylight, he put his head through the rifle sling, positioning it across his back, and followed. He emerged into a small open area within a sea of waist-height ferns. No sooner had he got his head and shoulders out of the opening than he was grabbed by one of the raptors, dragged to one side and placed in a sitting position next to Sherri. Everyone else was also sitting or crouched down below the level of the fern tops.

Blinking fast, Sam watched as David and Callum

were given the same treatment. Nathan was talking to Edison in raptor language. He clicked and growled with unmistakable urgency. Edison appeared to be arguing, but Nathan looked adamant. Newton emerged from the hole. A distant burst of muffled gunfire came from below. It sounded so much further away than it had in the tunnel. How far behind was the rearguard?

'Each of you climb on one of the raptor's backs,' Nathan ordered. 'They can run far faster than we can. Edison will lead the way.'

'What about Mum?' Sam asked.

'She'll follow with Alex and Einstein. There's no time for discussion. Let's go!'

Nipper crouched down next to Sam and beckoned for him to climb up. Sam did as he was told, putting his arms round the raptor's neck and clamping his legs round his middle. Callum went with Grunt, who had picked up the two heavy ammunition boxes again, and Newton took David. The would-be aviator looked deathly pale. Nathan teamed with Edison and Sherri with Crick. There was more gunfire below. It sounded a little closer, but Nathan had no intention of waiting for them. He grunted and Edison set off at a bounding run through the ferns.

Nipper and the others followed and Sam realised

instantly that he was in for a most uncomfortable ride. The rifle he had slung across his back bounced with every footfall, banging hard against his back. Within a minute, he was wishing he'd never offered to carry one at all. Although it had provided a measure of comfort in the dark tunnels under the city, if they were attacked now it was more likely to prove a liability than an asset.

With their ultra-powerful legs, the raptors powered through the ferns as if they were no obstacle at all. Sam had ridden horses whose flat-out gallop had been slower than they were running and he was forced to wonder just how fast a raptor could run when unencumbered.

I wonder if they have races? he wondered. *A raptor version of the Olympics maybe? Now that would be a sight to see!*

He tried to look over his shoulder for any sign of his mother, but he couldn't turn his head far enough. They were covering ground at a tremendous rate and the hulking outer walls of the city were already less menacing. There was woodland ahead. Once they entered the trees, there would be no chance of seeing if the others were following.

Grunt suddenly gave one of the characteristic guttural noises that had earned him his nickname. Nipper gave a double-click response and as they reached the edge of the trees, both raptors stopped. Grunt dropped the two ammunition boxes and Nipper took a turn carrying them. While they did the exchange, Sam craned his neck round for one last look behind. He could see all the way to the city walls, but there was no sign of anyone following. Where were they?

'Come on, Mum!' he breathed. 'Please. You said you weren't going to lose me again. Don't break that promise!'

CHAPTER TWELVE

As she approached the corner at the rear of the house, Tessa stopped. She had intended to march round and pretend to be all hurt that they hadn't answered the doorbell, but instinct made her hesitate before she launched straight out into view. Instead, she paused and peeped first.

She was surprised to see another girl with them. Who was she? All Tessa could see was the back of her head, but it was instantly obvious that Tony had eyes for her. She ducked back out of sight.

'So that's the reason you ditched me in a hurry yesterday!' she muttered, her insides twisting with fury and her mind racing. 'You *blew me off for her. Well, that's it! I've had it with you, Tony Dale.*'

She turned to leave, but found she couldn't resist taking one last peek to see if she could get a better look at this mystery girlfriend of Tony's. Keeping down low, she peered round the corner again. All she could see was the girl's dark brown hair.

'Come on!' she muttered. 'Turn around. Let's get a proper look at you.'

Tony made a playful lunge towards the girl and she dived under the water in a bid to escape. Carrie was laughing with delight as he caught the girl by the ankle and hauled has backwards. She surfaced, spluttering, her hair covering her face. Suddenly she raked it back with her fingers and Tessa drew a sharp intake of breath as recognition dawned. She pulled back out of sight again.

'The English runaway!' she breathed.

She'd changed her hair colour, but there was no mistaking her. *So you were hiding her after all*, she thought, as her lips pulled tight into a malicious smile. *Well, that's a mistake you'll live to regret.*

Tessa reached into her pocket and pulled out her mobile. She flipped open the cover intending to dial the police, but then she paused. *No,* she thought. *They'll be able to trace the call back to me. I'll use the call box. Then the police can take her back to where she belongs.*

Smiling to herself, she backed away from the corner, turned and strode away with a spring in her step.

'OK, OK!' Niamh laughed. 'I give in. Stop trying to drown me. How about telling us about this thing you were looking at on YouTube?'

'Oh, yeah, the Hutchison Effect,' Tony drawled. 'It's pretty freaky stuff. I didn't watch much, but I'm goin' to take a look at some more when we go back in. This Hutchison guy had set up an area where he could create intense electromagnetic fields and he was puttin' different materials into it to see what it would do. There was stuff levitatin', metal bars twistin' and fracturin', one type of material fusin' with another, but in a weird way. And he mentioned stuff disappearin' altogether, but I didn't see that happen, which made me think about the Philadelphia project and the disappearin' ship.'

'What? You mean you didn't wait to see the end of the clip?' Carrie taunted.

'It was long. . .'

'And somethin' more interestin' caught your eye?'

Niamh blushed and looked away after Tony glanced across at her just as her eyes turned towards him.

'Ignore her, Niamh,' he said, apparently not at all embarrassed by his sister's suggestion. 'She's a big tease. But if it'll make you feel better, sis, then yes, someone much more interestin' caught my eye. Do you have a problem with that?'

'Not at all,' Carrie giggled. 'Just wanted to hear you say it, that's all.'

'Maybe we should go back in and take a look at this clip,' Niamh suggested, trying to divert the conversation. 'It sounds like it might have possibilities.'

'Sure,' Tony agreed. 'I glanced in the notes as well. Your dad's written quite a lot about Hutchison. He cross-referenced him with stuff to do with Atlantis as well.'

'Atlantis?' Snatches of things her father had said in passing about the mythical city flashed into Niamh's mind. 'I remember Dad telling me there was some evidence that Atlantis might have been somewhere near the Bahamas.'

'Well, I don't know about that,' Tony replied. 'But since you turned up on Monkey Island, this summer vacation's gotten a whole lot more interestin'. Disappearin' boats, UFOs, electromagnetic experiments, Atlantis – if it gets much weirder, I think I'm gonna totally freak out.'

'Yeah, 'n' we'd notice the difference because…?' Carrie teased.

'Listen, Carrie, I'm not joking,' Niamh said, her excitement rising. 'Dad's tried to tell me about something called the Bimini Road a couple of times, but I didn't pay much attention because he frequently gets excited about stuff to do with the Triangle. I don't know why, but the hairs on the back of my neck are prickling. What if there *is* something linking all this stuff together? Electromagnetism, Atlantis, the UFOs . . . all of it.'

Carrie sighed. 'I guess that's recess over with then.'

'Would you like me to sound the bell for you?' Niamh suggested. 'I do a pretty good bell. . . !'

Carrie scooped a wave of water over Niamh with both hands and all three of them laughed. They swam to the edge of the pool and climbed from the water. Niamh grabbed her towel from where she'd left it on a sunbed and wrapped it round her shoulders. Although it was steaming hot outside, she knew that the moment she stepped through the door back into the air-conditioned living area of the house, she'd be shivering. The lure of the sunbed was strong, but as nice as it would be to lie out and let the hot sun do the work of drying her body, she really felt like they might be on to something. Maybe she was getting closer to discovering the truth about what had happened to Sam and Callum, and maybe even about her mother's disappearance.

Sure enough, as she crossed the threshold into the house, she shuddered. It was like stepping inside a walk-in refrigerator.

'Race you to the shower!' Carrie challenged.

'No. It's your shower. You go first,' Niamh replied.

'OK, I'll be quick.'

'You'd better be or I'll lob a jug of iced water over the top of the door.'

'You wouldn't!'

Tony laughed at Carrie's shocked expression. 'You know what, sis? I think she just might.'

A few minutes later, Carrie announced the shower was free. Niamh smiled to herself, shaking her head and wondering if the threat of the cold water had actually made Carrie shower faster. She stepped under the powerful jets of hot water and the luxurious heat of the power shower set her body alight and tingling all over. Again, the temptation to linger was strong, but she concentrated on rinsing her hair and body clean of the chemical-rich pool water as efficiently as possible.

When she had dried and dressed, she walked back through to the living area where she found Tony already at his laptop and Carrie bustling around the kitchen preparing food.

'Pizza OK?'

'More than OK with me,' Niamh replied, giving Carrie a broad smile of approval.

She looked at the clock on the wall and was surprised to find it was nearly two in the afternoon.

No wonder she was hungry. The day was fast disappearing, but between them they had managed to scan through a lot of her father's notes. There were huge sections that they had not opened yet, but she could not help feeling they had made some progress.

I wonder what Dad would think if he could see us now, she mused.

Thinking about him made her heart sink. He would be back in England now. Would the police be holding him in a cell or would he be allowed to go home? Niamh had a horrible feeling that it would be the former. What would it be like in a police cell? She had only ever seen them on TV shows and the cells she had seen were always bleak, soulless places. She could only imagine what it would feel like to have to spend any time in such a place.

She shuddered. *Poor Dad,* she thought. *And he's probably worried sick about me on top of everything else. While here I am – having fun and living in comfort with friends. If only there was some way of letting him know that I'm safe and well and doing my best to get him out of there.*

'I've found that thing you were talkin' about, Niamh,' Tony announced, startling her from her morose thoughts. 'The Bimini Road – discovered by some oceanography professor dude called Valentine.' He looked up at the ceiling and tapped his temples

155

with his forefingers before looking round at Niamh. 'It says here that Valentine was divin' in shallow water off somewhere called Paradise Point on the island of Bimini when he found a whole bunch of huge polyg... polygon... polygonal stones... jeez! That's a mouthful!'

'And that's supposed to be the remains of Atlantis?' Carrie asked. 'How's that help us?'

'There's something about a Bimini Wall here as well,' he added. 'But it doesn't claim they found Atlantis. I've not read it all yet. Hang on.'

'From what I remember Dad telling me, there's people that think the Atlanteans used an unusual form of energy that might have led to their eventual destruction,' Niamh recalled. 'Dad said something about a popular clairvoyant in the 1920s who made several predictions and readings about it that have proved spookily accurate. He also said something about energy from crystals, but I don't remember it clearly enough to see how it fits in with the Bimini stuff.'

'Hmm. I'm guessin' this cross-reference to someone called Edgar Cayce is what you're talkin' about,' Tony said.

'Cayce, that's it!' Niamh exclaimed.

'Interesting. . .' Tony murmured.

'What?'

'I've just flicked through to the bit about him and it seems he talked about the Atlanteans using electromagnetism and some sort of crystal energy source. Hutchison demonstrated takin' energy from a form of crystalline stone that he claimed would effectively last forever on that YouTube clip. We've started going in circles here.'

Niamh shook her head. 'No,' she said. 'I think we're on to something. I'm not sure exactly what, but something about this feels right. I read a few accounts this morning by those who have seen strange things, and of the last words from pilots before they vanished that mentioned compasses going crazy. A powerful electromagnetic force could cause that.'

'Accordin' to Hutchison, if the field is strong enough, it can damage metals, make different materials fuse together, cause strange electrical fogs and maybe even affect space and time,' Tony observed, his tone thoughtful. 'The notes say that he thought the potential power source could be enormous. If he's right and the Atlanteans tapped into somethin' they didn't understand well enough to control, you could see how they might have suffered a major disaster and wiped themselves out. But if somethin' from an ancient sunken city is causin' things and people to vanish, why would it affect such a massive area of ocean? I don't get it.'

'You're right, that doesn't make sense,' Niamh agreed, frowning. 'You'd expect it to be much more localised. Unless...'

'Unless?'

'Unless Atlantis was more than just one city,' she suggested. 'I mean, don't the legends talk of Atlantis as a civilisation, rather than just a city? A civilisation wouldn't live in a single city, would it?'

They all fell silent as they considered the implications of what Niamh was suggesting. The idea that there might be not one, but any number of sunken cities containing potentially dangerous sources of energy was mind-blowing.

A glorious waft of cooking pizza reached Niamh and she drew in a deep breath. Her stomach rumbled, but she was determined not to let the temptation of food distract her. They were close to a major breakthrough. She was sure of it.

A sudden loud knock at the front door made them all jump. They all looked at one another, the unspoken question *Who's that?* hanging in the air.

'You'd better get outta sight,' Carrie suggested in a hushed voice. 'Get into my room. Hurry!'

Niamh flitted across the living area towards the bedroom. As she went, she saw a shadow at the window and looked across straight into the eyes of a policeman. It was the same man that had followed her the day the police had taken her father in for questioning. Recognition sparked in his eyes immediately and Niamh froze. Her mind whirled with options. Going to the bedroom was now out of the question. It was a dead-end trap. Should she run out through the back? Was there time?

'It's her!' she heard the policeman call. 'She's inside. I saw her.'

She turned and started towards the glass doors to the pool area and then froze again. Another policeman had appeared there as well. The *thump, thump, thump* at the front door was repeated. It was no good. There was no way out.

'There's cops all round the house!' Tony exclaimed. 'What should I do?'

'There's nothing you can do,' Niamh sighed. 'It's over. You'd better go and answer the door before they decide to force it open. I'll have to go with them.'

'No! We can tell them you're a friend stayin' with us. . .' Carrie said.

'The cop at the front window recognised me, Carrie,' Niamh said, giving her a grateful smile. 'They're not going to leave without me. Don't get into any more trouble on my behalf. Don't worry. I'll be fine. They're not going to hurt me.'

Carrie ran across and threw her arms round

Niamh in a dramatic hug. Niamh laughed and hugged her back. She couldn't imagine Beth being so flamboyant with her emotions. Tony went to the door and answered it.

'Hello, officer. What can I do for you?'

'We've come to collect Miss Niamh Cutler,' he replied. 'I understand she's inside.'

'I'm coming,' Niamh called out. 'Give me a moment.'

She gave Carrie one last squeeze and eased free of her embrace. They walked together to the front door. Tony's expression was one of helplessness.

'Thanks for everything,' she said to Tony and Carrie. 'I'll email you both when I get home.' She turned to the policeman at the door. 'I don't suppose you'd let me stay long enough to eat some of the pizza, would you?'

He did not look amused. 'No tricks this time, miss,' he said, shaking his head. 'You've caused a lot of trouble and wasted a lot of police time. Don't make things worse.'

'Thought not,' she said, pursing her lips. 'There is just one quick thing I need to do before we go though.'

She stepped up to Tony and kissed him. It was not a long kiss, but it was full on the lips. He barely had time to respond before it was over. When she stepped back, she nearly laughed at his mixed expression of surprise and pleasure.

'Until next time,' she said, and stepped out through the door.

CHAPTER THIRTEEN

It was like something out of an Enid Blyton adventure story, Sam decided, peering around the cave – but not as comfortable.

'Cool place!' Callum announced, sounding excited as he stepped into the cavern, squeezing past Sam. 'Not as stylish as the HQ, but it has a certain atmosphere.'

'You mean it's damp, dark and cold,' Sherri observed, sounding grumpy.

'I was looking at the positives,' he replied with a shrug. 'It's certainly well hidden.'

'With no back door to escape out of if they do find us,' she replied.

'Do you really think the Imperium are likely to find us here? What sort of tracking abilities do they have?'

'No more than any other raptors, I suppose – just an enhanced sense of smell and a hunter's instinct,' she said coldly.

Callum had no answer to that.

Just then a ball of light began to glow at the back of the cave and Sam looked over to see Newton busily tinkering with some odd-looking machinery that was emitting the glimmer. Under the gently brightening artificial light, the full extent of the cave became clear. It extended some way back, though the area that was habitable was limited. The stream that had carved out the cavern bubbled through the centre to the front wall of rock, where it dropped into a dark hole with a constant rushing, splashing sound, only to emerge again through the tumble of rocks at the base of the valley about twenty-five metres below. Two sets of flat-topped stepping stones had been carefully placed to form paths across the water.

Sam estimated the roof of the cave to be about three times his height across most of the width and length of the open space, which meant comfortable headroom even for the raptors. The floor to either side of the stream was by no means flat, with both sides gently sloping down towards the water. However, the lumps and bumps across the floor had been worn smooth, presumably by the running water.

163

Access to the cave was concealed behind a tongue of rock halfway up the valley's end wall. Getting up to the entrance had involved a tricky climb for the humans. The raptors had made it look easy, but had not wanted to risk carrying the rest of the party up.

Unlike the main HQ, this place had been furnished with the absolute bare essentials, which apparently did not include any form of beds that Sam could see. He wondered how long it would take Callum to spot that. He would not mind betting that David noticed it before Callum did.

Rather than heading into the cave with the others, Sam returned to the entrance where Nipper was crouched, keeping watch.

'Any sign of Mum and the others?' he asked, taking care to pronounce his words clearly.

Nipper shook his head.

'Sssssam imm,' the raptor said, pointing inside. He then pointed at himself and at his eyes. Sam understood perfectly.

'OK,' he said. 'I'll go inside while you keep watch for them. Thanks again, Nipper . . . for everything. Let me know when you see them, OK?'

The raptor bared his pointed teeth in a grin that a few days before would have terrified the life out of him. Now Sam found it reassuring. Nipper had gone out of his way to help Sam and Callum from the first time they had met. Sam was still not sure he understood why, but he felt deeply grateful for the raptor's unwavering support.

Feeling better, Sam went back into the cave. To his surprise, he found David and Callum warming themselves by an electric fire and Sherri heating water on what looked like a basic electric hob.

'Look at this, Sam,' Callum said enthusiastically. 'Heaters, light and everything! I thought we'd be roasting food over an open fire, but no. According to Nathan, they've got their own mini-generator outside concealed among the rocks. It's one of those magnetic energy converters that we saw from the train on the way to the city, but smaller. You've got to hand it to the raptors. Some of their tech is seriously clever.'

'Don't get too excited,' Sherri grumbled. 'There's not much in the way of food stored here, and I've never managed to find a comfortable spot to sleep yet. Does anyone else want a drink?'

'Do you have any coffee?' David asked.

'What do you think this is? A café? No, we don't have coffee. I can make you an approximation of tea, though I don't recommend it personally. Otherwise, it's hot water or a hot fruit drink, which

165

is slightly more palatable than the tea. I do have some sweetener here if you find it too tart.'

'I'll try the fruit drink then, please,' David said.

Sam opted for hot water, while Callum followed David's lead. Nathan declined all options, preferring instead to sip something from a hip flask that he had attached to his belt. Although Sam did not know for sure, he felt it a fair bet that whatever was in the flask had a high alcohol content.

While Sherri was preparing the drinks, Edison and Crick were busy fiddling with another strange piece of technology. They were clicking and growling at each other in a conversation that sounded distinctly argumentative. Sam listened and watched the body language of the two as they bickered like two old women until Newton intervened with a loud grunt that set Nathan choking. He had been in the process of taking a sip from his flask, but whatever Newton had said set him coughing and laughing simultaneously.

Newton strode over to the piece of technology that the other two raptors had been tinkering with, shoved them out of the way and gave the box an almighty thump with the side of his fist. Something flickered in the air at the back of the cave. He hit it again and the flicker solidified. It was a holographic image similar to the one they had seen in the station.

Newton glared at Edison and Crick for a moment, gave another grunt, turned and left them to play with the settings. Even without a translation, Sam found himself grinning. Nathan was reduced to fits of laughter, but Edison and Crick ignored him. Sam did not need to be an expert in raptor body language to know they were not amused.

'It's hard not to like Newton's style,' Callum commented. 'If in doubt, give it a clout!'

'I know,' Sam agreed, chuckling. 'He's my sort of scientist!'

'Look! It's the news,' David said, his eyes fixed on the holographic image. 'My abduction seems to be the main story,' he said, sounding pleased. 'As I suspected, the High Council of the Imperium have condemned it in the strongest terms. They have sworn to exact revenge on those who broke into the Imperium labs.'

'Is the newsreader saying anything about our fight under the city?' Callum asked.

'No,' David replied, shaking his head. 'It's all about how important my work is and the negative impact of the rebel group on raptor society. The Imperium are painting your group in the darkest possible light.'

'*Your* group?' Sam asked. 'So, after all you've seen and heard, you don't feel ready to join us?'

'I'm not sure,' David admitted, his eyes darting nervously around the cave. He seemed to be looking everywhere and anywhere to avoid making eye contact. 'I understand what Claire believes, though I'm not totally convinced by her explanation of how the crossing points between worlds are formed or that they're definitely being caused by the raptor technology. Why does it have to be something in this world that's causing it? From what I hear of the world you come from, the human population are doing some bad things to their environment. I still think the crossings may be due to something that's happening there.'

'It's true that our world isn't perfect and that humans are having an impact on the weather systems there, but when we crossed, the weather was fine in our world and we arrived in this world into the eye of a hurricane,' Sam said firmly. 'Everyone we've spoken to who has crossed appears to have arrived under similar circumstances. The evidence of those accounts alone makes it difficult to see another reason for the crossing points. They only seem to form at the eye of powerful storms in this world – not in ours.'

'Nevertheless,' David said, his defiance unwavering, 'I'm not ready to believe it yet. Until I can see it for myself, please forgive me for remaining sceptical.'

168

'So where do they keep your flying machine anyway?' Callum asked, changing the subject. 'I'd love to have a go at flying it.'

'Really? Have you flown before?' David asked, dodging the question.

'I've done some gliding.'

'Yeah,' Sam chuckled, 'but you should have seen him quaking in his seat when we took off out of Heathrow! Anyone would have thought it was his first time in the air.'

'Well, it was the first time I'd been up in a jet,' Callum said defensively. 'There's a world of difference between flying a glider and flying in something that's so big and heavy that it's difficult to see how it can possibly get off the ground. I was surprised at just how nervous it made me to be taking off without a control column to hold on to. Gliding's brilliant fun. No engines, just long wings and very basic controls. I'd love to go solo, but I'm not allowed until I'm sixteen.'

'Ah, yes! Gliding,' David said, a spark verging on fanaticism lighting in his eyes. Suddenly, he was more animated than Sam had yet seen him. 'I'm familiar with the principles. What type of launch system were you using? Bungee? Winch? Aerotow?'

'Most of my flights were winch-launched,'

Callum said. 'Which is a pretty spectacular way to get into the air. You climb really steeply. I've had a couple of aerotows as well. The club at Bicester had a tug, but it was more expensive so Dad didn't let me do it very often.'

'Fascinating,' David said. 'And did you manage to soar your machine?'

'Yeah, quite a few times. The longest I managed to stay up was nearly two hours.'

'Two hours of unpowered flight! Amazing!'

'Sorry, guys,' Sam interrupted. 'Winch-launch? Soar? Would you mind filling me in a bit? I lost you somewhere back at the start of this conversation.'

'Because it has no power source of its own, a glider can only fly if it is launched high enough into the air to make use of the air currents,' Callum explained. 'A winch-launch system is probably the most common. The glider is attached to a long cable, the far end of which is connected to a power-ful winch. When the glider is ready to get airborne, the winch operator winds the cable on to a huge drum, pulling the glider towards it very quickly. With the speed it gains from being pulled toward the winch, the glider is able to take off and convert the speed into height.'

Sam thought about that for a moment. 'But surely

the glider will eventually be pulled downward and crash into the winch if it's attached by a cable,' he observed.

Callum laughed. 'That would ruin your day, wouldn't it? There's a release mechanism in the cockpit and a fail-safe release to stop that from happening,' he explained. 'When you can't gain any more height, you release the cable and start looking for rising air currents called thermals. Catch one of those and you can ride it to gain more height – which is called soaring.'

'Really? Rising air currents are strong enough to lift an aircraft?' Sam asked, amazed.

'More than strong enough if the aircraft design is right,' David explained. 'Some updraughts, particularly around storm clouds, can be strong enough to hurl aircraft skyward with such force that they can be torn to pieces. But my latest design is superior to any glider. It makes use of both air currents and the natural magnetic field, allowing you to use both to generate lift and forward speed. So if there's no rising air, you can fall back on the electromagnetic generators to drive the fan on the back, which will keep you in the air and travelling fast enough that you can climb further if you wish.'

'Clever,' Callum acknowledged, pursing his lips thoughtfully and nodding. 'From what I saw, the design looked similar to some of the microlights we have back home, but the engine doesn't have the same irritating whine.'

'You say your *latest design,*' Sam noted. 'So how many different ones have you built?'

'Just two so far,' David replied. 'The first one flew well enough, but it struggled for power with the weight of a raptor underneath it. I had designed it with a human pilot in mind. It was only when we came to the test-flight stage that I discovered the raptor scientists had no intention of letting me pilot my flying machine.'

'And these flying machines are both kept in the same place?'

'Yes. In a purpose-built hangar just outside the main city wall.'

Sam looked at Callum, who looked back and nodded. 'It would be the next logical step,' he said.

'What?' David asked. 'What next logical step?'

'Stealing the machines of course,' Sam explained.

'But that's madness! They'll be expecting you for sure! You'd be walking straight into a trap!'

'True,' Sam agreed. 'But only if they think that we're not expecting a trap. But we *are* expecting a trap. So because we know that they know we'll be after the flying machines next, if we plan it well, we'll be able to allow for them knowing and still gain the advantage of surprise.'

David's brow furrowed as he tried to follow Sam's logic.

'Of course we'll have to wait until Mum gets back before we even begin to think about doing anything. Where *are* they, I wonder? I would have thought they would be here by now. I'm going to go and find Nipper again and see if there's any sign of them.'

'Sam. . .' Callum said slowly, his eyes wide and a note of horror in his voice.

'What?'

Callum pointed towards the back of the cave and the glowing light of the holographic projection. The colours of the moving images had a ghoulish green tinge to them, casting a sickly glow around the back of the cavern. Sam's breath caught in his throat as he recognised the setting. An angry mob of raptors was roaring and jostling towards the central tower at the middle of the City of the Imperium. Were they going to attack? Had the raptors turned against their leaders? Then it dawned on him – the crowd wasn't angry. They were roaring with wild triumph.

'No!' he breathed.

Three sorry-looking figures were being dragged along in the midst of the great pack of celebrating raptors. A cold chill ran through him and for a moment he thought he was going to be sick as a snake of fear twisted inside his belly. There was no mistaking the faces of Alex, Einstein and his mother. They had been captured.

CHAPTER FOURTEEN

Niamh's breath caught in her throat as she felt herself soaring through the air high above the ground. For a moment, it was as if the aircraft had vanished from around her and she was flying through the air without it, but the perspective was wrong. She was high up, but not flying-in-an-aircraft high. A rooftop was approaching fast and there were figures poised waiting to catch her as she raced through the air towards them. As suddenly as it had begun, so the feeling and image faded. She opened her eyes.

'Wow!' she breathed. 'What was that?'

It was most certainly not a memory and she had done nothing that she could think of to trigger that sort of image. It had to be another vision through her link to Sam. What on earth was he doing? She closed her eyes again and tried to reconnect her consciousness to Sam's, but it was no good. The clarity had gone and the details were already slipping away from her. The moment had passed. She glanced at her watch. They were only two hours into the flight and there was a very long way to go. She glanced out of the window and ground her teeth in frustration.

'I don't know what on earth you're doing, Sam,' she whispered. 'But please don't go getting yourself killed before I find you!'

For some time afterwards, Niamh tried reading a book, but found she couldn't concentrate on it. There was nothing on the in-flight entertainment system that she fancied watching or playing. It was going to be a long flight home to England. In the end, closing her eyes and with little expectation of success, she tried to sleep.

When she woke, her neck was stiff and her mouth was so dry that she felt sure someone must have drawn all her saliva out with tissues while she slept. The aircraft was descending. The pressure change in her ears must have been what had woken her, she realised.

The American police officer escort had barely spoken to Niamh during the entire flight back to England. Not that she had wanted conversation with him, but after an eight-hour overnight journey, dry mouth or not, she found she was itching to talk.

'So what happens to me now?' she asked him as the aircraft taxied towards the Heathrow terminal. 'Do I get handed over to the British police?'

'No,' he replied, without looking at her. 'One of your relatives is gonna meet you and take you home.'

'Oh joy!' she replied, piling as much sarcasm into the two words as she could manage. 'Can't you hand me over to the police instead?'

The policeman ignored her.

Niamh had no need to ask who would be collecting her. She didn't have many relatives to choose from. The one grandparent she had left alive on this side of the Atlantic was Grandma Cutler, and she didn't drive, so that ruled her out. This left one other close relative – Aunt Agatha – or Aunt Aggie, as she preferred to be called. Agatha was her dad's younger sister. She was nice enough, but every time Niamh saw her, she felt as if she was being inspected and there was always something in her aunt's expression that made Niamh feel she didn't meet her expectations. Her aunt's manner was almost, but not quite, sneering. As for Aunt Aggie's thirteen-year-old son, Archie, he was a pompous jerk of the highest order. The idea of living in the same house as him sent a shudder down Niamh's spine.

Agatha's husband Edward was lovely, but he was rarely at home. He was a high-flying businessman who spent more time jetting around the world to meetings and conferences than he did at home. Niamh didn't know exactly what he did, but there was no mistaking that he was successful and wealthy. Aunt Aggie's house was huge and she always seemed to be wearing the latest designer clothes. Archie never wanted for anything.

Niamh fell quiet again as she considered the likelihood that she would have to spend the rest of the summer holidays living with her aunt and her obnoxious cousin. The more she thought about it, the more her heart sank. Under normal circumstances, it would be unpleasant enough, but she had to continue searching for the truth about Sam and Callum's disappearance and she knew exactly what her aunt's response to that idea would be. In her eyes, searching would be the job of professionals and Niamh would be forced to stay at the house and be *ladylike*. The prospect of living with her strict aunt was unbearable. There had to be some way out of spending the rest of the summer with them. There *had* to be.

The aircraft came to a halt and before long Niamh was walking through the monstrous walkways of Heathrow, following the signs to Baggage Reclaim.

She found it quietly amusing that the man from the Monroe County Sheriff's Office insisted she stay in front of him at all times. She had told him on several occasions that she had no intention of running away again, but it appeared she had a reputation now and he was taking no chances.

For once, her bags were among the first to appear on the conveyor belt. She loaded them on to a baggage trolley and was then ushered through Customs to the Arrivals Lounge. Sure enough, Aunt Aggie was there waiting.

'Hello, Niamh.'

'Aunt Aggie!' she said, doing her best to sound pleased. 'Thanks for coming to collect me.' She gave her aunt a hug and then stood to one side to allow the policeman to check Agatha's identification. Once he was satisfied that everything was in order, he politely wished them a good day and left, walking off in the direction of Departures. Niamh did not envy him the flight home. Her back was stiff and while her bottom was not exactly numb, it felt strangely lifeless after sitting for so long.

'So what's all this I hear about you running away from the police, Niamh?' Agatha asked, as she led the way out of the terminal towards one of the nearby short-stay multi-storey car parks. 'What on

179

earth possessed you? Surely Matthew brought you up to know better than that?'

'Yes, he did,' said Niamh, keeping her voice humble. 'But I overheard the policemen who came to arrest him. They were talking as if Dad had murdered the boys and I know he didn't. I thought I could find Sam and Callum and prove Dad's innocence.'

'And what made you think you were any more qualified to do that than the police or the coast-guard, dear?' Agatha asked, her voice thick with condescension. 'Honestly! You could have been seriously hurt, or abducted, or . . . well, any number of horrible things might have happened to you. It doesn't bear thinking about. Especially with your poor brother already missing! And to steal a neigh-bour's boat! I thought you were the sensible one. I couldn't believe it when they told me. Now I want you to promise me that you won't do anything ridic-ulous like that while you're staying with me. No madcap adventures, Niamh. Your father is worried enough about your brother and everything that's happened since; he doesn't need a wayward daugh-ter to contend with too.'

'Yes, Aunt Aggie,' Niamh mumbled, keeping her head down and her eyes straight ahead as they entered the steel box of the car-park lift. 'I promise. How is Dad? Have you seen him? Can I go and visit?'

'I have seen him and I suppose he is as well as can be expected under the circumstances. The police are still holding him in custody while they question him. As far as I know, they've not charged him with anything yet, but there's no sign that they are ready to release him, and believe me, the prison where he's being held is no place for a young lady, Niamh.'

'I don't care if it's suitable, Aunt Aggie. I just want to see that he's all right.'

'Well, we'll see,' she said. 'Let's get you settled in first and then maybe we can talk about it again.' Her tone left Niamh in no doubt that what she actually meant was, 'Not over my dead body!'

'Do you think they will charge him? He's not done anything wrong. You know Dad. He wouldn't hurt anyone and especially not Sam.'

'I know. Perhaps you can tell the police that when they question you tomorrow.'

'Me?' Niamh squeaked. 'Will I have to go into a police station?'

'No. Nothing like that,' Agatha reassured her. 'They're going to come to the house tomorrow. Don't worry, Niamh. The detectives just want to hear your side of what happened, that's all.'

'But what if they twist what I say and use it against Dad?'

'Why would they want to do that?'

'I don't know, but I've seen them do things like that on TV sometimes.'

Agatha let out a bark of laughter and gave her a reproving look. 'I'm sorry, Niamh. I don't mean to mock you, but you really shouldn't believe everything you see on the television. Especially some of those police dramas. The police have no reason to frame Matthew. They're just trying to establish the facts, that's all.'

'Oh, OK then,' Niamh replied, realising that her aunt was never going to take her fears seriously. 'Will you be there? I'd rather not do it on my own.'

'I can be there if you want. I'm sure that will be fine.'

Agatha pressed the button for the fifth floor and the doors closed behind them. They emerged again in silence and she led them along the rows of cars. Fishing a set of keys out of her handbag, she pressed the remote central-locking button on the ignition key. There was a *beep* and the hazards on a large shiny green jaguar flashed once.

The car looked like it was new, but the personalised number plate, which read AGG 13, gave no clues as to exactly how new. *What a waste of money!* Niamh thought. *What does Aunt Aggie need a car like this for? It's ridiculous.*

Waste of money or not, having loaded her

suitcase into the boot, Niamh could not help admiring the soft leather as she settled into the passenger seat. She ran her fingertips over the material either side of her legs, enjoying the texture. She inhaled deeply. There was nothing quite like the scent of leather.

Agatha started the engine and the initial deep growl it gave as it fired into life dropped instantly to a soft purr that was barely audible. It was not hard to see how someone used to this sort of luxury would find Niamh's recent choice to become a fugitive so strange.

A high-pitched squeaky voice announced from her pocket, 'You have a text message. A tiny text message. Please read it.'

Aunt Aggie raised an eyebrow, but said nothing as Niamh pulled out her phone. It was from Beth. Texting her friend had been the first thing she'd done when the police had returned her phone to her just before they had left the US; she'd needed to check she'd not got her friend into trouble with the police for being in the Cutler house. But luckily, Beth had been quick enough to sneak out without being noticed – and, in fact, it had seemed to Niamh that she'd quite enjoyed the adventure!

Speak soon? Bx

Fingers flying around the keys, Niamh typed a quick response. *L8r. Just landed. Nx*

* * *

An hour later, they turned in through the black wrought-iron gates and drove up the sweeping gravel driveway to Aunt Aggie's house. The huge six-bedroomed property on the outskirts of Banbury was situated in an acre of landscaped gardens. Niamh had always enjoyed playing here with Sam when they were younger, as there were so many mature trees and bushes to climb and hide in. Where the drive split into a loop in front of the house, three large statues adorned the central island. But while they had looked impressive to her in the past, she now regarded them with a cynical eye.

Ridiculous and pretentious, she thought. *Who do they think they're impressing with this stuff? It's so over the top, it's laughable.* A smile spread across her face as she remembered the time Sam had convinced Archie that one of the statues was really a stone angel monster like the ones on *Doctor Who*. Poor Archie had spent the entire afternoon trying not to take his eyes off the statue in case it stole his life force and sent him back in time to live out his life in obscurity and poverty.

I wonder if he had nightmares about that afterwards, she thought, feeling a tiny seed of guilt deep inside for having not intervened. Sam could be mean at times, and Niamh had often found herself acting as his conscience. Mentally crushing the sensation of guilt under an imaginary foot, she rationalised that if anyone deserved to be the butt of one of her brother's pranks, it was the pretentious and annoying Archie.

Agatha swung the car round the loop and pulled to a stop in front of the wide stone steps that led up to the front door. They climbed out of the car and Niamh hauled her heavy case out of the boot. She had to carry it across to the steps, as the wheels were useless on the gravel. As she approached the front door, it opened and there was Archie with a big grin that exposed the heavy metal braces across his teeth. He had developed a nasty case of acne since she had last seen him, which made his hawkish face more unappealing than ever.

What planet does he think he's on? Niamh wondered as she realised she was staring at her cousin's clothing. He was wearing a pair of neatly pressed beige slacks, a thin green turtleneck pullover and what she could only describe as a plum-purple jacket over the top. His dark ginger hair had been slicked back with gel, presumably in an attempt to make him look sophisticated. The attempt had failed. He looked ridiculous.

'Hi, Archie. Nice threads,' she said, trying her best to sound genuine.

'Hello, Niamh. Thanks. It's good to see you again.'

The worst thing was, he sounded as if he meant it. She had hoped he would show no interest in her being here, but apparently, she was not going to get that lucky.

'Can I take your bag for you? It looks heavy.'

'Thanks, Archie, but I can manage.'

'Nonsense, Niamh!' Aunt Aggie interrupted. 'A young lady doesn't turn down a gentlemanly offer like that. Good boy, Archie. That was very polite of you. Please do take Niamh's bag for her and show her up to her room. Doubtless, she will want to have a wash after her long journey, so don't delay her with idle chatter, please. You can play together after she's had a chance to freshen up and change.'

Play together? Niamh thought, so incredulous that she was unable to keep her eyebrows from momentarily rising in disbelief. *You've got to be kidding! What do you think I am, five years old or something?* It took all her willpower to bite her tongue and hold back from pointing out that she was not interested in playing anything – especially with Archie. *Stay calm*, she told herself. *Keep a low profile. Alienating them will only make staying here worse.*

'A shower would be nice,' she admitted. 'Lead on, Archie. I can hear the water calling me.'

'And don't drag the case across the wooden floor, Archie,' Agatha warned. 'I don't want to find scratches later.'

'Don't worry, Mummy. I won't.'

Mummy? Niamh nearly choked. *Archie still calls his mother 'Mummy'! He dresses like some wannabe adult from the 1950s, yet he hasn't progressed his language past that of a little kid!* She lowered her gaze, covered her mouth with her hand and bit her lower lip to hide her amusement. *Maybe it's not his fault,* she thought. *It could be that he's not been allowed to grow up. Aunt Aggie is such a control freak.*

'It will have to be a bath, rather than a shower, I'm afraid,' he continued, extending the 'a' sound in the word 'bath' so much, it sounded like 'baaarth'. 'We don't have a shower in the guest bathroom yet. Daddy has talked about getting one fitted, but he's not got round to it. There should be plenty of hot water though.'

Oblivious to her amusement, he struggled along the hallway and up the stairs with her heavy case.

Poor Archie, she thought. *What have they done to you? You always were a pain in the backside, but the posh accent and the clothes are just too much. Sam and his friends would be merciless if they saw you now.*

'Not to worry,' she assured him. 'A bath will be fine.' She couldn't resist extending the 'a' sound a little to parody his accent, but if he noticed the mimicry, he showed no sign of it.

'Jolly good,' he grunted, heaving the case up the final steps to the long landing. 'Here you go. Second door on the right. Could you open it for me, please? Thanks. It's a nice room. The bathroom is opposite. Towels are on the end of the bed. Give me a shout when you're done. I'd love to hear about your adventures in America.' He looked over his shoulder and lowered his voice. 'Mummy says you stole a boat! Is that true?'

Niamh sighed and nodded. 'Yes, it's true,' she confirmed.

'Wow! How absolutely wizard!'

Wizard? Are you still overdosing on Biggles or is it The Famous Five?

'If you say so,' she said aloud. Archie put the case down at the end of the bed and looked at her expectantly like a dog waiting to be fed. 'Right. I'll see you later then,' she added in a not so subtle hint for him to go away.

'Yes. Yes, of course. Righty ho then. Cheerio for now.'

As the door closed behind him, Niamh fell back on to the bed and heaved a deep sigh. She stared at the ceiling for a moment and then closed her eyes and tried to reach into the part of her mind where she normally sensed her brother. 'Where are you, Sam?' she breathed. 'Come on! Hurry up and get found so I can get my life back.'

No sooner had the words spilled from her lips than she felt a wave of guilt wash through her. Sam was lost and in danger, her dad was in a cell and here she was, moaning about living in luxury with rich relatives.

'Get a sense of perspective, Niamh,' she muttered. 'You've got it easy.' But despite feelings of guilt burning inside her, the tight knot of selfish anger stubbornly refused to unwind. Why was she feeling guilty? It wasn't as if this was her fault. It was Sam's pig-headedness about taking the boat out that had caused all this. Despite being worried for him, she couldn't help being angry with him at the same time. If he'd listened to her in the first place, they would still be in Florida soaking up the sun and relaxing by the pool. Dad wouldn't be in prison and she would not have come within a hundred miles of Aunt Aggie and her nerdy son.

On the other hand, she probably wouldn't have met Tony either. A fleeting image of the look on Tony's face after their parting kiss flashed through her mind, bringing a brief smile to her lips. But even that positive had been short-lived. There were thousands of miles of ocean between them now. Why did life have to be so complicated? It was time to ring Beth. She probably wouldn't have any answers to the difficult questions, but it would be good to catch up.

'Sam, I promise that when I find you, I'm going to hug you and punch you really hard . . . not necessarily in that order.'

CHAPTER FIFTEEN

Sitting with his head in his hands, Sam didn't flinch as he felt a hand squeeze his shoulder.

'I'm sorry, mate. I don't know what to say.'

'Thanks, Cal,' he answered without looking up. 'I don't think there is anything to say. I just can't believe that Nathan won't do anything to save her.'

'What sort of thing did you have in mind? Storming the capital? Come on, Sam! There's only a handful of us. Your mum and the others are in the middle of the City of the Imperium. There must be tens of thousands of raptors in there baying for her blood. You've got to admit that Nathan's got a point. Any attempt at a rescue wouldn't stand much chance of success.'

'I know,' Sam sighed. 'But they're going to publicly execute her, Cal. How can I just give up? I can't sit back and let my mother die without trying to do something. I've only just got to know her again. There has to be a way. There *has* to be.'

Callum was silent for a moment. 'You can't blame yourself, Sam. Sometimes there really isn't a way. It's not your fault. There's simply no time to even plan something. Sherri says the executions are going to be held in just a few hours. It would take a miracle to get them out of there.'

'Then perhaps you'd better start praying for one,' Sam said, climbing slowly to his feet. 'I can't sit here any longer. I'm going back to the city. I know it's crazy, but I've got to do something.'

'Ssssamm. Sssstay.' It was Nipper. Neither Sam nor Callum had heard him approach. 'I 'o,' he said, pointing first at his own chest and then towards the cave entrance.

'You go?' Sam asked, his heart suddenly racing. 'Have you got a plan? What are you going to do?'

Nipper turned and said something in raptor speech that made no sense to Sam. His clicking, growling speech was loud enough to draw everyone's attention.

'What!' Nathan exclaimed. 'Are you sure?'

'What? What did he say?' Sam begged.

Nipper spoke again and everyone in the chamber listened, though Sam and Callum had no idea what he was talking about. Sam could sense excitement rising among the rest of the party, but he couldn't tell what was happening. It was David who explained.

'It appears your friend plans to claim the right of ritual challenge on behalf of Claire and the others,' he explained.

'Ritual challenge?' Sam asked. 'What does that mean?'

'If the Council of the Imperium agree to it, then it means he will fight the Imperium's champion for the lives of the captives. Apparently it's an ancient law among the raptors. He thinks they will have little choice but to accept his right of challenge.'

'So if he wins, the Imperium will just let them go?' Callum said, amazed. 'I find that hard to believe.'

'They'll have no choice,' David explained. 'It's that or break one of the longest-held traditions of the raptor world. That would not sit well with the wider raptor population. If the Council do not allow the challenge, they would risk a possible backlash.'

'And if Nipper loses?' Sam asked. 'What will they do to him if he loses?'

'They won't do anything to him. He'll be dead.'

'The ritual challenge is to the death?' Callum gasped.

Sam reached out and touched Nipper on the arm. He stared into the cold reptilian eyes of the raptor, searching for something that would explain the raptor's offer. 'You would do this? You would fight to the death to save Mum and the others?' He shook his head as he tried to understand the raptor's motivation. 'Why?' he asked. 'I don't understand. You have shown Callum and me nothing but kindness since we were stranded here. Why would you do this?'

Nipper turned to David and uttered a quick sequence of clicks and growls.

'He says it's the raptor way,' David explained. 'When a raptor finds prey, he faces a choice: to kill or to adopt. Not adopt in the way humans do, making you a full member of your family, but sort of a step up from a loved pet or a slave. I suppose you get a sort of half-status in his family. Nipper adopted you, as he has adopted other humans in the Reserve. When he did that, you became a part of his family. That makes your mother a part of his extended family, no matter how distant the relationship. Nipper takes his responsibilities seriously as head of his family. He sees this challenge as protecting his own.'

Sam drew a deep breath as he soaked up the answer.

'Can I come with you, Nipper?' Sam asked. 'I want to come.'

The raptor shook his head. 'Sssssam sssstay,' he repeated, pointing at the floor of the cave with the central claw on his right hand. 'Ssssaaafffer.'

'Please, Nipper! I don't want to be safe! I want to help save Mum.'

'Listen to him, Sam,' Callum urged. 'Don't be an idiot! If you go with him, you'll only be in his way.'

'How do you know?' Sam snapped back. 'I could help. I could. . .'

'What? What could you do?'

'I don't know,' he admitted, his shoulders sagging. 'I don't know what I could do. I just want to help, that's all.'

'We all want to help,' Nathan said. 'I've known Claire a long time now. I probably know her better than you do. I want to help, but I think this is something that your friend is going to have to do without us. He needs to move swiftly if he's going to do this – faster than any human.'

Nipper looked across at Nathan and chattered something at him quickly in raptor. Nathan nodded and replied with a short series of clicks and growls.

'He says Grunt is going with him to act as his second,' he explained to the boys. 'I'm not sure what that involves, but I've wished him well and thanked them both.'

Sam nodded. He turned again to Nipper. For a

moment, he struggled for words. 'Thank you,' he said finally. 'Fight well and don't die. Look after him, Grunt.'

'Urghh,' Grunt replied, baring his teeth in a wide grin.

The two raptors turned, and the boys watched as they leapt lightly across the stream and disappeared outside at a loping run. How long would it take them to reach the city? It was a fair distance and they would surely arrive there tired. After carrying the boys and the ammunition boxes all the way to the cave and running all the way back to the city, how could Nipper hope to be in any condition to fight a raptor champion? Sam knew Nipper was strong, but that sort of sustained exercise would surely take a heavy toll. His friend was going to be at a huge disadvantage if he had to fight straight away.

From the instant Nipper left, every minute dragged, laden with worries. Questions went round and round in Sam's head as he sat staring into the fire. Each led back in circular fashion to the central question. Could Nipper do it? Could he successfully challenge for the lives of Claire, Alex and Einstein?

Surprisingly, it was David who broke the morose atmosphere with a suggestion that suddenly triggered heated debate.

'Nathan, your people risked a lot to get me out of

196

the Imperium science labs,' he began. 'But I'm not going to be a lot of use to you without significant resources.'

'Tell me something I don't know,' the bearded man growled.

David looked down at the floor for a moment as if questioning the wisdom of what he wanted to say. Then he lifted his head again.

'I've been thinking about what the boys here were talking to me about earlier,' he said. 'Forgive me if I'm out of line, but having risked so much to get me, don't you now have the perfect diversion to complete the job and steal my flying machines as well?'

'What do you mean?'

'Well, Sam said you'd have to wait for Claire before making a move on the aircraft, but every raptor eye in the continent is going to be focused on the news this afternoon. Your mother is infamous, Sam. The execution of the human rebel leader is an event that will captivate the raptor world. If ever there was a perfect time to commit to another strike, it's now. They'll never expect you to make such an outrageous move in the face of such a major disaster to your cause.'

'He's right, Nathan,' Sherri said, her voice carrying a note of excitement. 'And it's exactly what Claire would want us to do.'

Newton growled and nodded his head.

'But we're all beat,' Nathan pointed out. 'We don't have a plan and we don't even know where the machines are.'

'I do,' David said. 'And the more I think about it, the more I think I can get us inside without much of a fight. If you can take out the guards once we're in, then I think we could pull it off.'

'*We?*' Callum asked. 'So you've made the decision to join us then?'

'I guess I have,' he replied, a strange light burning in his eyes. 'I'll be honest – I have an ulterior motive. If joining you means I get a chance to fly one of my machines, the risk is worth it. But I can't fly them both and why steal just one? What do you think, Callum? Would you be willing to fly the other one?'

'Does it have a conventional joystick control?'

'Not exactly, but you've done some flying before, so I'm sure you'll pick it up quickly enough.'

'Quickly enough not to die in the first few seconds?'

'I don't think you need worry too much about that,' David replied with a chuckle. 'I can draw you a quick diagram of how the controls work. The principles are similar to those of a glider, but rather than a column control, you use a horizontal bar and there are no foot pedals. Don't worry. It's really simple.'

Callum thought for a moment. 'Count me in,' he said, looking across at Nathan. 'What do you think?'

'Are you crazy?' Sam butted in. 'You're not seriously considering this, Cal, are you?'

'It's no more crazy than your stunts on those cables last night,' Callum said. 'I'd love to have a go at flying one of those machines. And if it helps your mum's cause too, then why not?'

'And you really think you'd be able to get us inside?' Nathan asked David thoughtfully. He ran his fingers through his beard as he considered the proposal. 'How many raptors could we expect to face once we're in?'

'Well, normally there are only two,' David answered. 'But I imagine they increased the guard after you snatched me out of the science labs last night. The truth is I don't know, but I would guess eight to ten at most. There's no room to house any more than that. The machines are kept in an outbuilding that's not much more than a glorified shed.'

Nathan stared David in the eye, his gaze steady and unblinking as he considered the proposal. David matched his stare, his stance strong and defiant.

'I've got to admit, it's a tempting prospect,' Nathan admitted, chewing at his lower lip. 'And Sherri's right. It's exactly what Claire would want us to do, given half a chance. All right, fly-boy. You've got my attention. Where is this shed of yours?'

'Yes!' Callum yelled, pumping his fist as if he'd just won a crucial point in the Wimbledon final.

'Do you have a map of the city?' David asked. 'I'll show you. If we're going to do this, we're going to have to move quickly. Even if we leave now, it's going to be tight to get there in time to coincide with the scheduled executions.'

Sam could barely believe what he was hearing. It seemed like everyone had forgotten that his mum and two other members of their group were facing execution. He couldn't believe that they were now thinking of their impending deaths as a useful diversion. Anger swelled inside him like a vast black tide and he realised he had to get away before he exploded with the pressure of it. He scrambled to his feet and without a word, stomped off towards the cave entrance.

Sherri shot Callum a questioning look, but all he could do was shrug. He was as mystified as everyone else. 'I'll go,' he mouthed, gesturing that he would follow his friend. Sherri nodded, giving him an encouraging smile as everyone else gathered into a huddle to plan the new mission.

Callum crossed the cave, stepping lightly across the stones in the stream and striding out to catch up with his friend. He intercepted Sam at the cave mouth and placed a hand on his shoulder. Sam stopped and twisted hard to throw Callum's hand off.

'What do you want?' Sam snapped. 'I thought you'd want to plan your adventure.'

'Come on, Sam. Don't be like this. You know what David suggested makes perfect sense.'

'You've all written Mum off already like she's totally expendable. You don't care about her at all.'

Callum sighed. 'Don't be ridiculous! You know that's not true. Of course we care. Just because she's your mum doesn't mean that you're the only one who's upset. Nathan, Sherri and the others have been close friends with Claire for years. Don't you think they're worried about her – that they would help her if they could? I think your mum is possibly the coolest person I've ever met. She's amazing, Sam, but she's also in a situation that is totally beyond any of our abilities to help. Only Nipper and Grunt can do that now.'

'So you're just going to ignore the fact that the Imperium are going to execute her this afternoon and go play rebels instead.'

Callum stared at Sam for a moment. It was obvious to him that nothing he could say was going to dig Sam out of his current mood, but he felt he should at least try.

'You heard Sherri and Nathan,' he said. 'It's what your mum would want us to do. Do you think she'd rather we all sat in a dark corner and sulked? That's not the Claire Cutler that I met. I know you're hurting inside, Sam. But you're not thinking straight. When you see sense and snap out of your mood, come and join us inside. Just don't leave it too long. I imagine we'll be on the move again soon.'

Sam didn't reply. He stared out along the rocky valley as the quiet sound of Callum's retreating footsteps echoed lightly behind him. He felt bad about how he'd spoken to his friend, but he wasn't ready to apologise yet. Instead, he concentrated on trying to picture how far Nipper and Grunt might have been able to run by now. Could they have reached the city yet? It was probably too soon for that. They were quick, but he doubted even a raptor could cover ground that fast.

'Go, Nipper!' he breathed softly. 'Fight well and win . . . please win.'

CHAPTER SIXTEEN

Niamh's heart gave a flutter of excitement as Tony's image appeared on her laptop screen. *Whoever invented Skype is a genius!* she thought.

'Hey, Niamh! Great to see you. How was the flight home?' His voice came out of the speakers slightly out of synch with the lip movement on the screen image, but it was wonderful to hear his voice.

'Not bad, thanks. The cop they sent with me was about as chatty as a stone statue, but it was pretty uneventful. You OK? How's Carrie?'

'She's fine. She's in the other room at the moment, but she'll be through in a minute for a chat. I'm missin' you already. I just felt I'd started to get to know you when the cops came an' whisked you away. They wouldn't say who tipped them off, but

I'm sure it was Tessa. We had 'em round again today askin' questions.'

'Same here,' Niamh said. 'I had my first interview today.' She stared at Tony's face on her laptop screen. Even slightly distorted as he was by the laptop camera, he looked gorgeous. What she wouldn't give to be back in Florida with him and Carrie now!

'Really? How did it go?'

'It was no big deal,' she told him. 'It seemed to be a form-filling exercise. The real deal is going to be tomorrow. I've got to go somewhere in Banbury to a special police interview room. It's not at the police station, but apparently, an officer from the CID is going to do the questioning.'

'CID?'

'Criminal Investigation Department,' Niamh explained. 'Not the regular street police. I must admit, I'm a bit nervous. What if I say the wrong thing? I might get Dad into even more trouble.'

'Hey, don't think like that!' Tony said. 'You'll do fine. You know your dad's innocent, right?'

'Yes.'

'Well, that's what you tell 'em. Carrie and me're still lookin' through your dad's notes. There's loads of crazy stuff in there. You done any more?'

'No,' Niamh said, feeling instantly guilty. 'There's not been much time since I got here and I don't have them on my laptop. Can you talk me through getting them the way you did with Beth?'

'Sure. No problem. I'll copy them to online storage while we're chatting and talk you through pickin' 'em up before you go.'

'That would be great. Thanks. Have you found anything new?'

'Not really sure it's new, but your dad seems to have concentrated a lot on the reports of magnetic anomalies and incidents where the sea has been reported as lookin' different. In one of the files he's marked at the bottom *Note to self: what if it really was a different sea?* Not sure what he means by that. You?'

'I don't know,' Niamh replied. 'If I'm allowed to visit him, I'll ask.'

'Won't he be upset that we've been goin' through his personal files?'

'I doubt it,' Niamh said, giving him a smile. 'In fact, I'm sure he'll be pleased we're trying to help.'

'I hope so.'

Tony helped Niamh retrieve the files he'd posted online and then for the next ten minutes they revisited the topic of magnetic anomalies, the Hutchison Effect and the Philadelphia Project that had seemed so promising before the police had knocked at the Dales' door. Once again, the hairs on the back of Niamh's neck prickled. She felt sure they were on the right track, but she simply didn't know enough about the physics involved to construct any sort of working theory on how such forces might form or how it would help them find the boys.

Niamh fell silent, staring at Tony's image on the screen. Their discussion had gone round in circles and now that she could see no way forward with it, the sudden silence was stretching into the realms of awkwardness. Perhaps she should change the subject for a bit. What else could she talk about? She wanted to say something, but 'Boy, you look hot!' was all that kept coming to mind and she couldn't bring herself to say that!

'So is that your bedroom?' Tony asked.

'No,' Niamh said, looking round the room, grateful that he had introduced a new topic of conversation. 'At least, I'm not at home, if that's what you mean. My room at home is more colourful than this and nowhere near as tidy. I'm staying with my aunt at the moment.' She lifted the laptop and walked round the room, giving him a virtual tour. 'Her house is a bit like a mansion. It's comfortable, but I hardly dare to touch anything in case I break it.'

'Cool.'

'No. Definitely not cool.' She dropped her voice to a whisper and flicked a glance in the direction of the door. 'Especially as staying here means having to put up with Archie.'

'Archie?'

'My cousin.'

'Ah! The rich cousin. I'm jealous already.'

Niamh laughed. 'Believe me, you've got nothing to be jealous about,' she said, keeping her voice very low. She wouldn't put it past Archie to be listening at her door. He'd followed her around like a lapdog from the moment she'd arrived. 'If you met Archie, you'd know what I mean. He's a geek of the highest order.'

'He's there with you,' Tony replied. 'That's enough to make me jealous.'

'Aww! You say all the right things.'

The next forty minutes passed in a blur. Tony made conversation easy, continually finding new things to talk about. Carrie joined them after a few minutes and Niamh was amazed, and a little irritated, when Archie knocked on her door and called for her to join them for dinner. She looked at her watch, surprised to see how much time had passed.

'OK, Archie. I'll be right there,' she called over her shoulder. 'Listen, guys, it was great to chat,' she told them. 'Keep looking through the files for me, please? I'll do the same. I've got to go now, but I'll speak to you again late afternoon or early evening your time tomorrow.'

'Sure thing, Niamh. Good luck for tomorrow,' Tony said.

'Bye, Niamh,' Carrie added.

'Thanks, guys. Bye for now.'

Niamh broke the link and switched off her laptop. Pausing to take a quick look in the mirror to check her hair, she took a deep breath and opened the door. Archie was waiting for her on the landing outside. He was so upright and stiff he looked like a soldier on parade.

Perhaps Aunt Aggie puts extra starch in his clothes so he can't slouch, she thought, biting at her lower lip to keep from giggling. 'You OK, Archie?' she asked aloud, unable to meet his eye as she swept past him and headed for the stairs.

'Fine thanks,' he replied, half-running to catch up. 'So what were you doing? Did I hear you talking to someone?'

Niamh thought for a moment. She was tempted to say something like 'I was just rehearsing the pack of lies I'm going to tell the police tomorrow' or 'I was just arranging to hijack a jet so I can fly back out to Florida'. He was so gullible that he would probably take whatever she told him at face value, but she found she hadn't got the heart to wind him up.

'Yes, you did,' she said. 'If you must know, I was talking with my boyfriend and his sister.'

'Oh! Boyfriend. Of course. Wizard,' Archie said, his enthusiasm clearly forced. 'On your mobile?'

'Internet: Skype.'

'Super.'

And to Niamh's relief, her admission killed the conversation stone dead. *Is Tony my boyfriend?* she wondered. *It feels like he is, but we've not exactly gone out on dates or anything. We've had one proper kiss. Does that count? If nothing else, telling Archie I have a boyfriend should keep him from getting any daft ideas. He's the sort of dork who might see being my cousin as an advantage in winning my affection.* They descended the stairs in silence and then Archie rushed ahead to open the door to the dining room for her, standing bolt upright and staring ahead as she passed.

All he needs is the white gloves and he'd make a great butler, Niamh thought, thanking him. She took her place at the dining table. Checking her watch she saw it was exactly six o'clock. Was life always this regimented with Aunt Aggie? What must it have been like for Archie, growing up with her for a mother? She looked across at him and he immediately looked down at his place setting and busied himself making minute adjustments to his cutlery placement.

209

And I thought I was unsure of myself around boys, Niamh thought. *Archie is so shy!*

Making polite small talk over dinner was surprisingly easy. Aunt Aggie was well versed in dining-room etiquette, and she effortlessly steered the conversation through a string of innocuous and trivial subjects. An hour later, Niamh left the table and returned to her room.

Turning her laptop on, she opened her father's files on the Devil's Triangle. For several minutes she re-read the section on the Philadelphia Project, but after looking at the same few paragraphs several times, she realised that although her eyes were scanning the words, nothing was going into her head. She could recall almost nothing of what she'd been reading. Anxious feelings about the interview with the CID were destroying her powers of concentration.

Perhaps it would be better just to relax and get an early night, she thought. Hoping to distract herself, she picked up a book from her bedside table and climbed into bed. It turned out that she was more tired than she'd realised, because after only reading a few chapters she felt her eyes beginning to droop.

* * *

To her surprise, it seemed almost that she had blinked and it was morning. She sat up and looked around, momentarily confused. The clock next to

210

the bed read 07:35 – early, but not ridiculously so. As her mind oriented and placed her at her aunt's house, fleeting snatches of dreams hovered at the edges of her mind and she tensed. A momentary, ephemeral memory of running through magical gardens linked by strange gateways, being chased by police; bluebells in the woods; lying on a branch watching as a drip of sweat fell towards one of the policemen; a fight; one man dead with a knife in his chest.

No, she thought, remembering. *I'm mixing fact with fiction. The man killed by the knife was in the book I was reading. Come on, Niamh! Pull yourself together.*

More images surfaced: more running, this time through dark tunnels. She was breathless and anxious. They were after her, hunting her. Not police, but creatures – powerful creatures – incredibly fast and covered with scales, their mouths full of wickedly sharp teeth. She was trapped. They were everywhere. There was no way out. Terror! Terror in the dark.

She blinked a few times. That wasn't from the book. *Sam?* She closed her eyes and reached inside to the place she could normally feel him. Was he still alive? Her body was rigid with tension. Breathing in through her nose, she deliberately drew in a deep breath and held it for a moment before slowly

211

releasing it. Then she took another. He was still there. Faint, but definitely there.

Feeling light-headed with relief, she staggered out of bed and across to the bathroom to wash. Splashing her face first with hot water and then with cold, she lifted a towel from the rail and buried her face in it. For a moment, she held it still, then almost like a child playing peek-a-boo, she peered over the top and into the mirror above the sink. What would the police think if they saw her like this? There was a haunted look in her eyes that no amount of make-up was going to hide. If they saw her as she was now, they would think she was hiding something for sure!

'Calm down,' she breathed aloud, and thought. *Sam's alive. As long as he stays that way, there's hope of finding him. Concentrate on that.*

The interview was due to start at ten and Aunt Aggie had said it was only a ten minute drive to where it was going to be conducted. Niamh had about two hours to pull herself together. Crossing back to her room, she dressed quietly and then crept downstairs to the kitchen with the intention of foraging for some breakfast. To her surprise, Aunt Aggie was there already.

'Morning, Niamh. You're up bright and early. Nervous?'

'A bit,' she admitted.

'Don't worry, dear,' Aggie assured her. 'It'll be fine. You'll see. And I'll be right there with you.'

'You will?'

'Yes. I asked the constable the other day and he said it was fine for me to sit in on the interview if you want me to.'

'Thanks, Aunt Aggie. I appreciate that.'

Did she want Aggie there? Some of the things that seemed likely to come up in the interview would sound pretty outlandish. In particular, the mental link with her brother and some of the strange images she had been receiving from him. Niamh decided the best thing she could do was to give them the truth. What they made of it was their problem. However, she was concerned about what Aggie would think. If her aunt formed the impression that she was lying, Aggie was likely to then consider her untrustworthy. The implications of Aggie forming this opinion of her for the rest of the summer holidays could be considerable.

Niamh fretted about this as she toyed with a bowl of muesli, eventually binning half of it and retiring back up to her room where she picked up her book again. Opening up to the bookmark, she skimmed back a few paragraphs to refresh her memory and quickly found herself embroiled in the story once more. Before she knew it, Aggie was calling her name and a glance at the clock showed it was time to go. There were precious few pages of the book left and the murderer was surely about to be revealed. Unwilling to leave it, she tucked the bookmark back in and slipped the book into her handbag.

'Coming,' she called. Then she added under her breath, 'Let's get this over with.'

CHAPTER SEVENTEEN

By raptor standards, the building Sam was approaching looked positively ramshackle. There was certainly nothing that marked its importance. It was a plain, boring oblong structure, made of the same structural materials as the rest of the city. David's description of it as a shed appeared surprisingly accurate.

'Not very impressive, is it?' David whispered, grinning at the boys.

'It's not going to win any architectural awards, that's for sure,' Callum muttered back. 'But I was always taught never to judge a book by its cover.'

'A wise philosophy.'

'Cut the chatter,' Nathan hissed over his shoulder. 'We're getting close. Concentrate.'

Sam didn't care if the guards heard them coming or not. He was carrying the rifle again. This time not only was it loaded, but he had more ammunition in a pouch attached to his belt. The way he felt at the moment, he would welcome a fight. All he needed was an excuse to flick off the safety catch and start shooting. Previously, he might have been a bit wary of actually shooting at raptors, but he'd wanted to hurt something, or someone, almost from the moment he had discovered his mother had been captured.

He watched as David gave a shrug and nodded at the bearded rebel leader. As far as Sam and the others knew, there were no audio or proximity sensors around the building. Nathan was simply being ultra-cautious.

David had briefed them all on the raptor security system before they had left the cave. The main problem for the rebels if they had tried this raid on any other day would have been the DNA sensor on the door, but luckily David's was one of the few whose patterns would be recognised. Assuming the raptors hadn't amended their security protocols immediately after his abduction the night before, they were approaching through one of the blind spots in the security camera network and should be able to sneak through undetected. At the briefing, David had been confident that the chances of their being seen during this phase of their approach were remote.

The group closed in on the building until they reached the wall. Then they turned left and, staying tight to the wall, sank down and crawled until they reached a small service door.

'Ready?' David whispered.

Nathan nodded.

Sam's hands instinctively tightened round the stock of the rifle and he drew in a deep breath. If there were more than a handful of raptors on the far side of that door, the plan would likely go horribly wrong in a hurry.

David lifted his hand to the sensor pad.

This was it. They were going in.

Nipper and Grunt had entered the city and taken a ride in one of the multitude of cabin cars heading for the plaza in front of the Imperium Tower. Nipper's muscles tingled constantly with the after-burn of prolonged exercise. Although he did not feel particularly weary, he knew he would not be at his peak for the challenge ahead. In his favour, he had made more kills in the wild than most city-born raptors. He was counting on his experience and strong hunting instincts today. If they failed him, he would die.

For raptors like Nipper, death held no fear. He was content that if it was his time, he would die a worthy death. Defending his adopted humans felt natural. Sam and Callum were younglings and Nipper felt a keen sense of responsibility for them. He had not yet forgiven himself for the Brad-human's death on the train when they had first travelled from the Reserve to the city. Although the man had been fully grown, Nipper had been protecting him for some years. The Brad-human had been special. Unlike most, Brad had taken the time to learn the raptor language and to understand many of the raptor ways. That another raptor had killed him without observing the rites of the hunt was wrong. None of Brad's flesh had been consumed and the killing had appeared to be an act of bloodlust or plain prejudice against humans. Neither of which sat well with Nipper.

Although human ethics were different, and there were many things about them that Nipper still did not understand, he had come to admire much about them. He had observed that humans could be every bit as honourable as raptors. They were physically fragile and their ways were strange, but humans had subtle strengths and he did not doubt their intelligence. Killing them for no reason was an act without honour: an act not worthy of a raptor.

Nipper growled his frustration as the cabin car came to an abrupt halt. The tracks ahead were jammed solid. Everyone, it seemed, was trying to reach the Central Plaza. Some raptors were already abandoning the cars to walk the final stretch. He glanced at Grunt and with unspoken agreement, they elected to join the crowds on foot. Time was running short. They had to reach the plaza and get to the front of the crowds before the executions. For the first time since they left the cave, Nipper felt a pang of unease as he realised this might not be as easy to achieve as he had first thought.

Nipper had never seen so many raptors in one place before. Shoving through the crowd was likely to spark confrontations and he needed to conserve his strength now for the challenge. Meaningless spats would be dangerous. He turned to Grunt.

'Clear me a path,' he ordered.

Grunt bared his teeth in a grin of pleasure. Stepping in front of Nipper, he took a deep breath and began to growl. But this was no ordinary growl that rasped in the throat; it emanated from deep within the raptor's chest, reverberating and penetrating. It was a sound that oozed danger. The nearest translation in a human tongue would be: *Get out of my way or I'll tear you limb from limb*. It was not a threat that a raptor used lightly, nor was it ever treated with anything other than the utmost respect by others unless they actively sought confrontation. Grunt knew there was always a chance he might meet a raptor who was spoiling for a fight, but he felt this less likely among the city-dwelling raptors than it would have been if he'd tried it back in the Reserve.

He was right. The crowd parted ahead of him and raptors fell silent, moving aside as he approached, all giving him wary looks as he passed. Nipper followed tight in his wake.

As the two raptors entered the square, they could see that a gigantic holo-projection in front of the spire was showing a picture of the spire doors. Nipper grunted. The Council must have set it up to ensure even those furthest from the main action could see what was happening. It was clear they wanted as many as possible to bear witness to the deaths of the rebels.

The closer they got to the front of the crowd, the more closely packed the multitude of raptors became. But even here, Grunt's menacing warning penetrated and the bubble of space around him, though smaller now, carried them right through to the barriers that had been erected to keep the very centre of the square clear.

The two raptors arrived not a moment too soon. As they reached the barriers, the doors to the spire at the heart of the City of the Imperium slid open and Claire, Alex and Einstein were led out and down the steps into the Central Plaza. The three captives had their hands bound in front of them. The heads of Alex and Einstein hung down on their chests, but despite showing signs of having taken a severe physical beating, Claire's head was up, eyes flashing with defiance. A phalanx of raptors from the Imperium Guard followed them, spreading out on either side as they descended the steps. On a raised dais in the centre of the square three sharpened impaling posts had been erected, each about two metres high.

The main doors to the spire, having closed behind the party of prisoners and guards, opened again and two by two, the eight raptors that formed the High Council of the Imperium emerged and arranged themselves in a line at the top of the steps, resplendent in their ceremonial garb. Nipper looked up at them and a burning knot of anger ignited inside him. It was these eight raptors who were responsible for hiding the true reason for the appearance of humans in this world. It was they, through their iron control over the holographic news network, who insinuated blame and shaped anti-human public thinking. Yet they were also quick to use human technology and intelligence when it suited them.

He looked first at the Council, bloated with self-importance and power, and then at Claire Cutler walking upright and undeterred towards certain death. It was little wonder that some of the top raptor scientists had chosen to follow this female human's lead. She had admirable qualities, worthy of the greatest of raptor hunters.

The crowd around Nipper and Grunt were beginning a rhythmic chant, calling for blood, baying for the death of the rebels.

'Try to get the crowd behind me,' Nipper growled, preparing to make his move.

'Fight well and live,' Grunt responded.

Nipper could delay no longer. In a single enormous bound, he leapt over the barriers and roared. His mighty challenge cut through the chanting of the crowd like a claw through soft belly flesh. Stillness and silence spread through the raptors in an outward ripple and Nipper repeated his roar, calling out the ritual raptor challenge with every fibre of his being.

'Blood for blood. Life for life. I demand the right to challenge.'

Raptor guards sprang to surround him, but Nipper stood firm, looking up to the Council for a response.

He felt taut. He felt strong. Any doubts he had harboured about making this challenge had gone. This was the right thing to do. Not just for Sam and Claire, but for all of raptor-kind. Unless voices like those of Claire Cutler were heard, the High Council would continue to manipulate public opinion unchecked. They had wielded ultimate power unquestioned for too long. It was time for someone to test them.

The Council turned to one another, speaking quickly in low voices. At the front of the crowd, Grunt began a simple new chant.

'Challenge! Challenge! Challenge!'

Raptors around him picked up on it, adding their growls to his, and the chant spread until it thundered around the plaza. Nipper bared his teeth in an expression of satisfaction. The Council would have little choice. This was too traditional a ritual for them to ignore. The crowd had witnessed the challenge and supported it.

The holo-cube cut to the face of the Voice of the Council. The giant image looked down with contempt over the crowd.

'Silence!' it ordered, the voice so amplified that it boomed like thunder round the city centre. The eyes of the Voice flashed with anger as he waited for compliance. 'What right do you have to challenge here, citizen? These rebels are traitors. They have defied the Imperium and committed acts of terrorism. They are justly scheduled for execution. Do you wish to join them?'

Nipper took a deep breath. He was preparing to shout his response when he realised that the holographic image above him had changed. The holo-camera had been trained in on him. He could only assume his voice would be amplified as that of the Voice had been. It was.

'They are my kindred,' he said, his voice sounding sure and unwavering. 'I adopted the humans, and the raptor you hold captive is my blood brother. We have hunted together. I claim family justice as is my right by tradition. I am the head of my house. I claim my right to judge and to set my own punishment for their crimes.'

The crowd murmured their approval and somewhere in the middle, the chant began again.

'Challenge! Challenge! Challenge!'

It spread quickly. The High Council gathered into a huddle at the top of the steps. They did not discuss the matter for long. The voice of the crowd could not be denied. The chant was echoing around the Central Plaza with one gigantic voice. They could do little but concede to tradition.

The Voice of the Council called once again for silence, the gigantic hologram of his face staring out over the crowd from above the plaza. Slowly, the chant died away.

'We will honour your right of challenge,

youngling. Is there one who would fight for the Imperium?'

'I will,' barked a raptor voice from near the base of the steps. 'I will accept this human-lover's challenge and see justice done here today.'

Nipper looked round to see where the voice had come from, but he didn't need to find the source to know who had uttered the words. Sure enough, out from among the lines of guards at the base of the spire stepped a familiar figure. Large, with dark scales and a line of puncture scars across his thighs, it was the raptor from the train: the one from the Imperium's secret police; the one Nipper suspected had killed the Brad-human.

A low, menacing wave of growls raced through the crowd as they saw who was stepping forward. It appeared Scar, as the boys had named this fearsome raptor on their first meeting, had a reputation in the city.

The Voice of the Imperium nodded his approval. 'Thank you, Captain. I'm confident you will ensure the will of the Imperium is upheld. Continue.'

Nipper glanced across at the prisoners. Claire Cutler mouthed the words 'Thank you' but he did nothing to acknowledge her. He could not afford to demonstrate anything other than righteous anger until this was over. The guards ushered the prisoners to the side of the execution platform and changed formation to clear a large square area in the plaza for the two combatants to face off in.

Scar strode forward and entered the open square. He looked strong and powerful. Nipper could see instantly that his opponent would have the advantage of weight and reach, but Nipper remained calm and focused as he assessed his enemy. This was no soft city raptor that knew nothing of the hunt. He was lined in many places with the scars of combat. Nipper had no doubt that this raptor had done little but fight all his life. Would he have areas of weakness? Maybe the legs with the line of puncture scars? He did not seem to favour one or the other, but given their nature, Nipper found it difficult to believe Scar had not suffered lasting effects from those injuries.

Stepping forward into the square, Nipper moved to face off against his opponent. Scar's eyes were shining with anticipation and he was baring his teeth in a broad grin. The air was alive with the chants of the raptor crowd, urging the combatants forward as the gigantic holographic projection overhead displayed them on a scale that made them appear like titans. Nipper knew better than to be distracted by such things. He ignored Scar's face and blanked out the tumultuous noise and the shifting images overhead, concentrating instead on a point in the centre of his enemy's chest. At a spacing of about five paces, they began to circle, each assessing the other for signs of weakness.

From the top of the steps, the Voice of the Imperium barked a single word.

'Begin!'

CHAPTER EIGHTEEN

Niamh was surprised when her Aunt Aggie pulled up outside a nondescript building. Was this really the place? It looked more like a social services centre or a doctor's surgery. She gave her aunt a quizzical look.

'This is the address I was given,' Agatha confirmed, unfolding a sheet of paper from her pocket to double-check. She nodded. 'Yes. This is it. Come along. Let's not be late.'

She climbed out of the car and Niamh followed suit. Her aunt looked particularly chic today in a designer outfit that had no doubt been chosen especially to make her look the very image of prosperity and respectability. From the moment Niamh had seen Agatha in the hallway, she had felt positively underdressed. Agatha had raised her eyebrows at her choice: jeans, ankle boots, a T-shirt and a short leather jacket; but had not said anything. Adjusting her jacket, Niamh had thought for a moment about changing, but decided against it. She knew she did not look particularly smart, but at least she was comfortable. What image was she portraying with her choice of clothes? She had never consciously considered using her clothing to shape people's perceptions of her before, but looking at her aunt, it was easy to see that it worked.

Agatha blipped the car with the remote locking device on her key and led Niamh up to the door. A smart young woman met them there. For an instant, Niamh was tempted to turn and run. Gritting her teeth, she fought down the panic she felt welling inside.

'Agatha Barrington?'

'Yes, that's right.'

'And this must be Niamh.'

The woman's smile as she held out a hand for Niamh to shake was warm and friendly. Was this a front? Would her dark side emerge once they were inside? She was petite and smartly dressed with her shoulder-length blonde hair backcombed and held neatly in place with a black hairband.

'Please, do come inside. Niamh, I'm sure you're

probably nervous about today, but there really isn't any reason to be scared. I'm Detective Constable Kathryn White. I know I don't look much like a police officer dressed like this, but I can assure you I am. Here, let me show you around.'

Niamh followed her aunt through the front door and into a corridor with several doors along each side. Eyes roving, she scanned the interior. The first doors on either wall were open and the detective constable was indicating for them to go into the room to the left.

'This is where we'll be having our chat.'

Niamh tentatively stepped inside. The small room was furnished with three comfortable, cream-coloured chairs decorated with loose cushions covered with childish animal designs. There was a small coffee table in the centre of the room and a big open-topped box of toys in the corner. Mounted high on two walls were cameras on top of which were perched toy monkeys. DC White saw Niamh take in the cameras.

'Do you know what those are, Niamh?'

'Cameras. . .' she answered, feeling slightly patronised. 'I'm sorry. What do I call you? Constable? Ms White?'

The policewoman laughed.

'Detective Constable White is a bit of a

mouthful, isn't it? Just call me Kitty, Niamh. That's what my friends call me and, as nicknames go, I think it's quite nice. And is it all right if I call you Niamh or do you prefer something else?'

'Niamh is fine, Kitty,' Niamh repeated, saying the detective's nickname shyly. Despite being alert with nervous energy, she found that the woman's easy manner was seductively relaxing. She would have to be careful if she was going to avoid saying things that could be twisted and used against her dad.

'Great. Now, Niamh, I know some of the questions I'm going to ask today might seem a bit silly to an intelligent girl like you, but please bear with me. It's an important part of my job to make sure you understand exactly what's happening, so when we begin, I will run through some simple things for the record. Those cameras up there will transmit everything we talk about today through to that room over there where it will be recorded. Let me introduce you to my colleague, Detective Constable Colin Barker, who will be monitoring us throughout. Kitty and Barker . . . sounds like a kids' TV show, doesn't it?'

Niamh smiled. 'I guess it does a bit.'

The room on the far side of the corridor was the same size as the interview room, but this one was dominated by a desk with a couple of TV screens and a DVD recorder.

'If you'd like to follow me, I'll show you the rest of the place,' Kitty said, leading them out into the corridor again.

There was a toilet, a small kitchen, a waiting room and a medical examination room that had everything in it that you would expect to find in a doctor's surgery. Niamh didn't want to think too much about the reasons for having this room. It was a stark reminder of the sort of crime victims that would be brought to this place.

When they had finished the tour, they returned to the interview room.

'Now, Niamh, where would you like to sit?'

'Here's fine,' she replied, taking the chair nearest to the door.

'And would you like your aunt to sit in with us or would you prefer it to be just the two of us? It is totally your choice. Whatever you feel more comfortable with.'

Niamh thought about it for a moment. 'I think I'll be OK on my own, but what would you prefer, Aunt Aggie? I don't mind.'

'I'd like to sit in, if that's all right,' Aggie replied. 'At least for a little while.'

'That's fine, Mrs Barrington,' Kitty assured her.

'In fact, if you could just be filling out this consent form for me, I'll check with Colin that we're all set and we can get going.'

DC White nipped across the corridor and back again, closing the door behind her and taking the remaining chair in the corner of the room. She had a folder of papers in her hand and proceeded to leaf through them until she found the form she wanted. Taking out a pen, she checked her watch and made a couple of notes on the top of the form. Agatha finished filling in the form she had been given and handed it over. Kitty checked it, nodded and thanked her before turning her attention back to Niamh.

'Right, Niamh, for the tape I'd just like to repeat a couple of things. Firstly, I'm Detective Constable Kathryn White, though you can call me Kitty. You know we're here today to have a bit of a chat about what's been going on recently. I'm a police officer from Banbury Police Station, so you know who I am and you know what I do. Now, before we start talking, I have to do a bit of an introduction. So if you could just listen to what I have to say, then we can talk, OK?'

'Yes, that's fine,' Niamh said, feeling a twinge of nervousness again.

'Great. It's Thursday 5th August, and by my watch

I make it eight minutes past ten. I'm in an interview room with Niamh Cutler. That's correct, isn't it?'

'Yes, that's right.'

'And Niamh's aunty – would you like to introduce yourself?'

'Certainly. I'm Agatha Barrington, the sister of Niamh's father, Matthew Cutler.'

'Thank you, Mrs Barrington. My job here is to have a bit of chat with you, Niamh. We've already talked briefly about what's going to happen, so you know what's going on today. As you understand, you're not in a police station and you're not in any trouble. You're actually here today to help me do my job, and if you have any problems or concerns at any time during this chat, feel free to tell me, OK?'

'Yes, sure.'

'You've had a good look around and met my colleague, DC Barker, in the monitoring room. Are you happy with everything you've seen?'

'Yes.'

'Brilliant. If you need a break at any point, to go to the toilet, or to get a drink, or some food, or for anything else for that matter, will you let me know?'

'Yes, sure.'

For the next five minutes or more, DC White explained in painstaking detail what was happening and checked with Niamh that she understood exactly what was going on. Niamh quickly realised that Kitty was working from a checklist and there were going to be no short cuts. Kitty took time to establish, through telling a simple story, that Niamh understood the difference between truth and lies, and the importance of telling the truth to prevent any possibility of the investigation being misdirected. She explained that she would be taking some notes for her own benefit and that if Niamh didn't understand any of the questions she was asked, she should make it clear so that the question could be rephrased in a way she did understand.

The introduction seemed to go on and on, and Niamh began to wonder just how long it would be before she was asked any meaningful questions.

'So, Niamh, in your own words, can you tell me why we're here today?'

After the extended preamble, the question took Niamh by surprise. She thought for a moment before voicing her reply.

'I guess we're here because you . . . the police think that my dad murdered my brother and his friend.'

'Right. . .'

Niamh waited, expecting another question. It didn't come. After a moment of silence, she realised that Kitty was waiting for her to explain in more detail. She took a deep breath. Where to start?

'Well, we were on holiday in the Florida Keys: Dad, Sam, me and Callum, Sam's friend from school. Dad insists we go there every year, because he's still a bit obsessed with finding out what happened to Mum after she disappeared nine years ago. He'd gone out looking for clues one day when the boys . . . well, Sam actually, decided to borrow Dad's boat to go out fishing. That's when they disappeared. Dad didn't have anything to do with them disappearing. He wasn't even there when it happened.'

'So you were on holiday in the Florida Keys with your dad, your brother and his friend. Your dad went out and the two boys took your dad's boat to go fishing. Why do you think your brother took your father's boat out?'

'I don't know what got into him. He's never done anything quite so idiotic before. I think he was bored and a bit hacked off with Dad for going off and leaving us with nothing to do. Dad had promised to take Sam and Callum out fishing, but then he went off in the car on his own instead.'

Kitty nodded. 'So tell me a bit about your dad, Niamh. What's he like?'

For the next two hours, Niamh talked. To begin with, it was all about the family relationships. Kitty

236

seemed to have endless patience and interest, exploring many of Niamh's family memories. Time and again, she would repeat cogent points back and use them to raise yet more questions.

When she talked about her mental link with her brother, Niamh noted that Kitty's eyes widened. Aggie let out a snort of disbelief, but Kitty gave her a look that stopped her from interrupting. Lots of questions followed about the link that Niamh struggled to answer. It was not an easy thing to put into words.

'So can you feel him now?' Kitty asked eventually.

Niamh closed her eyes for a moment and concentrated. 'Not clearly,' she said after a long pause. 'All I can tell you about him right now is that he's alive, but wherever he is, Sam has been in danger several times since he and Callum disappeared. That's when I feel him most clearly – when he is experiencing particularly strong emotions like extreme fear. Believe me, I wish I could tell you where he was, but I can't.'

They moved on to talking about Sam's decision to take the boat out, going over and over every last detail that Niamh could remember about what was said and who was where. Eventually, it was Kitty who called for the break.

'Niamh, you've been brilliant so far. Thank you.

Let's take a break for a bit. We'll have a bite to eat and a drink and come back to it fresh in about half an hour. Is that OK?'

'Is there much more to talk about?' she asked. 'I'm sorry, but I don't see how this is really helping to find the boys.'

'Well, there are some more areas that I'd like to cover,' Kitty said, neatly dodging the question. 'Don't worry though. You're doing absolutely fine and the more people who look at the details of what happened, the more chance there is of someone seeing a clue that the rest of us may have missed.'

When they resumed, Aunt Aggie elected not to come in with her and waited in the other room. Niamh quickly realised that there was a lot more to come, as Kitty started diving into all sorts of tangential lines of questioning: who was this Geoff that her father had gone flying with? When had the family friendship with Moira and Mitch begun? Where had her father bought the boat and when? Details, details, details. It seemed endless, and Niamh was more than a little relieved when a halt was finally called at nearly six in the evening.

'Are we all done then?' she asked, eager to get away.

'I think so,' Kitty replied, stepping forward and shaking Niamh's hand. 'Thank you for being so brilliant about answering all my questions today, Niamh. If I missed anything, we'll get back to you. It'll take a while to go back through the tapes and collate the information properly, but I think we managed to cover most things pretty well. Try not to worry too much about the boys. Everyone is still searching for them out in Florida and the US coastguards are a very thorough lot. If you're right and the boys are alive, I'm sure someone will find them soon. Is there anything you want to ask me?'

'Thanks, Kitty,' she replied. 'There is just one thing. Can you tell me where Dad is being held? My aunt doesn't want to tell me for some reason.'

Kitty looked at her for a moment, considering the request.

'I don't see why not,' she said thoughtfully. 'He's in Woodhill High Security Prison in Milton Keynes. Why won't your aunt tell you?'

'She doesn't want me to visit him. Apparently, prison isn't a suitable place for young ladies to visit,' Niamh said, mimicking her aunt's voice.

Kitty laughed. 'She does have a point. It's not pleasant and you won't be able to visit without her, you know. You need to have an adult with you if you're planning to go and see him. What about your uncle? Wouldn't he take you?'

'Good idea. I'll try talking to him,' Niamh replied,

smoothly glossing over the fact that her uncle had been away the entire time since she had returned to the UK.

* * *

Niamh felt incredibly stiff as she walked out to the car with her aunt. Although the chair had been comfortable, she was not used to sitting still for such long periods of time. It seemed amazing to think the interview had taken nearly as long as the flight to America. Despite having talked all day, Niamh felt an overwhelming desire to ring Beth and tell her all about what had happened. She missed having her best friend around to share things with. In fact, she'd never felt so alone in her life. Perhaps she could arrange to go and see her, or Beth could come and visit. Beth was lovely and even Aunt Aggie would have difficulty finding fault with her.

'I'm afraid dinner will be a little late this evening,' Aggie said as they climbed into the car. The way she said it made a late dinner sound like a heinous crime in itself. What was more, it appeared Aggie placed the blame for this on Niamh for being so long in the interview room.

Oh, great! she thought. *That's all I need! Now I've messed up her routine. She'll never forgive me for that!*

'Not to worry, Aunt Aggie,' she said. 'Why don't we do something quick like noodles or something? We can do that by seven easily. I can help if you like.'

Judging by the stony look she received at her suggestion, Niamh realised that she was not making things any better.

'Don't talk nonsense, Niamh! After a day like that you need more than noodles to eat, young lady. No, I'll cook you a proper meal when we get home, but we'll just have to reschedule eating this evening, that's all.'

Don't talk nonsense, Niamh, she mimicked silently. *Don't be so silly. Do this. Don't do that. No wonder poor Archie is the way he is.*

The traffic lights ahead turned red and Aggie brought the car gently to a stop. For a moment, Niamh was tempted to jump out of the car and make a run for it. It would be easier for her to survive on the run here in England than it had been in America. She had places she could go, friends she could stay with. Maybe she could even find a way of getting back across to the United States and continuing the search there.

Use your common sense, the voice inside her head chided. *Wait. There will be a better time.*

Biting her lip, the voice of the old, sensible Niamh won her over. She would just have to bide her time living at Aunt Aggie's. Besides, now that she knew where he was, the most important thing was to find a way to visit her dad and tell him about her theories on Sam's disappearance. She was sure he would know what to do. But how could she find a way to see him when her aunt was so against the idea?

CHAPTER NINETEEN

The door hissed open at David's touch. Nathan and Sherri were through it in a flash, followed closely by Callum and Sam. The raptors, Newton, Edison and Crick, went next, with David last to enter.

No sooner had Nathan and Sherri crossed the threshold than their guns began spitting death. The two raptor guards nearest the door went down instantly, pounded to the ground by a hail of bullets. The rebels split. Nathan went forward and left, angling towards the flying machines in the middle of the large open space inside. Sherri went right with Sam and the others behind her. She hugged the wall of the building and fired one short burst after another at three more incoming raptors.

Callum's heart raced as he followed Nathan, his

rifle butt held tight into his shoulder. He'd released the safety catch, but made no attempt to shoot at anything as he ran. That would be a last resort, he decided. As far as possible, he would leave the fighting to those better suited to it; unlike Sam, he hadn't quite come around to the idea of shooting a gun at a living target.

'Don't shoot at the machines!' David warned everyone as he sprinted in through the door and chased after Callum and Nathan. 'If you damage them, I can't guarantee they'll fly.'

Callum ran round the wing of the nearest machine and dropped to a crouch. He glanced back just in time to see Sam lift his rifle to his shoulder and loose a volley of bullets at an incoming raptor guard. The expression on his face held a mixture of anger and determination. He looked different from the friend that Callum knew; this was a harder, stronger Sam and if he was afraid, he was showing no outward sign of it. It was scary to think how quickly circumstances here had changed Sam, and Callum couldn't help but wonder if he would have reacted the same way if Claire had been his mother. The thought of shooting to kill still turned Callum's stomach, but Sam appeared to have lost all inhibition and it was perhaps just as well that he had. The raptor twisted as Sam's bullets hit, but it did not stop. It snarled, exposing its teeth, and launched into a flying leap at the boy.

Callum took a sharp intake of breath. No number of bullets from Sam's gun could possibly stop the momentum of a leaping raptor, but just as it looked certain that Sam would be mauled, Newton intercepted the incoming guard with a flying attack of his own. He impacted the guard shoulder to shoulder at an angle that deflected him away from Sam and sent him sprawling across the floor and into the wall. Before the guard had a chance to regain his feet, Newton touched a black fork-like device against his torso. There was a blinding flash that left Callum seeing spots. When he looked back, the raptor guard was writhing on the floor in a rapid series of violent, jerking convulsions.

It was then that Callum noticed Crick and Edison were holding similar devices. Judging by what he had just seen, he guessed they were something akin to tasers. The raptor scientists were not fighters like Nipper and Grunt, but it appeared they had thought to create technology that would give them an edge in any close-quarters confrontation.

The hangar was nowhere near as large as ones that Callum had visited with his dad when they had gone gliding, nor was the roof as high, but it was still a sizeable building. The two small aircraft looked almost lost in the middle of the large open space.

'OK, Callum. Let's get you set to go,' David said, taking him by surprise. The young man looked more animated than Callum had ever seen him.

'But the guards. . .'

'Are not our problem,' David interrupted. 'Quickly. Put that gun down and climb into the harness. Let's get you strapped in. Here're your goggles. Put them on over your glasses if you must, but they are important. They'll give you more protection against the wind.'

Callum did as he was told. It was a struggle to settle them over his glasses in a way that was comfortable, but he decided that a bit of discomfort was probably better than not being able to see properly. 'How do I get in?'

Gunfire blazed behind him. It was hard to concentrate, but Callum did his best to focus on the job at hand.

'It's a bit awkward the first time. Use the steps to get to the harness. That's it. Now turn your body round to face the front of the machine and reach back with your right foot until you feel the harness. Great. Now, slide yourself back until your arms fit comfortably through these loops,' David directed. 'It should mould to your body. That's it. Don't worry. I'll adjust the straps for you. They're set for a raptor at the moment. It'll take me a moment to get you comfortable. Feet back a bit more – that's it.'

A thrill of excitement ran through Callum as he settled into the harness. He looked at the structure around him and the shining, silver-coloured wings above and below. Suspended in front of him was a small panel with three instruments on it. One he recognised as an artificial horizon. The other two clearly measured something – probably speed and altitude, Callum decided, but without any clear units displayed, it was unclear as to which was which.

'How does that feel?' David asked, his eyes shining.

'Fine. I don't feel as though I'm going to fall out.'

'Good. OK, very simply, this is the control bar,' he said, putting Callum's hands on to a parallel bar just in front of and below his face. 'It acts in the same way as a column: pull back to go up, push forward for down. Move it left and right to turn in the usual way.'

'Cool. I think I can cope with that. So what makes the fan go?'

'These two switches turn on the magnetic converters,' David explained. 'Don't put them on yet, because they also have a built-in battery pack to get you moving. Wait for Nathan to open the doors.

They work in the same way as the rest of the raptor technology, by converting magnetic energy into electricity. The electricity drives the fan. I installed limiters on them, because the faster you go, the more lines of magnetic force you cut and the more electricity you generate. Without the limiters, the fan would just accelerate to destruction.'

'OK. I recognise this instrument showing the artificial horizon, but what are the other two?'

'Yes, the artificial horizon was recovered from a crashed Cessna and converted. This one here is your altimeter. The unit of measurement is one devised by the raptors, but a rough conversion would be one complete revolution of the large needle is approximately 600 metres. . .'

'Which is somewhere between 800 and 2000 feet,' Callum calculated.

'If you say so. So long as you have a rough idea. You zero it using this knob like this. Just remember that having set zero on the gauge before take-off, because it's a static pressure instrument, it doesn't measure how high you are above the ground; it simply tells you how high you are above the zero-line pressure you set before take-off.'

'Got it. Exactly the same as the ones we use in gliders. And this one?'

'That's your airspeed indicator,' David said.

'Again, the measurement won't mean a lot to you, which is why I coloured it with a green zone for the raptors. As a basic rule, so long as you keep the needle in the green zone, you won't fall out of the sky. If you manoeuvre hard, then it is possible to stall the machine even with the needle in the green. For cruising, stay in the middle to top end of the zone, but when you want to land, turn off the magnetic converters and as you get close to the ground, try to stay as low in the green zone as possible. Happy?'

'Yes, I think I've got it,' Callum said.

'Any questions?'

'About a million, but they can wait. I'll just try to follow you. Where are we flying to?'

'We'll head east, back towards the cave and look for somewhere sensible to land as close to it as we can. Good luck.'

'Thanks. You too.'

Callum watched as David sprinted the short distance to the second machine. Nathan followed him, scanning for any further signs of trouble. It was then that Callum realised the shooting had stopped. He had been so focused on what David had been telling him that he had not noticed. Looking over his shoulder, he could see the rest of the party gathering at the back of the hangar. They were watching the holo-projection flickering in the air there.

From what he could see, Sam and the others were all fine. He counted seven raptor bodies unmoving on the ground. Was that all of the guards down? Nathan and Sherri in particular still looked very alert. They were both scanning the hangar for signs of movement. Sam's attention was fixed on the glowing images of the holo-projection. It wasn't hard to work out what was being shown. Had Nipper made it to the capital in time to make his challenge? It was no good. No matter how hard he tried, Callum couldn't see the glimmering image clearly enough to see any detail.

David had crawled into the harness of the other machine and was busy adjusting the straps. Callum shivered as he watched. In a few minutes, he was going to take off and fly solo for the first time in a machine that was nothing like any aircraft he had ever seen before. Would his gliding experience be enough to keep him from crashing? Suddenly, he didn't feel so sure. He moved the control bar around, trying to get a feeling for how sensitive it was, but there was no way of telling until he got into the air. All he could do was wait until David gave the signal for them to go.

Callum didn't hear David tell Nathan to open

the doors, but he did see the bearded rebel suddenly get up from where he had been kneeling next to the other flying machine and run across to a panel to the left of the main doors. Throwing the large lever on the wall there, Nathan raised his gun back to his shoulder as electricity surged through the motors and with a loud rumble, the doors began to slide open.

'Switches on!' David called to Callum, reaching up and turning on his magnetic converters.

Callum flicked the two switches and felt the thrum of power surge through his machine as electricity began to flow. David's machine was already moving, accelerating slowly towards the opening doors. A few seconds later, Callum's began to creep forward as well.

'OK, steering this thing in the air I understand,' he muttered. 'But how the heck do I control it on the ground?'

It was one of the many questions he had neglected to ask and unless he changed direction soon, he would crash into the left door before it had a chance to open fully. Callum felt his heart begin to pound still harder, but he didn't panic. Instead, he looked to see what David was doing and began experimenting by shifting his weight around. He quickly realised that David was a clever designer. The control bar didn't do anything to change his direction, but the foot supports had somehow been linked to a nose-wheel steering mechanism, making directional control on the ground as instinctive as he knew it would be in the air. Stretch back with the left foot and he went left. Stretch back with the right and he went right. Easy.

He steered right until he was directly behind David's machine and followed him out through the doors and on to the grass meadow outside. The field was long and wide with the great wall of the city to the right, woodland to the left and scattered trees some distance ahead opening into another meadow beyond. As he left the building and trundled across the grass, the machine began to bounce and shake on the uneven ground, making his sling-like harness rock, twist and bounce uncomfortably.

Callum heard the shout behind him and another rattle of gunfire. He tried to look round, but it proved impossible. It was all he could do now to try to keep the flying machine accelerating in a straight line. Ahead, David's machine was picking up speed, fast. It bounced once, twice into the air only to drop back to earth. Then with a final skip, it pulled free of the ground more smoothly and eased skyward in a smooth, shallow climb.

A movement in the corner of Callum's eye caught

his attention and he realised what the shouting had been about. Two raptors were racing towards him from the right. There was another distant rattle of gunfire, but if the shots were aimed at the incoming raptors, they did not find their targets. The airspeed indicator needle had fluttered into life and was climbing in unsteady leaps towards the green zone. He looked across at the closing raptors. Could he get airborne before they intercepted him? It was going to be close.

Come on! Come on! he urged, willing his machine onward. Applying a gentle back pressure to the control bar, he attempted to ease it into the air. The whirr of the fan and the thrum of energy from the magnetic converters were reaching fever pitch. He was out of time. The nearest raptor was closing fast. The other was losing ground and no longer a threat.

The needle on the airspeed indicator surged up into the bottom of the green zone and Callum hauled back on the bar even as he saw the raptor launch into a flying leap towards him. The machine lurched about two metres into the air and the airspeed needle dipped back below the green. At the same time, the diving raptor caught hold of an undercarriage strut. The combination of the sudden impact from the right, the substantial increase in weight and drag, and the lack of speed caused the right wing to dip and the aircraft to drop back to the ground.

Wrenching the control bar to the left, Callum managed to prevent a crash, instead touching back down on to the meadow with the wings level. But despite being dragged along the ground, bouncing and flipping under the aircraft, the raptor clung on, stubbornly refusing to let go of its prey.

With a roar that sounded distinctly like a challenge the raptor twisted its body so that it could kick upward at Callum with its feet. Its first blow erupted through the silver fabric of the lower wing and caught Callum in the stomach, but fortunately, its power was severely limited by its awkward position, and the thick leather of the harness protected him from the creature's sharp claws.

'Let go you ugly son of a. . .'

Callum could do nothing to protect himself, nor reach to fight back in any way. All he could do was to concentrate on trying to get into the air. Again, the raptor kicked upward, tearing the hole still wider. This time the blow struck Callum in the groin. He groaned and writhed in pain. Snarling at the raptor, he spat at it, though his wad of spittle was whipped away by the wind.

In defiance of the extra drag of the raptor and the tattered hole in the lower wing, somehow the fan produced enough thrust to notch the aircraft's airspeed up into the green again. Callum pulled back on the control bar, lifting first the aircraft and then the determined raptor into the air. Gaining height was a problem. Having lifted the dangling raptor about three metres from the ground, the aircraft seemed to reach a barrier. It could no longer accelerate and it could no longer climb.

'Let go, damn you!' Callum yelled again. 'You're going to kill us both.'

It was unclear if the raptor understood him. However, the open meadow space was fast running out. Scattered trees loomed ahead. Without some very fancy flying, or a significant altitude gain, they were going to hit one of them very soon and there was no chance of climbing so long as the raptor remained clinging to the underside of the aircraft. Ahead, David was already safely above the treetops and soaring away in a turn to the east.

Callum turned left towards the biggest gap he could see between the trees, but he could not sustain a turn for long because the pendulum effect of the raptor dragged the wings back level.

He tried again, rolling the aircraft harder this time in an effort to throw the raptor clear. To no avail; the raptor clung on with the determination of a limpet and the pendulum effect simply became

255

more violent. It was at this moment that Callum realised what he had to do.

He had no choice.

He would have to deliberately fly into a tree.

CHAPTER TWENTY

At the Voice of the Imperium's starting order, Scar immediately took the offensive. His leaping attack was fast and vicious, forcing Nipper to evade. What surprised Nipper was not the power or the speed of Scar's attack. It was his ability to move without telegraphing his intention through his body. There was no coiling preparation for the leap. Scar's muscles barely seemed to bunch at all before he was flying in at Nipper, claws poised to slash.

There was no time to prepare a counter-strategy. All Nipper could do was attempt to sidestep and deflect Scar's attack. He dodged left, swinging his right arm out in a defensive block that impacted the side of his attacker's upper body with a satisfying thud. Scar's momentum carried him clear, but

Nipper felt the burn of a raking cut open across his side as Scar slashed at him in passing.

Nipper spun, hoping to take advantage of any momentary imbalance Scar might have on landing, but the big raptor rolled and twisted to his feet with effortless ease. The crowd roared around them, excited by the first lightning-fast exchange.

'I hope you're ready to die, youngling,' Scar snarled, baring his teeth in a vicious grin. 'I've killed many who were stronger, more experienced fighters than you. You cannot hope to win here.'

Nipper knew better than to rise to the taunt. He kept his focus on trying to read his opponent's body movements.

'What is it that you like about the humans?' Scar asked, beginning to circle again. 'They are soft and weak. They care nothing for raptor traditions.'

There was little warning of Scar's second attack, but Nipper read it better this time. Instead of shying away, he leapt to intercept and the two raptors clashed in mid-air. The change of tactic surprised the bigger raptor. He had been expecting Nipper to evade again, because his greater mass was always going to give him the advantage in any head-on collision. As it was, the clash came more quickly than he anticipated.

Nipper felt another slashing cut open across his

back as one of Scar's claws raked him again, but in the moment of brutal collision, he gained the satisfaction of sinking his teeth into Scar's right shoulder, biting deep into the flesh. Blood spurted into his mouth and as his momentum spun him clear, he raked the hooked central claw on his left hand across Scar's chest, while the claw on his right tore a hole in Scar's back. The bigger raptor roared in a mixture of pain and anger.

With the element of surprise gone, Nipper knew better than to try to repeat this tactic. Scar was unlikely to be caught off guard twice in the same way. All Nipper could do was to keep him guessing and hope that by being unpredictable, his opponent would leave openings he could exploit.

He leapt clear again, and the two protagonists resumed their stalking circles. What Nipper had to avoid at all costs was grappling. Scar was too big and strong for him to wrestle effectively. He'd need to use speed and cunning if he was going to survive. His best chance for a clean kill would be to open one of Scar's major arteries or to crush his windpipe. A raptor's vital organs were too well protected by bone and muscle to be easily damaged without some sort of heavy weapon. And Scar was clearly no stranger to injury. Nipper judged that the big raptor would not succumb to the pain of any number of minor injuries. It was going to take something much more substantial to take him down permanently.

Baring his bloodied teeth at Scar in a silent grin, Nipper tried a subtle taunt of his own. The bigger raptor snarled in reply. All around them the crowd was roaring and chanting for their favourite, but as far as the two fighters were concerned, they were alone. Everything else was blanked out as irrelevant.

The femoral artery in Scar's thigh was another possible target, Nipper realised. But the only point where it was close enough to the surface to present a realistic chance of severing it was at the groin. Neither the groin nor the throat were an easy target. Of the two, the throat was more open, but that's where Scar would be expecting him to focus his attacks. He would protect his throat at all costs, so what other options were there?

Scar attacked again. Not leaping this time, but charging. Nipper tried to dodge, but Scar was too fast. The big raptor cannoned into him and they both went down in a rolling frenzy of claws and teeth. Somehow, Nipper managed to scrabble clear before Scar gained enough purchase on him to bring his greater bulk to bear, but the exchange was costly. As he regained his distance, it became clear that the bigger raptor had inflicted more nasty cuts to

Nipper's body and arms. Blood was running freely from multiple wounds now, but more telling was the wave of fatigue that suddenly enveloped him. The initial pulsating energy that he had felt before the fight had passed and his body was now feeling the effects of his exertions earlier in the day.

All of Nipper's pre-fight confidence left him. The realisation that he was facing a superior foe who had the measure of him sent a cold shockwave through his chest. Was this the fear of which the humans spoke? It was not something he had ever felt before. At the Reserve he had always been the strongest, the fastest and most audacious of hunters. But fighting between raptors there was uncommon, and for all his experience at hunting other prey, this was not the Reserve and Scar was unlike any foe that Nipper had fought before.

Scar was back on his feet, his wide grin confident. Nipper looked the bigger raptor in the eye and could see the expectation of imminent victory in his expression. For an instant, he allowed his focus to shift on to the three prisoners nearby. The desperate hope in their eyes shot a bolt of renewed strength through him, but even such a brief glance away from his opponent was a mistake. Scar saw the opening and seized it. Before Nipper knew what had hit him, he was down and rolling. He lashed out wildly, but ineffectually, as Scar tore at him with teeth and claws. Pain erupted in Nipper's chest, his arms, across his back and the side of his head. For a moment, there seemed nothing he could do. The dark raptor was slicing him to pieces and it seemed only a matter of time before he struck a mortal blow.

With a surge of strength born of desperation, Nipper twisted free again and regained his feet, but Scar did not give him a chance to recover. The big raptor knew he was close to victory and he pressed home his advantage, charging after Nipper in another headlong attack. In the split second before Scar struck, Nipper had a moment of revelation and he suddenly realised what he had to do.

The image of Sam taking down Nathan three times in quick succession in the rebel HQ lounge flashed through Nipper's mind. His opponent was used to fighting raptor-style. It was unlikely he would know anything of human fighting tactics. As Scar's right hand whipped towards him in a slashing attack, he adopted the boy's most memorable first counter-attack. Swaying to the left, he swept the arm aside with a hooking grab. His claws found the purchase he wanted and, gripping Scar's wrist tightly, he twisted it over to the right. His execution of the move was not as slick as Sam's, but to his delight, the big raptor went down face first to the ground just as Nathan had, with his arm locked out straight. However, where Sam had stopped short of driving his weight down on Nathan's arm, Nipper showed no such mercy. His full weight dropped hard on to Scar's locked elbow and the resounding crack as the arm snapped at the joint was profoundly satisfying.

Scar roared with agony at the explosion of pain, but the roar was cut short. Before he had a chance to recover, Nipper had leapt on to his back, reached round his throat and torn it open with a single vicious slice from his central claw. Scar bucked and writhed beneath him, but Nipper rode out the frenzy with renewed calm. A large pool of blood spread rapidly beneath them and the mortally wounded raptor's efforts to escape faded fast.

Nipper could not resist giving Scar a parting comment. Keeping his weight firmly bearing down on his opponent, he put his mouth close to Scar's ear.

'That's one of the reasons I like humans,' he growled softly. 'If you take the time to observe them, you can learn many things: even new ways of fighting. You dishonoured raptor tradition with your kill on the train, Captain. The manner of your death today is fitting reward.'

Scar surged upward in one final futile effort to throw Nipper from his back, and then dropped limp to the ground. Nipper waited until he saw the life fade from his enemy's eyes before climbing slowly to his feet. Suddenly, the world spun and the pain of his wounds threatened to overwhelm him. His body felt slick with blood, most of it his own.

Then the noise of the crowd struck him. The roar of appreciation for his victory was unlike anything he'd ever imagined. It was as if the air was alive, hammering at him from every side. Beaten and bleeding as he was, the sensation was almost too much.

He could feel, rather than see, the titanic image of himself being projected into the air above the square. Would the technology pick out his voice from the tumultuous roars of the crowd? He drew in a deep breath.

'Blood for blood,' he growled, forcing out the ritual words. 'Life for life. Release the prisoners to me and I shall see justice served upon them.'

The High Council of the Imperium gathered at the top of the stairs and it appeared that a heated debate was taking place. What could they be arguing about? He had challenged and beaten their champion in fair combat. Thousands of city raptors had witnessed the fight. They could not deny him his right. It was a tradition that had been upheld for over a millennium.

The crowd began to chant in support of his victory. 'Re . . . lease. Re . . . lease. Re . . . lease.'

The chant grew in strength until it echoed from every quarter. Still the Council remained in their circle, ignoring the crowd and continuing their debate. After what seemed an age they broke and reformed their line at the top of the steps. Some of the Council did not look happy. The Voice stepped forward and raised his hands for silence. He got it. The chants died rapidly and all eyes focused on him or his projection.

'Blood for blood. . .' he repeated. A great roar of approval went up from the crowd, but the Voice held up his hands once more for silence. 'A life for *a* life,' he continued, emphasising the subtle change. 'The Council acknowledges your victory and releases your blood brother to you. However, we deem your adoption of the humans invalid. There is no precedent for a raptor championing humans under the old traditions. Therefore, it has been decided that in the greater interest of raptor-kind and the Imperium, we will not release them. They will meet Imperium justice for their traitorous acts as scheduled.'

'No!' Nipper roared. 'This is not justice! They are my family. They are mine by right of challenge. Every raptor here heard my challenge and your acceptance of it. You cannot change the rules because you lost.'

'Youngling, we are the High Council of the Imperium. We *are* the law. You do not dictate to us what we can and cannot do. We have decided.' He turned his head to address the leader of the guards. 'Do it,' he ordered.

'Blood for blood!' Nipper roared again. 'A life for a life. I challenge again for the lives of the humans. If I must fight for each of them in turn, I will. I refuse to leave them. They are my family.'

Even the act of issuing the new challenge made his head spin. Although he knew he had no real chance of winning, his gut burned with anger at the Council's decision. He would rather die than give up the humans without a fight now.

The Voice looked down at him, snarling with derision. 'Even if I wanted to assist your certain death by granting another challenge, I could not. The Council has decided, youngling. Your challenge is denied. Go. Take your blood brother and do not enter this city again. His acts of treason against the Imperium will not be forgotten. Neither he, nor you by association, are welcome here. Guards – get rid of them and execute the humans.'

Before he could respond further, Nipper was surrounded by raptor guards who led him firmly from the centre of the square to the barrier that held the crowd line. Einstein appeared next to him, also shepherded by several guards. He said nothing. Thanks would not have been appropriate at this point.

'No! No! Don't do this. Please. Let me go! Arrrggghhh!'

Alex's pleading voice, followed by the unmistakable sound of him being impaled sent a lance of white-hot fury through Nipper, but he did not look back. He could not bring himself to do it. The Council's decision was wrong. He felt the injustice of it through every fibre of his being, but he was powerless to stop them.

* * *

'NO!' Sam shouted, sinking to his knees as he stared at the holographic projection at the back of the hangar. 'NO! Nipper won. They can't do this. It's wrong. MUM! They can't! They can't!'

The sight of Alex being lifted and forced onto the gigantic spike made him retch. The impaling post drove into Alex's back and out through his chest as the raptors pulled his body down until he was almost on the ground. To Sam's horror, the man's scream did not cut off instantly and his arms and legs continued to move. Sam could see the look of shock and pain on Alex's face as he clutched in vain at the post. It looked as though he was torn between wanting to somehow attempt to remove it and yet not wanting to move, as every movement intensified the pain.

The guards removed Claire Cutler's chains and prepared to lift her. Unlike Alex, she did not beg for release. The holo-imager zoomed in on her, looking to capture her fear for those in the crowd too far from the centre to see. However, if Claire was scared, she had buried the emotion deep. Instead, sensing her chance, she calmly began to speak in the raptor language.

Sam turned to Sherri.

'Please,' he begged her. 'What's she saying?'

Sherri frowned with concentration and began to translate.

'We have tried to help you – perhaps now some of you will see the truth. Your High Council deceive you. Today they ignored one of your longest-held traditions, but that is far from their worst crime. Behind your backs they are destroying your world and blaming it on us humans. Remember my words. Test them. And would someone please send word to my family that I love them . . . and tell my son he should try to go home.'

The guards lifted Claire over another of the wicked spikes, but she did not struggle. Sam looked away, unable to watch. Tears filled his eyes and he sobbed. All strength left him. He felt as if his body weight had just doubled. He couldn't move. He gritted his teeth, tensed and clenched his eyelids tightly shut as he waited for his mother to cry out in pain. When after several seconds he had heard nothing, he made the mistake of opening his eyes and looking back at the screen.

CHAPTER TWENTY-ONE

'NO!' Niamh gasped, dropping to her knees on the lawn, her eyes filling with tears. 'Mum! Sam?'

'What's the matter, Niamh? Are you all right?'

Niamh ignored Archie's question. Her brother's presence inside her mind was the strongest she had felt since returning to England. His mind was reeling with shock. Something terrible was happening. At first, she thought he must be hurt, but then she realised his only hurt was emotional. She would have felt an echo of physical pain. This was not about him at all. It was something to do with their mother. What was going on that could get Sam into this sort of mental state? *Mum must be in serious trouble for him to be this worked up*, she thought. A keen sense of horror swept through her and she felt herself tense up inside.

Sam was holding a gun! It was as if she could feel the weight of it in her hands. *A gun! What was Sam doing with a gun?* Worse, she could feel he was experiencing a burning desire to use it – to kill. The sensation shocked her to the core. Her brother *wanted* to kill. And she could feel that this was no passing curiosity, no random thought about what it would be like to kill. He was filled with a burning desire to aim the rifle he was carrying at someone and pull the trigger. How could this be? This was not the brother she knew.

A hand on her shoulder brought her partly back to the present.

'Are you feeling ill? Shall I get Mother?'

'No, Archie,' she snapped. 'I'll be fine. Just give me a minute.'

But she was wrong. At that moment, an image entered her mind that would stay with her for the rest of her life. It was worse than her most horrible nightmare.

'Please God, no!' she gasped. 'It can't be. It can't! Oh, Sam! Mum! No!'

Darkness took her.

* * *

Niamh coughed, suddenly choking as she fought to surface from the nightmare. Confused images twisted through her mind. Mum impaled on a giant spike.

271

Monsters. Guns. Strange-looking flying machines. Panic.

An incredibly strong smell of ammonia flooded her nostrils, filling her sinuses with a burning sensation. She coughed again and struggled to pull away from the source.

'It's all right, Niamh. Relax,' Aggie soothed. 'You're fine. You just fainted, that's all. The smelling salts are to help bring you round. Archie says he came and found me as soon as you passed out. You've only been unconscious a minute or so. Two at the most.'

'Please, take it away,' she gagged. 'Too much.'

'OK, Niamh,' Aggie crooned. 'There you go. The lid's back on now. Just let me know if you think you need another dose. There now. What on earth brought this on? Are you prone to this sort of thing? Matt has never mentioned anything about you suffering fainting spells.'

'No, Aunt Aggie,' Niamh replied, struggling up into a sitting position. 'I don't make a habit of this sort of thing.'

'Archie says that just before you passed out you said something about Sam and your mother. . .'

The terrible image filled her mind's eye again and Niamh felt the blood draining from her face. She couldn't tell Aggie. She couldn't! Given her aunt's reaction to the possibility of a mental link with her brother during the interview the previous day, Aggie would never believe what she had seen anyway.

'He did? That's strange. I don't remember anything,' Niamh lied, closing her eyes as she pretended to concentrate. 'It's all a blank. I remember Archie was going to show me where we used to make dens when we were younger. We were walking across the lawn towards the trees and the next thing I knew my head was threatening to explode with the stench from those smelling salts.'

'Hmm. Perhaps you've not been drinking enough. A lack of fluids can make you light-headed sometimes. You sit here and I'll go and get you something. What would you like? Lemonade? Dinner is nearly ready. Some food will probably help as well.'

'A glass of lemonade would be lovely, thanks.'

As Aggie marched away towards the house clutching her jar of smelling salts, Archie gave Niamh a calculating look.

'You lied to her,' he said, a note of outrage in his voice. He kept his voice low so there was no chance his mother would hear. 'I watched you as you answered her question. You do remember what you said before you passed out, don't you? You remember perfectly.'

Niamh hesitated a moment before replying. Even looking at Archie, all she could see was the terrible picture of her mother in agony. Churning emotions raged within her and Archie's prying was making it worse. This was not something she wanted to share with him, but she got the feeling that he was going to worry at it like a dog with a toy unless she did something to distract him.

'I don't know what you mean, Archie,' Niamh replied, trying her best to sound innocent. 'Why would I lie to your mother?'

'I'm not sure,' he admitted. 'But it's not a good idea, you know. Mummy will find out the truth in the end. She always does.'

'Well it's a good thing there's nothing for her to find out then, isn't it? And Archie, I don't want to sound mean, but aren't you a little old to still be calling her *Mummy*?' she added, neatly changing the subject. 'If Sam was here, he'd be teasing you rotten about that, you know.'

It was a simple diversion, but it worked perfectly. Archie's chin tilted up and he set his mouth in a firm line of defiance. He glanced over his shoulder to see if his mother was within earshot. She wasn't. Agatha had gone into the house.

'It's what she likes to be called,' he said, as if that made it perfectly fine.

'Oh, well, that's all right then,' Niamh said, her voice dripping with sarcasm. 'I suppose it's not my place to tell you to grow up anyway. So long as you're OK with your mother insisting you play the little boy toff, it doesn't bother me. What do your school friends think of it?'

Archie looked away as he answered. 'My best friend Rupert does the same,' he said matter-of-factly. 'He doesn't have a problem with it either.'

Although he didn't say it, Niamh got the distinct impression from his body language that while he had told the truth, there was a lot he wasn't saying. If she was to guess, Archie would probably have been more accurate with his statement if he had exchanged 'best friend' with 'only friend'.

Aunt Aggie reappeared from the house bearing a small tray with two large glasses of sparkling lemonade perched on it. As she approached, Niamh noted the ice cubes, slice of lemon and two straws in each. *Perfectly presented, as ever*, she thought.

'There you go, Niamh darling. I'm sure you'll feel better once you've rehydrated. I brought one for you as well, Archie. Now, are you sure you're all right? If the drama's over, I'll get back to the dinner. Remember to bring the glasses in when you're done, please. Dinner should be ready in about half an hour.'

'Thanks for the drink, Aunt Aggie. I'll be fine,'

Niamh assured her. She took a glass from the tray and forced herself to smile. She hoped it didn't look as false as it felt. 'We'll come in and wash our hands in just a minute.'

Agatha nodded and turned to leave.

'Oh, Aunt Aggie? Before you go, there was just one thing I wanted to ask. . .' Niamh added.

'Yes?'

Archie glared at her, almost imperceptibly shaking his head. Niamh's smile broadened as it suddenly felt less false. He was probably expecting her to say something about him.

'I was wondering – remember we talked about my visiting Dad? Is there any way I could go and visit him soon?' she asked. 'I haven't seen him since the police took him from our house in the Keys and I really want to make sure that he's OK.'

Agatha looked down her nose at Niamh as if she had just suggested something disgusting.

'You seriously want to visit the prison?' she asked. 'Are you sure? It will be full of awful types, you know.'

'I don't care what the prison's like,' she insisted. 'Where Dad is won't change who he is.'

'No, of course not. It's just. . .'

Niamh looked her in the eye, waiting for her to finish the sentence. She didn't.

'Well, we'll see,' Aggie said in a way that signalled the end of the conversation. She turned away and headed back to the house. Niamh watched her until she went in through the door. She sipped her lemonade.

'Well, we'll see,' she repeated, mimicking her aunt. 'So, Archie, when your mother says "We'll see", what does that normally mean?'

'Generally, it means no,' he said.

'Thought so.' She took another sip of her lemonade.

Archie gave her a long look through narrowed eyes. 'You're going to get into trouble again, aren't you?'

'What? What makes you think that?'

Archie shrugged. 'Call it nerd's intuition. So what are you going to do? Run away again?'

'Nah! Don't be ridiculous! What good would that do? I guess I'm going to be stuck here for the rest of the summer unless someone finds the boys.'

Archie's eyes narrowed as he considered her response. 'So what do you want to do before dinner?'

'Actually, I think I'm just going to go up to my room and lie down until Aunt Aggie calls us. Is that OK?'

'It's fine. I'll see you later.'

Niamh took her lemonade to her room and

closed the door. She pulled out her laptop and her phone, and while the computer was warming up, she rang Beth.

'Come on. Come on! Pick up, Beth . . . Hi! Beth? Thank goodness. Listen. Something bad has happened and I need to tal. . .'

* * *

The house was dark and silent as Niamh crept out on to the landing. With utmost care, she eased her bedroom door closed behind her, wincing as the latch clicked back into place. She paused a moment, holding her breath and listening intently to see if the noise had disturbed anyone. Nothing.

It was just after 4 a.m. She had timed her exit to be sure that everyone else would be fast asleep. Her purse held enough money to get to Milton Keynes by train, but not much more. There was certainly not enough for a cab to Banbury Station. She would have to walk. It would take over an hour and she would have a bit of a wait when she got there, but the weather was fine, and she didn't mind walking. Her plan was to be on the train and away before Aggie or Archie noticed she was missing.

Dressed in jeans, trainers, a dark top and her leather jacket, she tiptoed down the stairs to the hallway feeling a bit like a burglar. As she reached the front door, she hesitated. Thinking of burglars made her wonder – was the alarm switched on? Niamh had noticed the box on the front of the house with its winking light, but had never thought to ask Aggie if it was activated in the evenings. There was only one way to find out.

Gritting her teeth and silently turning the key in the lock, Niamh's body tensed as she gently cracked the door open. To her relief, no blaring siren split the night. She let out a long, low sigh of relief and edged out of the door, closing it silently behind her. Walking along to the edge of the steps, she leapt lightly over the flower bed and on to the lawn. The last thing she wanted to do was to crunch her way along the full length of the gravel driveway, but to her dismay, as she landed on the grass, a motion-triggered security light clicked on, bathing her in a harsh yellow light.

Niamh instinctively launched into a run, dashing across the lawn towards the deep shadows of the trees at the far side. *So much for a stealthy exit*, she thought as she hurdled over another flower bed and sprinted across the open ground.

Heart thudding hard against her ribcage, she slowed as she reached the safety of the shadows and looked round to see if she had aroused any attention. As far as she could see, no internal lights had been switched on in the house.

'Phew!' she sighed. 'OK, Niamh – Milton Keynes, here we come.'

She turned towards where she knew the pedestrian gate through the outer hedge would be, but as she did so, a movement in her peripheral vision caused her to freeze.

'No!' she breathed. 'It can't be.'

A shadowy figure was creeping round the side of the house and looked to be about to strike out across the open ground towards the same area of shadow she had run to. Was it a burglar? The figure seemed to be wearing dark clothes and she could make out the unmistakable bulge of a small rucksack.

The front security lights chose that moment to time out, plunging the front of the house back into darkness and Niamh found she could see virtually nothing, her night vision having been ruined by the bright lights.

Whoever was out there, Niamh had no desire to meet them here in the dark. Doing her best to move swiftly and silently, she crept through the dark towards the gate. Seconds later, she reached and unlatched it, easing it open. As it swung, the hinges moaned a horrible, unearthly groan of metal on metal and the sound triggered an instant response from behind her. A sudden and unmistakable rhythmic sound of running feet sent Niamh into a panic.

Without thinking, she turned left and sprinted away along the lane as fast as she could. After about two dozen paces, she realised she should have turned right if she was going to head towards Banbury and her blind sprint stuttered to a momentary stop as she hesitated, wondering if there was still time to double back without encountering the stranger. A second groan from the gate decided it. She had to keep going.

'Damn it!' she cursed as she pumped her arms to help gain momentum.

There was very little light, but she could just make out enough to see where she was going. Her breathing was too loud for her to be able to tell if the stranger was following her and she didn't dare try to look back for fear of tripping.

'Niamh! Niamh, stop! Wait!'

The voice was Archie's. For a split second, Niamh considered continuing, but she knew it was no good. She had been caught. Archie would go to Aggie for sure and she would be found and brought back before she got anywhere near Banbury Station. She slowed to a walk and then stopped altogether. A moment later, Archie caught up with her.

'What do you think you're doing out here, Archie?' she asked. 'And how did you catch up with me so fast?'

'I was expecting you to try something like this, so I rigged your door with a simple contact-breaker that set off an alarm in my room,' he said, sounding very pleased with himself. 'There are some advantages to being a rich nerdy type, you know. I've got all sorts of cool gadgets to play with. I went to sleep in my clothes, so when the alarm triggered, I just nipped down the back stairs and out of the back door.'

'Great. Very clever, I'm sure. Now, why don't you go back to your room and play with your gadgets? I'm sure you don't want to get in trouble with your mummy and I'd appreciate it if you forgot you ever saw me.'

'You're planning to go and see your dad, aren't you?' he replied.

Niamh sighed and shrugged her shoulders. 'Yes, Archie,' she admitted. 'And nothing you say is going to stop me. Now, go home.'

'No way! I'm going to come with you. It'll be a wizard adventure! Besides, you need me.'

'Really, Archie? And how did you figure that out?'

'Look, Niamh,' he said confidently. 'I might be needy, nerdy and all the other labels you want to add, but I'm also resource-rich. You booked a visit for 2.30 p.m. this afternoon, right?'

'Yes. How'd you know?' Niamh asked, astonished. 'Have you bugged my phone as well?'

'No, but it wasn't hard to find out,' he said. 'I also know that you booked in my mother as well, because you can't get into the prison without an adult to accompany you. How did you plan to get in without her? You won't be able to blag it, you know?'

'How do you know what I can and can't do?'

'Trust me, Niamh. They'll never let you in to see your dad without an adult.'

'So you're saying I should just give up? No way!'

'No, I didn't say that at all,' he continued, looking around nervously. 'But I took the liberty of altering your booking slightly. Come back to the house and I'll explain. It's a bit creepy out here.'

'I'm not going anywhere until you tell me exactly what you've done, Archie,' she snapped, hands on hips and bristling with anger. 'You've got no idea how important this is. I've got to see Dad. I have to!' The horrible image of her mother on the spike entered her mind again and she blinked back tears. A lump formed in her throat.

'Listen,' he told her. 'There's no need to get angry. If we do this my way, we'll get a lift into Banbury with Mu— my mother, we'll have an adult to

283

accompany us and mother will never even realise what she helped us to do.'

Niamh stared at him in the dark. She couldn't really see him very well, even now that her eyes were beginning to adjust. He sounded remarkably sure of himself, and so far he'd demonstrated a lot of sense.

'OK, Archie,' she said slowly. 'You've got my attention. What's your idea?'

'So you'll let me come along? Wiz—'

'Stop!'

'What?'

'If you want to come with me, then you're going to have to promise that nothing we do will be wizard, spiffing, simply splendid or any other sort of toffee-nosed archaic nonsense,' Niamh insisted.

'I'll try my best, I promise.'

'Good.'

'So I *can* come then?'

She sighed and clenched her teeth together for a moment. *Is involving Archie a mistake?* she wondered. *Do I have a choice? If I do, he could be helpful. He's already shown more initiative than I would have believed possible of him. If I don't, then he could sink my plan in seconds by running to his mother.* He had her backed into a corner and she knew it.

'I'm almost certainly going to regret this, but I suppose so,' she conceded.

'Wiz— I mean brilliant!' he exclaimed, punching the air and dancing around with excitement. 'This is going to be so much fun! Listen. This is what we're going to do.'

CHAPTER TWENTY-TWO

'This is going to hurt!' Callum muttered, tensing his body as he drove the aircraft directly at the tree ahead. He glanced down through the tattered hole in the lower wing to where the raptor dangling from the undercarriage strut was trying to manoeuvre its body into a position to strike at him again. 'But I'm hoping it'll hurt you much more than it will hurt me.'

The raptor suddenly went still as it realised what was about to happen. They were not high enough for the raptor to be concerned about jumping and for a moment, Callum thought it might let go before the inevitable impact and drop to safety. He had witnessed first-hand how far a raptor could safely fall without injury during his first escape from the clutches of the Imperium with Nipper and Grunt. Unfortunately, this raptor chose to stay with its prey.

The tree loomed closer and closer until Callum dared leave it no longer. At the last possible second, he forced the control bar as far left as it would go and pulled back hard. The left wing dropped fast, and as the aircraft cranked around into a hard turn, the raptor swung out wide, deep into the foliage of the tree. Unfortunately, the aircraft did not respond with the immediacy of the gliders that Callum had been used to flying and the entire lower structure of the flying machine also ploughed into the thin outer branches.

Twigs and leaves whipped at Callum's head, shoulders, arms and hands as he fought to maintain the turn. The caged fan momentarily sounded like a lawnmower chewing on a pile of sticks. In the space of no more than a second, there was a rapid sequence of cracks and a solid-sounding thud. The aircraft lurched and there was a final particularly loud CRACK before it found its way into clear air.

Later, Callum could not work out how the aircraft had retained enough momentum to stay airborne, especially given that it did not have a lot to begin with. Almost as if it was sticking two fingers up at the laws of physics, it stayed stubbornly clear of the ground and Callum fought the control bar to keep it that way.

Once clear of the tree, a glance down through

the hole beneath him revealed the raptor had gone. Unfortunately, so had more than half of the under-carriage! As far as he could tell, the nose and right main wheels were missing, as was most of the tubular structure that had supported them. Several more tears had also appeared in the lower wing fabric at different points along the wing. Now it was in clear air, the abrupt lightening of the machine combined with the reduction of drag from the raptor and the brush with the tree resulted in a surge of acceleration.

Callum could feel the blood pounding in his ears as he struggled to retain control. As the airspeed indicator needle climbed rapidly into the heart of the green sector, panic and fear gave way to relief and excitement. Finally, he was in familiar territory. Miraculously, the machine was responding normally and felt like something he could fly.

Easing back on the bar, he tightened the turn, hauling what was left of the aircraft around until he was pointing back along the field towards the hangar. With the wings level, he pressured the control bar forward, deliberately entering a shallow dive. Down he flew, lower and lower, until it felt as if the remaining wheel must almost be skimming the top of the grass as he converted what little height he had gained into yet more speed.

A movement to his left caught his eye and he looked over to see another raptor racing across the meadow towards him, but at this speed the raptor had no chance of catching him. With a whoop of joy, Callum eased the control bar back again and soared up high into the air, well beyond any raptor's reach. The exhilaration he felt as the ground dropped away beneath him was heightened beyond anything he had ever experienced in a glider.

Yowser! This is fantastic! Dad's going to totally freak out when I tell him about flying this beastie, he thought, laughing aloud as a sensation of sheer joy swept through him. The gentle *thrum* of the caged fan was accompanied by a slight rattle that had not been there when he had first started the machine, but it didn't sound bad, so Callum chose to ignore it.

Looking down as he swept over the roof of the hangar, he saw a patrol of half a dozen raptors approaching the open main hangar doors. From his vantage point, he could also see the rebels exiting through the back door. They would not have much of a head start on the patrol, but there was nothing Callum could do from up here, except perhaps attempt to distract the hunters if it came to a chase.

Suddenly, he saw David in the other flying machine come into view on his right. He was over-taking Callum, descending past him in a dive and rocking his machine rapidly left and right. Callum understood instantly. David was asking Callum to follow him.

Giving a gentle wing rock of his own to acknowledge the message, Callum gently turned his machine to the right and began to follow. Did David know where he was going? Callum knew from experience that navigating in the air was totally different from navigating on the ground. The different perspective made judging distances hard, and things that were great landmarks for finding your way when you were on foot were often not so obvious from the air.

From what Callum could tell, David had set a course almost directly towards the secret rebel cave. But Callum wondered if flying in a straight line to where they were going to land was a good idea. The raptor patrol was sure to try to track them and the last thing they wanted was to make it easy for the Imperium to find them. If their initial heading was observed, any trackers could simply project forward the line of flight and keep going that way until they eventually caught up. It would be better to fly a more circuitous route to their destination. But how could he communicate this to David?

Callum thought for a moment as he settled his machine on to a parallel heading. *What would I give for a radio now?* he thought, clenching the control bar with frustration. *Think, Callum! How else can you communicate?* At the gliding club they sent simple messages to airborne pilots with coloured lights. Ships used to talk to one another using different-coloured flags. Neither of these methods was any more available than a radio.

I could try hand signals, but even if I could get close enough to get his attention, what signals do I make with my hands to get my message across? I'd do just as well by shouting.

It was then that he remembered a strange phenomenon he had noticed one day while gliding. On days like today when there was very little wind, sounds from the ground carried into the air with remarkable clarity. He had sat one day, circling high above a cricket match, and he distinctly remembered the surprise he had felt as he was able to listen in on conversations being held such a long way below. That was it! He was right. He *would* do just as well by shouting. What he needed to do was to get below and slightly ahead of David's machine and yell to him.

Although the idea was simple, it proved impossible to execute. Even though it was now in a steady climb up towards the top of the ridge surrounding the bowl-like valley, David's undamaged machine was flying faster than Callum's. Try as he might by holding his altitude and even descending a little, he could not catch the other machine.

'OK,' he muttered aloud. 'If I can't catch you, David, I'll just have to do my best to throw them off our trail on my own. With luck, you'll catch on to what I'm doing.'

He turned to the left, enjoying the breathtaking view as he headed back towards the spectacular city. For a moment, he was tempted to climb his aircraft so that he could go and circle round the central spire, but he decided better of it. Instead, he concentrated on returning to the hangar area. There was no sign of Sam and the others now, but he spotted the raptor patrol straight away. They were leaving the hangar, clearly looking to pick up the trail of the rebels.

'Let's see if I can't distract you a little,' he breathed, grinning as he drove his machine back down towards them. *Wish I had something to throw!*

Closer and closer he flew, narrowing his eyes and imagining he had a machine gun mounted in front of him. '*Dacka-dacka-dacka-dacka*,YAHOOOO!' he yelled, pulling up over the hangar roof and rolling left again. His body felt heavy against the harness as he manoeuvred hard and there were some ominous creaks from the lower wing structure. A momentary vision of the aircraft wings folding up made him ease off the back pressure on the control bar. He had no way of knowing how strong the machine was – especially as damaged as it was. The raptor patrol was still next to the hangar and every one of them was looking up at him.

Kid gloves from here on, he thought. *No more flying like a hooligan. Come on now. Here, raptor, raptor, raptor! Come follow me. You know you want to.*

Rolling out of the turn, he settled the machine on to a heading about twenty degrees to the right of where his friends would be going. Close enough to be believable, but far enough from the true heading to give the ground party a good chance of getting away. In the far distance, he saw David disappearing behind the ridge at the edge of the valley. Had the raptor patrol noted his path? It was impossible to tell. As far as Callum could tell, he had gained their undivided attention, but there was no guarantee.

He settled the machine into a climb, keeping the airspeed as low in the green sector as he could. He wanted to give the patrol as much opportunity to follow him as possible, but at the same time, he knew he had to give himself a small margin of safety. The damaged lower wing would not be generating as much lift as the designer intended and he did not want to stall at low altitude. As he climbed, he eased a few more degrees to the right, subtly steering the trackers away from his final destination.

The ridge ahead climbed steadily and to begin with, Callum wondered if his damaged machine was going to climb fast enough to clear the top without building in a greater ground track by zigzagging or circling. Although circling would have allowed the hunters a better chance of following him, he did not want to have them so close on his tail that he couldn't lose them on the other side of the ridge.

'Come on, baby,' he urged as the ground crept closer and closer. 'You can do it.'

It was close, but he squeaked over the ridge, all but skimming the treetops as he flew first out of the valley and then out of sight of the City of the Imperium. The ground dropped away again on the far side of the ridge and the rich green countryside spread out like a gently rucked carpet below.

All that was left to do was to fly in a wide triangle to confuse the hunters and then land. For the first time since smashing through the tree, Callum gave thought to landing. With only the left main wheel intact, landing without destroying the rest of the aircraft was unlikely to be easy. He was used to landing gliders on a single central wheel and allowing a wing to drop as the aircraft ran out of forward energy, but what would it be like to land on a single wheel that was offset to one side? With the bottom wing so close to the ground on landing, there was little likelihood of cartwheeling, but Callum was keen not to damage the machine any further. It represented his chance to get home, and now that he had got it away from the raptors, he had no intention of destroying it.

He looked around for any sign of David's machine, but could not see it anywhere. It seemed likely that David had already landed, as it was only a few miles to the hidden cave. No doubt the inventor would be wondering why there was no sign of Callum and the second machine by now, but that could not be helped.

For the next half an hour, Callum flew in a huge triangle, only turning for the second leg of the circuit when he could use the contours of the land to hide his course change from the raptor patrol that he hoped was following him. Dropping down, he flew lower and lower until he was almost skimming the treetops. Once he was sure he would be invisible to his pursuers, he turned north and then eventually back south-west, looping back towards his intended landing ground.

Flying so low meant that he didn't see the landing site approaching until he was virtually on top of it. David was standing in the open waving to him as he flew over. There was no sign of his machine. Callum circled the field once in an effort to determine the direction of the surface wind, but as far as he could tell, there was none here. The air was still, which was not ideal for his purposes.

'Come on, Callum,' he ordered himself. 'Chin up. You can do this. Time to turn off the power and get back into familiar territory.'

He reached up to the two electromagnetic converter switches and flicked them off in quick succession. The hum of the fan died to a whisper and suddenly, the only sound was the gentle rushing of the wind and the flapping of the torn fabric beneath him. Watching the airspeed indicator closely, he felt for the correct glide angle with the control bar. He lowered the front of the aircraft gently further and further until the needle stabilised in the bottom of the green sector. The glide angle was steeper than he was expecting, but then he realised why. The big fan propeller now idling behind him had gone from being a power source to a gigantic airbrake, generating a huge amount of drag.

'This is going to be a bit hairy,' he muttered.

Diving at the ground, he knew he could not afford to level out early. If he did, he would float briefly, run out of airspeed and stall – dropping whatever distance was left to the ground at a bone-crushing rate of descent. He considered flicking one of the power switches back on to reduce the descent angle, but realised there was no time. The ground was rushing up to meet him fast. He had to concentrate on maintaining the approach and airspeed if he was going to make a safe landing.

'Look well ahead,' he coached himself, his heart thumping against his chest like a jackhammer. 'Wait for the ground to swell round your ears and then ease her level.'

How many times had his gliding instructor repeated those words to him? His approach and preparation for landing were perfect, but as the aircraft touched down he discovered the field was far from flat and the resulting bounce was not pretty. The aircraft bucked a metre back up into the air again, the airspeed bleeding off so fast that before he could even think to try to force the aircraft back down on the ground, it went of its own accord. In a moment of inspired quick thinking, Callum threw the control bar left, forcing all the weight on to the remaining wheel. Somehow the structure withstood the firm impact and this time the aircraft stayed on the ground, though even with the control bar fully left, he could not stop the right wing from dropping and catching on the ground.

Slewing round to the right, the aircraft came to a

dizzying and abrupt halt. Callum swung from side to side in the harness for a moment until that, too, came to rest.

Moments later, David arrived at a run. 'Where the hell have you been?' he panted. 'And what have you done to my poor machine? I thought you knew how to fly?'

'I do,' Callum replied, a wave of relief and elation rushing through his body as the reality of what he'd just done struck home. He looked David in the eyes and grinned. 'I've been leading the raptor hunting party a merry dance round the countryside to put them off our trail. As for your machine, I thought it could do with a few modifications. Your version had far too many wheels and I decided a downward facing window or two would make great new features.'

David's mouth opened and closed as he tried to articulate an answer. No words came.

'Can you give me a hand?' Callum asked, trying to keep his voice casual. 'I'd hate to damage anything as I get out.'

CHAPTER TWENTY-THREE

'No! Leave me alone!'

'There's no time, Sam. We'll all grieve when we're safely away from here. There's a raptor patrol approaching across the meadow. We've got to get out of here.'

Nathan put a hand on Sam's shoulder, but the boy shook it free and continued staring at the holo-projection, tears flooding down his face.

'Don't make me do something I'll regret later, Sam,' he warned. 'We need to leave. *Now!*'

Sam could hear Nathan, but his words were like the distant echo of a dream. He was reliving the moment in the heart of the Central Plaza. His mother was still alive, impaled on the spike, dying, but not yet dead. How could he leave? She was not struggling, but he could see she was speaking. Even though the camera shot was far from being a close-up, he could see her lips moving. What was she saying? He wanted to know.

At the edge of the camera shot there was a disturbance. Raptors were struggling against raptors. What was happening? Suddenly, the picture shifted to focus on the Raptor Council retreating in a stately procession through the main doors of the Imperium Tower.

'Sam! Listen to Nathan.' It was Sherri. Her voice was pleading. 'Do you think your mother would want you to die here? Come on, Sam! We've got to go now. Watch it later if you have to. Newton's recorded the transmission back at the cave. If we don't get away from here, how will we ever hope to avenge her?'

Vengeance. The concept acted like the trigger of a gun inside his head. No sooner had Sherri squeezed it than Sam fired into action. His blood seemed to ignite and burn through his veins like liquid fire. Without a word, he turned and ran for the door.

'Finally!' he heard Nathan mutter.

Crick and Edison were waiting. They stared at him with their cold reptilian eyes. Sam got the distinct impression that they were trying to convey emotion to him – sympathy maybe, but if they were, he could not read their raptor expressions well enough to understand them. He looked away, searching for Newton. The raptor scientist was holding position near the main doors, keeping watch on the approaching patrol. Nathan signalled him to join them and he came running at a sprint. There was a whooshing noise, accompanied by the gentle whine of a propeller overhead as one of the flying machines made a low fly-past over the top of the building.

'David and Callum are on their way. Now it's our turn,' Nathan announced, his voice urgent. 'Let's get the hell out of here. Crick – take point with Sherri. Newton, you're rearguard with me. We know they're gonna come after us, but let's try to get a bit of a head start. And when they come, let's make them wish they hadn't. Edison – stay with Sam. Keep him moving and don't leave him, no matter what.'

A simple push button opened the door from the inside. The Imperium science team was clearly more interested in keeping intruders out than keeping them in. Sam checked his weapon again. He was tempted to leave the safety catch off, but his mother's voice intruded in his mind, warning him of the dangers.

'Always make sure the safety catch is on when you carry a gun, Sam. Only switch it to fire when you're ready to shoot. When possible, take a rough aim first,

flick off the safety, refine your aim and then fire. That way you will only hit the things you intend to shoot at. If you run round with the safety off, all it would take is one slip of the finger and you could shoot me, or Callum, and none of us want that, do we?'

With one final glance back towards the holographic projection, he thumbed the catch to safe and followed Sherri and Crick out through the door. They set off at a run, quickly traversing the open area and taking to the cover of the trees.

One of the flying machines circled round and passed overhead again just after they had made the relative safety of the trees. Sam looked up, but he couldn't see if it was David or Callum flying it. Whoever it was appeared to have the attention of the approaching raptors. They were all following its progress as if hypnotised. The pilot was drawing them away, flying off on a diverging course.

'Genius!' he breathed.

Sam prided himself on his fitness, but it had been a long day and he was amazed by how quickly weariness set in. Within a few minutes, the rifle he was carrying felt as if it had doubled in weight, his lungs burned and his legs reached the leaden state he normally felt at the end of a long cross-country run.

Sam found the next hour a living hell. Periods of sprinting across open ground alternated with tough stints of forcing his way through thick undergrowth beneath the trees. The constant fear of pursuit drove them onward, though if hunters were tracking them, they did not show themselves. They were well out of the city vale before Nathan called a rest stop.

'Do you think they managed to fly those machines and land them safely, Nathan?' Sherri asked.

'It doesn't really matter either way,' he replied with a shrug. 'If they have, we've gained ourselves some flying machines. If they didn't and they wrecked them, then the raptors no longer have flying machines. As far as I'm concerned, it's a win-win situation.'

Sam's breath caught in his throat. If Nathan had a heart, he was good at hiding it. The man was the most callous individual Sam had ever come across. A flush of guilt rushed through him. He had been so caught up with the fate of his mother that he had totally forgotten about his best friend, Callum. What if his friend had crashed in that crazy-looking thing David had designed? He might be dead or badly injured and Sam had not spared him a thought in the last hour.

Then there was David. Sam closed his eyes and pictured the young inventor's face for a moment. He hadn't even wanted to be a part of this.

Suddenly, everything seemed so real; this wasn't

an adventure any more, it was real people he cared about getting hurt. *God, please not Callum!* he thought. *I couldn't bear to lose him and Mum in the same day.*

The image of his mother impaled on the spike filled his mind again. More tears welled and his chest tightened with emotion. He opened his eyes and dashed the tears away with the back of his hand. A tight knot of anger in his gut squeezed and twisted as he thought about what he would like to do to the raptors on the High Council. A quick death was too good for them after what they had done to his mother.

'That's a bit harsh, Nathan,' Sherri told him, glancing across at Sam to see how he had reacted. 'I would be thankful that it wasn't your job to fly one, if I were you.'

'That would have guaranteed a wreck,' he growled.

'Exactly!'

Nathan grunted and took a swig from his water bottle. 'Has everyone had a drink?' he asked. 'If not, take one now. We move again in one minute.'

Sam groaned. It seemed as if they had only just stopped. He ached all over. How far was there still to go? He couldn't remember. The day had been a blur since they were chased from the underground HQ this morning. Had it really only been this morning? So much had happened.

Glancing across at Nathan, Sam experienced a surge of bitterness and anger. *Why did Mum choose him to be her second-in-command?* he wondered. *Why not Alex or Sherri? Nathan's no leader. He just likes to order people around and doesn't care who gets hurt. Without Mum to keep him in line, he's going to be unbearable. If he stays in charge, the rebel group will die a quick death. He'll kill it with his attitude in no time.*

Nathan began talking with Newton – clicking, growling and grunting in the raptor language. He looked troubled and Newton was shaking his head. What was going on now? Sam had no way of telling, but whatever it was, it didn't look good. This whole language barrier thing was so frustrating.

Sherri was sitting nearby, so Sam leaned towards her. 'What's that all about?' he asked in a low voice.

'Nathan's just asking Newton if he's seen any sign of the hunters,' she replied. 'I must admit, I expected them to catch up with us long before now.'

'But surely it's a good thing that they haven't, isn't it?'

'I'm not sure,' she said, glancing across at Nathan and Newton who were still clicking and growling fiercely at one another. 'Just because they haven't attacked doesn't mean they're not there. They might be deliberately shadowing us, waiting to find our hideout so they can return in force later. Nathan is suggesting that we take a more roundabout route to the cave.'

Sam groaned.

'I know how you feel, Sam, but think about the alternative. We take pains to lose them now or we get cornered by a horde of Imperium raptors later. I know which I would prefer.'

'Rest stop over,' Nathan announced. 'On your feet, everyone. Let's press on.'

* * *

Night had fallen by the time they finally reached the cave. Sam was dead on his feet, mindlessly putting one foot in front of the other. Drained of every last drop of physical and emotional energy, even seeing the shadowy figures of Callum and David sitting by a tiny campfire on the far side of the stream failed to spark life into his spirit. An empty shell, he stumbled across the stepping stones to his blanket where he sank to the ground without a word.

'So what kept you guys?' Callum asked cheerily. 'You look beat.'

'Glad to see you made it back in one piece, Callum,' Sherri replied. 'But it's not really a time for levity. The Imperium executed Claire and Alex.'

'Oh, God!' he gasped, getting to his feet and walking swiftly to where his friend was lying. 'Sam, I'm so sorry. I had no idea.'

Sam didn't respond. Inside he was delighted to see Callum alive and well, but he was so exhausted that he was beyond expressing emotion. He looked at Callum for a moment with unseeing eyes and then his eyelids dropped down over his eyes like storm shutters.

Callum stood over Sam feeling helpless. He wanted to offer his friend sympathy, but had no idea how to do it. What could he do at a time like this? There were no words that were sufficient. After a moment of silence, he crouched down and placed his hand on Sam's shoulder. Giving a single squeeze, he tried with all his heart to convey something of how he felt.

'And Nipper?' he asked, standing up and looking back to where Sherri was sinking down next to the fire. 'What happened to Nipper?'

'As far as we know, he's alive,' Sherri answered, depositing a lump of wood into the heart of the ashes and staring as flames immediately started licking around it. 'By chance, we arrived in time to see him kill the Imperium's champion on the holo-projector in the hangar, but after the fight, the Imperium Council decided to change the rules to suit their own purpose. They only released Einstein.'

Callum hesitated, torn between wanting to be close to his friend and wanting to leave him to rest and mourn in peace.

'I'd kill for a hot drink right now,' Sherri hinted.

'I'll sort that,' David offered, getting to his feet.

'Thanks.'

'But I don't get it,' Callum said, walking slowly back across to the fireside and throwing frequent glances back at Sam. 'How could the Council change the rules *after* the fight? Surely, as the leaders of raptor society, they're supposed to be the heart and conscience of their people.'

Nathan gave a sudden bark of scoffing laughter. 'You're attributing human ethics to them, boy, but don't forget that human history has not been without its share of atrocities. Raptors play by a different set of rules. Their mentality is totally different. There's no Geneva Convention here. The Council of the Imperium can do whatever they want to do; kill who they want to kill. They rule with absolute power and that is accepted without question. If they want to change the law, they do it as and when they want to.'

'Then their days could be numbered,' Callum replied. 'If there's one thing that history has shown, it's that ruling a population by fear will often result in a revolution.'

'I'll say it again, lad: among humans that might be true,' Nathan said, shaking his head. 'But the Imperium has controlled raptor society for centuries. The iron fist style of government seems to suit the raptor mentality. There have been no revolts. The Imperium is accepted and the Council is the unquestioned law.'

'So what about these guys?' Callum asked, pointing at Newton and Crick. 'What do you think they're doing? I'd call them rebels. A small stone can sometimes trigger an avalanche, you know.'

'Don't presume to preach at me, boy,' Nathan growled. 'I've been living among raptors for over twenty years. You think I don't know what I'm talking about? Since Claire came along and organised us, we've been a thorn in the side of the Imperium – yes. But it would take more than us few to take them down.'

Edison suddenly gave a loud grunt from over near the cave entrance. He followed it with a loud sequence of clicks and growls.

'Damn!' Nathan swore. 'That's all I need!' He picked up his gun again and ran across the stepping stones, his weariness apparent in his gait.

'What is it?' Callum asked. 'What's going on?'

'We've got company,' Sherri told him. 'Edison says there's a large party of raptors approaching along the base of the valley.'

'You were followed?'

'Must have been,' she replied through gritted teeth. 'But how they did it, I've no idea. Nathan's pretty good at throwing off pursuit and he used every trick going today. How a group could be that close behind us without our detecting them, I really don't know. Grab a weapon and as much ammunition as you can carry. You too, David. Get up, Sam! We're going to need everyone who can hold a weapon.'

Callum ran to where the small stack of rifles was leaning against the wall, grabbed one and scooped several pre-loaded magazines from the open box next to them. By the time he got across the stepping stones, only David and Sam were behind him. He reached the cave entrance and jostled for a position where he could see out.

The valley below was dark, but the darker shadows moving alongside the stream towards them were unmistakable.

'Blimey! There's loads of them!' Callum breathed.

'At least a hundred, boy,' Nathan growled. 'And we're in no state to run again. I guess this is it – the last stand. Anyone who feels up to it had better leave now, but I'm tired of running and hiding. I'm gonna take down as many as I can before they get up here. Who's with me?'

CHAPTER TWENTY-FOUR

Staring at the entrance to the visitor centre at Woodhill High Security Prison, Niamh had mixed feelings about going inside. She felt both scared and excited at the same time, and the mixture of emotions was playing havoc with her stomach, which felt as though it was churning and turning inside her like a bag of live eels.

'Why do I feel like a bad person just being here?' she asked aloud.

'Perhaps because mu— mother would have a fit if she knew we were here,' Archie suggested.

'No, I don't mean that. Just being here somehow makes me feel as if anyone looking at me will think that I'm a criminal.'

'Well, technically you are, Niamh. You did steal a boat after all.'

'You're not helping, Archie.'

'No. Sorry.'

'Don't you feel it?'

Archie thought for a moment. 'Actually, no,' he said eventually, giving her a nervous smile. 'I just think today has been amazing so far. I've never done anything like this before. And we're going to see inside a high security prison. I can't wait to tell Rupert about this.'

Niamh shook her head and sighed. Archie had shown aspects of himself in the past twenty-four hours that Niamh would never have believed possible had she not seen it with her own eyes. It transpired he was both a remarkably efficient organiser and a convincing liar. She had been amazed to see him deceive his mother without hesitation.

Archie had anticipated Niamh's plan, phoned the prison, altered her booking and had memorised the entire visiting procedure. Where Niamh would have met with a brick wall on arrival by coming without an adult, Archie had not taken any chances.

He rang Ben Jacobs, a local eighteen-year-old who had been working part-time as a gardener for his mother, and offered to pay him if he would accompany them for the day. Archie's money bought Ben's cooperation with ease. Given the choice between a day of hard labour and taking a paid trip to Milton Keynes was a no-brainer as far as Ben was concerned. He had spent all summer taking on all manner of work so that he could save some money before starting university in the autumn. He was not going to turn down a cushy job like this. Niamh nearly choked when Archie told her he'd booked Ben in as their guardian.

Archie also planned their journey in detail. Having looked at buses and trains, he had come to the same conclusion as Niamh that the easiest way to Milton Keynes was by train, changing at Coventry where they would pick up a London-bound train that stopped at Milton Keynes. Niamh had been more than a little impressed. Annoying geek or not, Archie had proved his worth today.

When Archie had given a stellar performance, pretending to arrange a meeting with his friend Rupert at the shopping centre in Banbury, his mother had not so much as raised an eyebrow. Niamh had no doubt that when Aunt Aggie dropped them in town, she was completely in the dark about their true plans.

'Have you got your passport?' Archie asked, taking his from his inside jacket pocket.

'Yes, Archie,' she sighed. 'For the *third* time, I've got my passport. Look.'

Niamh fished through her handbag, pulled out

313

her passport and waved it under his nose. No sooner had she done it than she felt bad. Although the irritation factor of his talking at her incessantly since they left Banbury was high, she knew she could not have done this without his help.

'Just checking,' he mumbled, putting his passport back in his pocket. 'We won't get in without the correct ID, you know.'

'I know, Archie. I'm sorry. I didn't mean to snap. I'm just a bit nervous, that's all.'

'That's OK. I know how you feel. I've never *seen* a prison before, let alone gone inside one.'

Niamh looked at her watch – twenty past one. Perfect. Their visit was booked for two o'clock and the prison website had said to allow at least half an hour for the check-in procedure. She looked across at Ben and then at Archie. Ben was wearing scruffy jeans and a T-shirt, while Archie was in immaculate slacks, a collared shirt and a jacket. Would anyone really believe he was Archie's guardian?

'Time to act like a grown-up,' she announced, pulling the earphone of Ben's iPod from his right ear and giving him a meaningful look. 'I said. . .'

'I heard,' he interrupted, taking out the other earpiece. 'Come on then. Let's go inside.'

They went in through the door and up to the desk.

'Hello. Who are you here to see today?'

The lady on the counter did give Ben a strange look when Archie did all the talking, but after confirming with her records that they were expected, she directed them to take a seat. And so the procedure began. Niamh jumped when their names were called. First their ID was checked and the boys were photographed and had their index fingerprints taken on an electronic scanner. Next they, and all of the other visitors in the group, were directed to put all of their belongings into a locker. Not so much as a scrap of loose paper could be taken into the prison. The only things allowed were the locker key and loose change up to the value of twenty pounds.

A prison officer led them from the visitor centre and into the main prison building where they had to remove shoes, belts and jackets to be put through a scanner while another officer conducted a wand search of each of them in turn. Once they were done, it was another wait in an enormous holding room before a door eventually opened into a corridor and everyone was ushered in. Only when everyone was in the corridor did the door close behind them and a sequenced door opened ahead, allowing them to progress across a courtyard and into another gigantic room with lines of chairs bolted to the floor, where they were asked to wait again.

Niamh was completely overawed by the experience. She passed through the entire procedure in a daze. When they were finally called to a table, she was on the point of tears. It was unthinkable that her father was being held in this place. Prison officers dressed in black trousers, white shirts and black jumpers with black ties watched everything. The sheer greyness of the place was overwhelming. All around the room were dozens of security cameras. Every possible angle was covered. There was no way anyone could so much as twitch without at least two cameras recording it. Privacy was impossible. How could her dad stand it? Would he have changed? How could he not have been changed by a place like this?

Niamh folded her arms tightly across her chest as she waited to be called forward. Despite the room being at a comfortable temperature, her body felt tight and chilled through to the bone. There was something about the bleak interior of the prison that seemed to emanate an unnerving coldness.

Again, Niamh started as she heard her name called. They were directed to a specific table where three blue chairs were solidly bolted to the floor on one side and a yellow chair was equally secured on the other. The table between the chairs was barely thirty centimetres wide, with a raised section in the middle to prevent anything from being slid from one side to the other. Matthew Cutler was led across the hall to them. He had a huge smile on his face. To her surprise, he was in his own clothing and he looked exactly as he always did.

'Niamh!'

'Dad!'

Without thought for the guards, or any rules she might be breaking, she ran to him and threw her arms round him in a huge hug. To her delight, the guards did not intervene, but allowed them their moment of intimacy. The intensity of the meeting was immense and the floodgates burst. Before she realised she was doing it, she was sobbing uncontrollably.

'Hey! Steady on there,' Matt soothed, stroking her hair and holding her close. 'There's no need for all that. I'm fine. Everything's OK. Come on. We can have our hug for a moment, but then you'd better sit down. How come you're here today? I nearly fell off my bunk with shock when they told me you were coming. Aggie told me she wasn't going to let you come and see me. I told her you'd be fine coming here, but she was very insistent. My sister can be a bit of a pain at times, but at least I knew you'd be safe with her.'

Niamh laughed through her tears at her dad's assessment of his sister. Archie laughed too.

'Good to see you too, Archie. Thanks for coming today. I have to say I'm equally surprised to see you here given your mother's feelings about the trouble I'm in.'

'It's super to see you too, Uncle Matthew,' Archie replied, reaching over and shaking his hand. 'Don't worry. I don't believe for one second that you're guilty.'

'That's good to hear,' Matt replied, giving him a warm smile. He eased Niamh loose from her bear hug. 'The guards are twitching, Niamh. You'd better take a seat. Now this must be Ben?'

'That's right.'

'And you're their *guardian*, I hear.'

Ben looked embarrassed. 'Sort of,' he said. 'Guardian for the day, you might say.'

'Agatha has no idea you're here, does she?' Matt asked, fixing first Niamh and then Archie with a reproving look.

Niamh and Archie looked at one another, their guilty glances saying it all.

'She was never going to let us come,' Niamh complained. 'I wanted to see if you were all right, and there are some things I really need to talk to you about. So I decided to come by myself. But Archie guessed what I was planning and asked to come along. Actually, Archie arranged the whole visit. He was brilliant.'

Archie flushed bright red.

'Well, you've put me in a tricky position – both of you. I'm not going to tell you off for coming, because if truth be told, I'm delighted to see you. But you do realise, Archie, that your mother will flip when she finds out.'

'Are you going to tell on us, Uncle Matthew?' Archie asked, looking at Matt with pleading eyes.

'No, you don't need to worry about that, but one way or another these things always seem to get found out eventually, and when they do. . .' He left them to imagine the consequences. 'After the police took me in that day back on Summerland Key, they did keep me updated on some of your exploits, Niamh, and your aunt told me a little more. Tell me, did you really steal Mitch's boat?'

'Steal's a bit of a strong word, Dad,' Niamh replied, suddenly unable to look him in the eye. 'But I did sort of borrow it for a bit, yes.'

'I can't believe you'd be so irresponsible!' he exclaimed, his tone full of reproof. 'What were you thinking, Niamh? Anything could have happened to you. I thought you were the sensible one. Did you ever stop to think how worried I'd be?'

Niamh looked into his eyes and the hurt she saw there stabbed like a dagger to her heart.

'Yes, Dad,' she said, tears welling in her eyes. 'I

thought about it often, but I didn't feel I had a choice. When the police came to take you away, I realised that I was the only one left with a real need to find the boys. Everyone else would just be going through the motions of a search. You made that point to me several times when I asked you about Mum.'

'And that made it OK to commit a serious crime and possibly alienate one of our family friends? You're very lucky that Mitch didn't press charges.'

'I'm sorry. No, Dad,' she said, unable to maintain eye contact. 'Of course it didn't make it OK. But I didn't feel as if I had much choice. I *know* Sam's alive. You know how close we are, Dad. I really believe we could find him if you weren't stuck in here, but there's not much hope of doing it unless we can get back to Florida.'

She looked up at him again and his eyes bored into hers as he considered her words.

'Apology accepted,' he said eventually, his expression softening. 'But please don't do anything like that again, Niamh. I don't think my poor heart will take much more. Now, can you fill in some blanks for me? Tell me what happened after you ran.'

Niamh went through an abridged account of her adventures in the Florida Keys and Matt's eyes were not the only ones that were wide as she described her tangles with the police and how she evaded them for as long as she did. She omitted to say anything about her growing fondness for Tony, but she knew her father well enough to know that he would read between the lines. Ben stared at her in amazement throughout and Archie listened intently, soaking up each word.

'Dad, you know how I've always said that there are times when I can feel when Sam is in trouble or pain?'

'Yes.'

'Ever since the boys disappeared, I've been getting images in my mind that can only have come from Sam, Dad. He's been in a lot of danger, but he's definitely still alive. I really think some of your Devil's Triangle theories could be the key to finding him.'

'You're sure?' he asked, his eyes alight as he considered her story. 'I can't tell you how good that makes me feel. For years I've told myself over and over that Claire might still be alive somewhere, but it's been hard to hold on to that hope. Your link with your brother could prove to be the key to solving the mystery that has baffled the world for years. So you've been going through my notes. Have you reached any conclusions?'

At the mention of her mother, the horrifying image of her impaled on the spike flashed into her mind again and Niamh was glad that her father's eyes were distant at that moment as she felt sure that something of her reaction to that picture would surely show on her face. Should she conceal the image from him? Would he want to know? Could she tell him even if she wanted to? She decided to avoid the subject for now. He had enough to contend with.

'Dad, I really think you're on to something with the electromagnetic research you were doing.'

'Really?' he said excitedly. 'For a long time I thought that was a red herring, but in recent years, I've become progressively more interested in it. What drew you to that?'

'It's more of a feeling than anything else,' she said thoughtfully. 'Intuition. For some reason I can't explain, there is something about it that makes me feel that you're getting close to the truth. There's something else as well. A common theme that kept cropping up among the incidents where people didn't disappear was "the sea looking different". You wrote a comment in your notes that intrigued me: what if it really was a different sea? Do you think there could be a link between an electromagnetic field and the sea looking different? I didn't find anything more in your notes.'

'Well, there're lots of reasons why the sea might

look different. . .' Matt said thoughtfully. 'I can't remember what I was thinking when I wrote that note now. It must be an old one. I don't think electromagnetism could affect the appearance of the sea—'

'What about the Hutchison Effect?' Niamh interrupted. 'He appeared to move non-metallic materials with electromagnetic fields. Would water not be similarly affected?'

I suppose it's possible,' he admitted.

'Of course there is another possibility,' Niamh offered.

'Which is?'

'Your note might have been spot on. They could have been looking at an entirely different sea,' she said.

'A portal!' Archie exclaimed. 'Like the sort of things they found in *Star Trek*?'

'I wouldn't know about *Star Trek*, Archie, but yes, I suppose so,' she said. 'Sort of like looking through a window into another world.'

'A window to another world. . .' Matt repeated, his voice low and breathy. 'Could it be? Or a different dimension? A different universe? No! Surely not. That's just too far-fetched.'

'Is it?' Niamh asked. 'It would explain many of the most baffling mysteries. What was it that Sherlock

Holmes said about solving puzzles? When you have eliminated all other possibilities, whatever remains, no matter how improbable, must be the truth.'

'Sherlock Holmes wasn't a real detective, Niamh. He was a fictional character.'

'I know, but the principle seems sound to me.'

'Assuming for a moment that your hypothesis was correct, it would mean that the boys . . . and even Claire . . . might still be alive and, well, in another world.'

At the fresh mention of her mother, Niamh looked away again, but not quickly enough. Matt's gaze zeroed in on her and his eyes narrowed as he tried to interpret her expression.

'There's something important you're not telling me, isn't there? Come on, Niamh. No secrets. We need to help each other here.'

'Dad, wherever Sam is . . . I think he found Mum there.'

Matthew's eyes lit up, but then narrowed as he studied her face. 'I want to leap about and yell "I knew it!", but there's still something you're not telling me, isn't there? Something bad. I can see it in your eyes, Niamh. Out with it. Come on. Don't bottle it up. Trust me, it's for the best.'

Tears welled afresh in her eyes as she tried to form the words in her mouth. How could she tell him?

She knew how much Claire still meant to him, even after all this time.

'Is it about Sam? Or your mum?'

'It's Mum,' she murmured, her voice feeling so tight that she could suddenly barely speak. 'It's why I had to come and see you, Dad. It happened yesterday. I saw her through Sam's eyes. Dad, it was terrible! I saw her dying and I felt Sam's shock and anger as I viewed it through his eyes. I can't get the image out of my mind. It's horrible.'

All the colour drained from Matt's face.

'I'm so sorry, Dad,' she said, words suddenly spilling from her mouth in an accelerating torrent. 'All these years you were right to keep looking. I know it now. I'm sorry if me and Sam doubted you. There's something going on in the Devil's Triangle – something weird. I wish I'd tried to help more before it came to this. I'm so sorry.'

Matthew Cutler took a deep breath and let it out in a long sigh. Tears welled in his eyes as he met her gaze.

'No apologies, Niamh,' he said, shaking his head and dashing the tears away with the back of his hand. 'You and Sam have always been very patient with my obsession with finding your mum. But until I can prove she's dead, I can't give up on Claire. I've come too far. And I've not had a chance to begin searching in earnest for Sam and Callum. All I can hope for now is that your vision is just a bad dream.'

'It's OK, Dad,' Niamh replied, tears running freely down her cheeks. 'I understand. I'm sorry, but I had to tell you.'

'Of course you did, darling,' he soothed. 'Listen. We'll find them. OK? Somehow, someday, we'll find them all.' He paused, thinking. 'Actually, I've been thinking for a couple of years now that I should see if I can get something, an instrument or gadget of some kind, that will detect, measure and track electromagnetic disturbances. I don't even know if such a thing exists. But maybe something like that could help.'

'If it does exist, we'll find it, Uncle,' Archie volunteered. 'And if it doesn't, then we'll just have to find someone who can build us something to do the job.'

CHAPTER TWENTY-FIVE

'Everyone find a comfortable vantage spot with a good field of fire,' Nathan growled, his deep voice thick with frustration and anger. 'Don't fire until you're sure of your target. Make every shot count. When they attack, they'll come like a swarm of angry hornets. Try to stay calm and pick them off, starting with the closest first. Let's make them regret coming here.'

Sam moved out of the cave entrance and settled himself behind a large rock. Last stand or not, Sam felt surprisingly unafraid. Instead, a white-hot furnace of anticipation roared inside him. Using the rock as a rest to steady his aim, he fixed his focus on a point some distance down the winding path and waited.

The gloomy light of dusk was fading fast. Would the raptors wait for complete darkness, or would they attack straight away? They were little more than dark shadows already. Picking them out well enough to make each shot count in the full dark of night would be nearly impossible. Breathing in through his nose and out through his mouth, Sam attempted to calm the throbbing beat of his inner fury.

Callum appeared to his right and squatted down behind the rock next to his. 'Nathan sounds pretty hacked off,' he observed.

'Nathan always sounds hacked off,' Sam replied without humour. 'But I suppose he has good cause now. I imagine I would be pretty annoyed if I'd just led an army of raptors to my secret hideout. It was a pretty stupid thing to do.'

'I'm sure he didn't do it on purpose.'

'I know, but that doesn't stop it from being stupid,' Sam said, maintaining his focus through the sights of his rifle. 'Hello! What's this? It looks like they've stopped.'

Callum stood up to get a clearer view. Sam was reluctant to lose his focus and do likewise, but after a moment, his curiosity won him over.

'It looks like a single raptor is climbing up,' Callum noted. 'What do you think he wants?'

'Our surrender probably,' Sam replied coldly. Trying to remember everything his mother had taught him, he concentrated on aiming the rifle at the raptor's centre of mass. Almost as if the raptor heard what he had said, or sensed fingers tightening on triggers, it suddenly stopped and called out to them in a loud voice.

'Hold your fire, everyone,' Nathan ordered. 'Put your safety catches on. Newton, you're with me. I want to check this out. It could still be a trap.'

'What's going on?' Sam asked in a loud voice.

'The raptor claims to be Einstein,' Sherri answered, as Nathan and Newton jumped up and moved down the path to intercept the lone figure. 'It certainly sounds like him, but it's hard to be sure at this distance.'

'So what are all those other raptors doing here?'

'Patience, Sam,' Sherri replied. 'I don't know any more than you do on that front. Let's wait and see, shall we?'

When Nathan returned, he brought some familiar figures with him. Alongside Newton came Einstein and behind them Grunt supported a sorry-looking Nipper. His wounds had been smothered with a pungent ointment that had stopped the bleeding. He walked slowly and with a heaviness that was so out of character that Sam barely recognised him.

On seeing Sam, Nipper stopped and regarded him with a steady stare.

'Ssssamm. Ssssorry,' Nipper apologised and bowed his head.

'You don't need to apologise, Nipper,' Sam replied, tears trickling down his cheeks in steady rivulets. 'You did all you could. You risked your life trying to save my mother. I will never forget that.'

Nipper looked up and met Sam's gaze with his steady black eyes. For a moment he was silent and then the injured raptor turned to Sherri and spoke to her in his own language.

'Nipper says he would not be alive now if it was not for you, Sam,' she translated. 'He says you owe him nothing. Any debt you had was cancelled when you taught him the human fighting techniques he used to stay alive. He says he was proud to name Claire as a member of his family, just as he is proud to name you.'

'And I am proud to be named,' Sam replied, inclining his head in a gesture of respect.

It was clear that Nipper understood. Sherri addressed Nipper again, but it was Grunt who answered. Sam was curious to know what they were saying because whatever Grunt had answered clearly excited the diminutive woman.

'What is it?' he asked. 'What did Grunt say?'

'It seems the Council of the Imperium made a big miscalculation this afternoon,' she explained, her words spilling out in a bubbling torrent. 'Their decision to ignore tradition and continue with the execution of Alex and Claire this afternoon after Nipper's victory over their champion has angered large numbers of raptors. Nipper is now considered a wronged hero, and Alex and Claire, despite being human, have been hailed as martyrs. All those raptors down there have sworn oaths to follow Nipper and to defy the Imperium. Better still, it could be that they are the tip of the iceberg. This could be the start of a full-scale rebellion!'

Callum let out a long whistle as the implications of Sherri's words sank in.

Nathan led the four raptors inside the cave, Grunt supporting Nipper, and Newton and Einstein deep in conversation. David followed them inside holding his rifle awkwardly. His face wore an expression of profound relief. Edison was sent down to the valley to organise the crowd and set up hunting parties. They were going to need a lot of food if they were to feed everyone.

'It's strange the way fate works. Losing Claire, Alex and Watson today should have crippled us, yet as a result, we may have gained the force we need to have a real chance of trying to take down the entire global pumping programme permanently,' Sherri added, watching as Edison descended towards the small horde of raptors in the valley. 'Claire talked about this for years, but none of us ever thought we'd be in a position to try it. If I know Einstein, we're not going to see much of him for a while. He's going to be tinkering with his machines day and night until they're ready.'

'Machines? What machines?' Sam's voice stabbed like a stiletto blade. At the mention of his mother, his eyes had ignited with fierce intensity and now they bored into Sherri. 'If Einstein's planning to follow up on something Mum wanted, then I want in on it.'

'I don't pretend to understand them,' she replied with a shrug. 'All I can tell you is that they are sort of ray-guns. The machines shoot beams of invisible particles that apparently increase the mass of whatever they hit. Einstein wants to direct the machines at the nuclear waste pumping shafts. He thinks he can mess with the pressures there in a way that will result in the simultaneous destruction of every pumping station around the world.'

'God particles!' Callum exclaimed. 'You're talking about a machine that produces a coherent stream of God particles.'

'Erm . . . if you say so,' Sherri replied, clearly flummoxed.

'What *are* you talking about, Callum?' Sam asked, turning his stare on his friend.

'If it's what I think, it means that raptors have discovered something that scientists in our world only started to look for recently,' Callum replied excitedly. 'You know when there was a big deal in the news about the possibility of the world ending when they switched on the LHC in Switzerland?'

'LHC?' Sam's eyebrows twisted into a frown as he tried to work out what the letters meant.

'Large Hadron Collider,' Callum explained.

'Oh, yeah! The big bang and all that.'

'That's right! The scaremongers were saying that by trying to recreate the conditions that scientists believe existed at the beginning of the universe, they might actually cause a miniature black hole and destroy the world. Anyway, I thought it was really interesting and read up on a lot of stuff about the experiments. One of the things they're trying to do with the LHC is to prove the existence of a particle called the Higgs boson, which is supposed to add mass to matter.'

'OK, let's just assume for a moment that I followed all that, which is far from certain. . .' Sam looked down at the ground, his focus distant as he mentally played back what Callum had just explained. 'I still don't see why this Higgs thingy is such a big deal.'

'To be honest, I don't understand much of the physics behind it,' Callum admitted. 'But the idea of a machine that could create a coherent Higgs field for use as a weapon is terrifying. The effects would be devastating. Depending how strong the beam was and where you aimed it, you could produce destruction more extensive than the detonation of a nuclear bomb!'

Sam looked back up at Callum again and his eyes narrowed with disbelief. 'You're serious?'

'Completely!'

'What would the side-effects be?' Sam asked. 'Nuclear bombs can leave radiation that pollutes for millennia. What sort of after-effects would this Higgs particle weapon leave?'

'Not a clue,' Callum replied with a shrug. 'No one's even managed to confirm the existence of the particles in our world. You'd better ask Einstein that one.'

'I will.'

Callum gave his friend a calculating look. 'Sam, don't get too involved. Your mum wanted you to try to go home. Sherri told me what your mum said before . . . before she died. We've got two flying machines now. They're our ticket out of here. I just know they are. One of them's had a bit of damage, but it won't take much to fix and they're really easy to fly. I can teach you in no time. Let Nathan and the others deal with the Imperium. It's not our fight.'

'Not *your* fight maybe,' Sam replied, his eyes taking on a distant look again. 'But my mum died for this cause so I'm not going anywhere for a while. If she had a plan, then I want to see it through. I'm going to make the Imperium pay for taking her away from me.'

'Don't be stupid, Sam! That's your anger talking. If you let your feelings about what happened today rule you, then you're just going to get yourself killed.'

'And trying to fly into the eye of a hurricane in the next best thing to a box kite is going to be perfectly safe, I suppose? I don't think so.'

'Sam, you promised you would get me back.'

'What?'

'In the boat – when we crossed,' Callum said. 'You said you would get me back home. I'm going to hold you to your word, Sam. *You* got me into this. Now it's time to go home. We've got the means. I'm asking you to keep your promise and come with me.'

'You should listen to your friend, Sam,' Sherri interrupted. 'Nathan won't be happy about you taking the flying machines, but I'll support you. It was Claire's dying wish, after all, and we don't really need them. Stealing them was all about denying the Imperium the power of flight. I can't see Nathan strapping himself into one of those contraptions and I certainly don't want to do it.'

'What about David? He built the machines. He

has more claim on them than anyone,' Sam pointed out. 'Surely he should have a say in this? I know he wants to see the flying machines of our world. Why not take him with you, Cal? I'm sorry, but I'm not sure I'm ready to go home. Not yet.'

'Sam, I'm never going to forgive you if you don't come with me.'

'Don't say that, Cal,' Sam pleaded. 'It's not that I don't want to come with you. I meant what I said that day about getting you home, but that was before the Imperium killed Mum. Surely you can see how important this is to me. If Mum had a plan, then I want to finish what she started before I go home. If I don't, I'm not sure I'd be able to live with myself.'

Callum shook his head. 'I'm not ready to fall out with you. You're tired, hurt and not thinking straight,' he said. 'It's been a crazy day. Sleep on it. We'll talk in the morning.'

Sam nodded. 'Good idea.' He took a final look down at the raptors in the valley before heading into the cave. Callum and Sherri followed him inside. Despite the louder than usual conversations both Sam and Callum were wrapped in their blankets and asleep within just a few minutes. For Sam, however, sleep brought no escape from pain.

* * *

By the time day finally broke, Sam felt terrible. His eyes burned and his stomach ached from twisting and turning inside until it felt like it was knotted tight. Throughout the night he had been plagued by nightmares. Pursued by raptors through tunnels, woods and across fields, he had battled for survival again and again.

In some of his dreams he had stayed with his mother as she had held the rearguard during their flight from the Imperium search parties. In others he had gone with Nipper to the Central Square to challenge for her life, but every dream ended the same way: with the one image that burned in his mind with crystal clarity. Over and over he saw his mother being impaled. Now he was awake, the picture seemed to be imprinted on his retinas. No matter where he looked, he saw it. And every time he did, his eyes filled with tears.

Peeling off his blanket, he stretched and got up. He needed a distraction, something to focus on. Callum was still fast asleep. Sam stared at him for a moment and his chest tightened with emotion as he considered again if he should deliberately part company with his friend. It was hard to imagine not having him close by, especially after all the recent adventures they had shared. It wasn't just Callum either. He knew he was gambling with the chance of never seeing his father and sister again, which added a whole different dimension to his feelings of guilt. However, neither sleep, guilty sadness at breaking his promise to Callum nor the risk of never getting home served to change his mind. His resolve had hardened overnight. If Einstein had a way of destroying the pumping stations, then Sam was determined to stay and help make the plan work.

CHAPTER TWENTY-SIX

Niamh rolled on to her back, opened her eyes and stared upward. Although her body felt desperately tired, her mind was far too active to allow her the blissful descent into sleep. A hard line of light round her door made a stark contrast with the gentle moonlight seeping in round the edges of the curtains. The combination lit the room enough for Niamh to see the swirling Artex patterns across the ceiling. Forcing her body to relax still further, she concentrated on following the lines of the patterns with her eyes in an effort to clear her head of worries and unwanted images.

The visit to the prison today had been disturbing on many levels. She still felt degraded by the experience, although she knew it to be an unwarranted and irrational response. The thought of what her father was going through made her want to cry. It was not just the loss of freedom and privacy, but of so many other simple things that most took for granted. And what had he done to deserve it? Nothing! It was not fair. She wrapped her arms across her body and hugged herself, remembering again how good it had felt to hold and be held by him.

I'll get you out of there, Dad, she thought. *I don't know how yet, but I'll do it somehow.*

Perhaps worse than seeing her father in that awful place was the image of her mother that she couldn't get out of her mind. Was it real? Had Sam really seen it or was her imagination playing tricks on her? Much as she wanted to believe the latter, Niamh could not bring herself to believe it. It had been too vivid – too real. She had felt Sam's pain as if it was her own and although she did not understand his mix of emotions, she could also still feel the searing heat of his anger surging through her like a roaring flame. Her heart had reflected her brother's pain and sorrow like a mirror, though she felt no anger. It was this difference that convinced her she was not suffering from an overactive imagination.

Rolling over again, she reached down the side of her bed and felt around until she found her laptop. She lifted it on to the bed and shuffled up, twisting her top pillow upright and settling it behind her back so that she could sit up and lean back comfortably.

She opened the screen and pressed the start button. The sudden light from the screen seemed unnaturally bright in the dark room and she found herself forced to squint, nearly shutting her eyes to reduce the glare until they had a chance to adjust.

The boot-up sequence seemed to take forever. Niamh drummed her fingernails impatiently against the laptop until the wireless internet icon finally showed as connected. Moments later, she had logged into Facebook and her eyes went straight to the chat box at the bottom right of the screen. It showed just two of her friends online. The clock just below chat showed 02:04, which meant it was just after nine o'clock in the evening in Florida. She clicked on the box, praying that one of the two was Tony.

The list expanded up the page. His name was on the list, but the dot next to his name was grey, indicating he was not connected. Given his position on the list, it looked as though she had just missed him. For a moment, Niamh experienced an almost overwhelming sense of desperation and frustration. She closed her eyes and counted to ten. Why wasn't anything going her way today?

She opened her eyes and was ready to log off when she suddenly saw the dot next to Tony's name turn green, indicating he was online again. In a flash, she had clicked on his name, typed *Hi Tony* and hit send.

There was a brief pause and the little icon next to his name began to swirl, indicating he was typing a reply. The popping noise as his response arrived sent a thrill through her.

Hi Niamh. A bit late for you, isn't it? Can't sleep?

No. Visited Dad today and now I can't get the prison out of my head. Wish I was back in the Keys.

I wish you were here, too. Missing you.

Missing you too. But Dad says we'll be coming back at the first opportunity. There's going to be a preliminary court hearing soon and he says his lawyer will try to get the case dismissed for lack of evidence. I just hope he's successful.

Fingers crossed. From what you've told me about your Aunt Aggie, I'm surprised she let you go and see him.

She didn't.

Ah! Up to your old tricks again! What did you steal this time? A car? A train maybe?

Lol. Nothing like that. Aunt Aggie has no idea that I went. My cousin helped me and we got there and back without her realising.

The annoying one? Archie?

Yep. He might be an irritating geek, but it turns out he's a bit of a wizard at organising things.

Niamh nearly laughed out loud as she typed the word *wizard*. Given Archie's love of the word, she bet he would be delighted if he knew that someone had used it to describe him.

They continued with their typed conversation for some time, in particular discussing her father's notes and what her Dad had said about the possible link between the electromagnetic phenomenon and the possibility of a gateway to another world, but eventually Niamh's eyes grew so heavy that she decided to try sleeping again. Talking with Tony, even via a chat facility on the computer, had helped to restore calm to her sea of emotion. She signed off and placed the laptop back down next to the bed.

Although her mind was still active as she settled back down, this time sleep claimed her and if she dreamed, there were no remnants haunting her when she woke the next morning.

* * *

'Wow, Callum! What did you do to it?'

Sam looked at the tattered lower wing of the flying machine and the mangled remnants of the undercarriage in amazement as David made a closer study of the damage. Even with the three of them it had been a struggle to pull it out from where Callum and David had secreted it under the trees.

'I flew it through a tree. What does it look like?'

Callum replied, trying to make the statement sound as though this was an everyday occurrence.

'And you want to teach *me* how to fly?' Sam laughed. 'You've got to be kidding!'

'In my defence, I did fly through it deliberately,' he said huffily.

'Yes, of course you did,' Sam agreed, nodding sagely. 'I'm sure it's one of the first things you learn when you start flying.' He changed his voice to make it sound like an imaginary flying instructor. 'Now then chaps, make sure you fly through at least one tree today. Remember, it's an essential part of your nesting qualification. We don't want those pesky birds getting all superior and thinking they own the place, do we?'

Callum laughed. 'Perish the thought!' he added.

'I'm going to need some materials if I'm going to fix this mess,' David interrupted from underneath the machine. 'And tools. The damage is more extensive than I first thought, but it's not a total disaster. I'm going back to the cave to see if I can enlist the help of Einstein and Newton. Do you want to stay here and watch over the machine, or shall we push it back under the trees so you can come with me?'

'We'll come with you,' Sam decided. 'I doubt it's a good idea for any of us to travel even short distances alone at the moment.'

Directed by David, they lifted the machine and eased it out of the open and under the cover of the trees. They spent a few minutes attempting to camouflage it, but there was no way of completely covering the aircraft. All they could do was break up its outline and hope for the best.

'We should set up a guard round the machines,' David said. 'Having gone to the trouble of stealing them, it would be crazy to let the Imperium take them back at will.'

'Makes sense,' Sam agreed. 'I'll ask Nathan about it while you sort out what you need with Einstein and Newton. With all the new recruits we gained overnight, I doubt a guard will prove much of a problem.'

Sam was right. Nathan was glad to have a task that he could assign some of the new raptor recruits that would make them feel useful. The number of raptors in the valley did not seem anywhere near as large as they had been the previous evening, but this was because Nathan had already organised some into hunting parties and guard patrols. The new group of raptors was far too large to house in the cave, so he had appointed scouts and sent them out into the surrounding countryside to look for another concealed site that they could use as a base for so many raptors.

'We're going to need some sort of a screening process for new recruits,' Nathan growled as he prowled up and down at the base of the waterfall. Every now and then he threw a glance at the remaining crowd of raptors camped in the base of the valley. 'I'm fairly confident there won't be any Imperium spies among this lot. The Council clearly didn't anticipate this response to what happened in the plaza yesterday, so they had no time to organise infiltrators. They won't take long though. The Council of the Imperium are no fools. I wish your mother was here, kid. She was great at organising stuff like this.'

Sam winced at the mention of his mum, but if Nathan noticed, he showed no sign of it. 'You're doing a good job, Nathan,' Sam replied, choking the words out. 'I'm sure Mum would be pleased with the way you're setting things up. So you're OK with setting up a guard and sending some of the new raptors out to scavenge parts for David?'

'Yeah, well, I'm not so sure about doing a good job, but you can leave organising a watch for the machines with me. In fact, I'll get Edison to go and set something up right now. Grunt can take a few of the newcomers to look for David's materials. I'll send him over to find out what they're looking for next time I see him. If I had my way, I'd destroy the ruddy things. As far as I can see, they're a liability, but if David and Callum are crazy enough to want to fly them again, they might yet prove useful.'

For a moment, Sam considered telling Nathan about Callum's plan to try to return home, but he decided against it. There was no telling how the man would react and although Sam knew his mother had trusted Nathan implicitly, he still could not find it in himself to share that confidence.

Will David be willing to go with Callum if I don't? Sam wondered. The thought of Callum attempting the journey on his own filled Sam with dread. As far as anyone in this world knew, no one had ever managed to cross back to modern Earth. Also, if anyone had done it, then the crossing had never become public knowledge in either world. Most felt trying to reach the eye of a powerful storm in this world to be a path to certain death. *So why do I feel better at the idea of David going along? Surely it's worse that they both fly to their deaths?* There was no justification for his feeling. It stemmed from a selfish desire to put a surrogate in his place.

Callum was right. Sam had promised to get him home and now he felt like a traitor for even contemplating breaking that promise. He was torn. He didn't want to abandon his friend, but equally, he had sworn an oath to himself that he would honour his mother's memory by completing the task to which she had dedicated the last years of her life: a task that would benefit not just one world, but two. One way or the other, he would have to break a promise. Which was worse? He thought he had made up his mind last night, but now he wasn't so sure. Dad and Niamh would be devastated if they ever found out and the thought of possibly never seeing them again wrenched at his heart. It was a terrible dilemma. Whatever choice he made, Sam knew he would look back at his decision and ask the question, 'What if?'

CHAPTER TWENTY-SEVEN

'Are you sure it will fly in that state?' Sam asked Callum, looking at the patchwork repairs and the mismatched wheels on the flying machine.

'It flew with a bloomin' great hole in the bottom wing and more than half of the undercarriage missing, Sam. I'm pretty confident that she'll fly a lot better now that we've put that right.'

Sam checked over both shoulders to see if anyone was in earshot and lowered his voice to barely more than a whisper. 'And David is still keen on trying to cross with you?'

'As mustard,' Callum replied, eyeing his friend for any sign of a change of heart. 'But you could still come, you know. This thing was designed to carry the weight of a raptor. It would easily carry both of us. I could get David to help me adapt the harness. It wouldn't take. . .'

'No,' Sam interrupted. 'I'm sorry, Cal, but my mind is made up. I'm going to see Mum's plan through. When I've done that, I'll find a way to come home. I won't be far behind you. Einstein expects to have his machines up and running within the next few weeks.'

Callum shook his head, feeling the cold sting of rejection inside. 'I wish I could say I understood, but I don't. Your mum wanted you to go home, Sam. This is our chance. What you're doing is madness. Leave Nathan and the others to do it. They're far more geared up for all this rebellion stuff.'

'I'm sorry, Cal. I know I promised to get you home, but I have to do this.'

'No. You don't. That's just the point. Let Nathan and Einstein destroy the pumping stations. If their plan is going to work, it will work with or without you. Please come with me. There's nothing here for either of us now. If you won't do it for me, then think about Niamh and your dad.'

For a moment, Callum thought he had got through to his friend, but even as hope flared within him, he saw the resolve harden again in Sam's eyes, as if slamming shut a cell door to deliberately lock himself inside. It was clear now that there was nothing he could say to change Sam's mind. Anger and frustration coursed through his gut, but he clamped down the emotions. Sam had been his friend since day one of secondary school. This might be their last conversation, and he had no intention of parting on anything other than friendly terms.

'Sorry, Cal. I can't do it.'

'OK. In that case, all I can say is good luck and give the Imperium hell,' he said. 'Try to get back before the start of term, won't you? I'm not sure I'd have the heart to wind up Mr Morris without you.'

'I'll do my best,' Sam replied, giving him a weak smile.

'I know you will.'

Callum turned so the breeze was blowing into his face and looked up as if surveying the sky. Blinking several times, he managed to keep the tears welling in his eyes from escaping down his cheeks. He turned again to climb into the aircraft harness, but before he had a chance to step up, he felt Sam's hand grip his shoulder and the next thing he knew they were hugging one another.

'Good luck, Cal. Fly safe. Tell Dad and Niamh what I'm doing. I think Niamh will understand even if Dad doesn't. Tell them I'm going to come home just as soon as I can.'

He wanted to say more, but his throat was

threatening to clamp shut with emotion and he couldn't articulate just how bad he felt.

'I will. I'm glad none of our other friends are here,' Callum said, squeezing his friend close and patting his back. 'We'd never hear the last of this if word got out that we'd been hugging each other.'

'I won't tell if you don't.'

'Not a chance. Be careful, mate. Don't do anything stupid like getting yourself killed. If Niall Rowlands takes your place as captain of the school football team, it'll be a disaster of unimaginable proportions.'

'I'll do my best,' Sam replied, smiling despite himself.

They broke from the embrace and both instinctively brushed themselves down as if clearing their bodies of the memory. Callum climbed the aircraft's ladder steps and settled into the harness, drawing the steps up and securing them on their rail beneath him. He pulled his goggles down, settling them over the top of his glasses and adjusting the straps to get them comfortable. Looking across at David, he gave him the thumbs-up signal and they both switched on their electromagnetic converters.

He waved at Sam as he stepped to one side as the gentle humming of the converters was followed quickly by the buzz of the caged fan propeller

352

accelerating and his machine began to gently trundle forward. His goggles began to steam up immediately as tears formed in his eyes.

'Damn it!' he cursed, tilting the goggles from his cheeks with his left hand to allow air to circulate and clear the fog while keeping the machine straight with his right. It was not easy. The ground here was not as flat as the meadow outside the city where the raptors had flown from. Even at a slow speed the machine bounced and the wings flexed alarmingly. As the acceleration built, the bumping run became progressively more violent until, with one final bone-jarring jolt, the wheels left the ground and hung in the air.

For a moment, the airspeed indicator needle fluctuated in and out of the green sector as the aircraft appeared undecided as to whether it was ready to be in the air. Gritting his teeth, Callum held the control bar steady and willed the airspeed to climb. To his relief, the steady increase of power from the converters did their job and little by little, the machine staggered away from the ground and established a slow but steady climb.

A glance to his right revealed David was climbing alongside him and slowly accelerating ahead in the other aircraft. There was no doubt that the newer machine had the edge when it came to power, but

353

Callum did not mind. Having seen the punishment this one could take and still remain airborne, he was perfectly happy to be flying the poor relation.

The ground slowly dropped away beneath him, quickly taking on the appearance of a complex tapestry. As prearranged with David, they climbed ahead to a safe altitude before turning through 180 degrees and overflying the open ground where Sam was waving enthusiastically at them. David extended ahead before turning, so that he could follow Callum's lead.

Callum rocked the wings in acknowledgement as he flew over his friend. To his right, he could see the rebel encampment in the valley near the cave. Avoiding it, he banked away to the left and set a south-easterly course that gave a good closing angle to the coast. Although he could no longer see David's machine, he assumed that the inventor was following.

The power difference between the machines and the difficulties in flying together had become apparent when they had stolen the machines. When Callum proposed taking the machines to attempt a crossing through the eye of a storm, David's eyes had lit up at the prospect. He had taken little convincing to make the attempt, but had quickly confessed that formation flying had never been a design consideration when he had built the machines. If it had, he would have given at least one of them the ability to vary the power output from the fan. As the newer machine was considerably more powerful than its predecessor, staying in formation was always going to be difficult, but it was Callum who had devised a working solution.

Flying behind Callum, David converted his excess power into height, climbing well above the lead machine. After a while, he turned off his magnetic converters and settled his machine into a fast glide, gradually descending until he was below Callum when he switched the converters back on and repeated the procedure. It was far from an ideal situation, as doing this required David to maintain unbroken concentration throughout the flight. Awareness of his speed and relative position to Callum's machine was essential if they were to avoid an inadvertent collision, but short of making complicated modifications to one or both of the machines, it seemed the most logical solution.

Callum climbed his aircraft to about a thousand feet, noted the needle position on the altimeter and then concentrated on maintaining his height and heading. He knew this flight was going to take a long time. The plan was to fly to the beach where they had first landed in the Reserve and launch into the next incoming storm from there. The train had taken over three hours to get to the City of the Imperium from the Reserve and that had been travelling at least three times as fast as he was flying. At best, Callum estimated they might just make it there before dark. It took a while for him to relax and the tension in his body quickly developed into pain. His back and shoulders were aching long before they reached the coastline and once they had begun hurting, there was to be no relief.

Time seemed to drag as the torment of muscle cramps and aches plagued him. It was just after midday when the danger struck. Distracted as he was by the discomfort of his position and the boredom of their apparent snail's pace, it took some time for Callum to become aware of the three black dots circling in the sky ahead. By the time he did notice, it was already too late.

Having witnessed raptors hunting in the jungle and encountered at least two large predators of the deep, it made sense that something would hunt the skies with equal ruthlessness, yet the thought had not crossed his mind until now. As a little boy, Callum had played with model pterodactyls and taken great joy in making them swoop down on unsuspecting toy soldiers who were then carried off to nests high on the bookshelves overlooking the battlefield that was his bedroom floor. They had been one of his favourite random battle factors. Playing those games, he had never once given thought to what it might be like to fall under the shadow of such huge wings.

The heart-stopping screech that carried on the air sent a wave of terror through Callum, as the first approaching black dot blossomed and resolved into a gigantic winged monster. All previous discomfort was instantly forgotten. Through blind panic, he wrenched the control bar to the right, tipping abruptly on to a wing tip and slicing the aircraft into a dive. In a manoeuvre born out of instinct, the creature climbed abruptly, screeching a second time as it passed overhead. Afterwards, Callum reasoned that the creature was probably as surprised as he was by their relative size, which was most likely what saved him from having his machine ripped apart there and then.

Two other creatures soared over his machine, both screeching as they went. From the brief glimpse that Callum got of the flyers, they were not so much like leathery-skinned pterodactyls as they were the legendary giant eagles known as rocs that he had read about in one of his books of myths and legends. However, although these creatures were feathered like a bird, they did not have hard beaks. Instead they had mouths that were elongated and full of needle-sharp teeth. Also, rather than the expected two legs, they had four and a split fan tail of huge feathers.

There was more screeching behind him. Callum craned his neck to see if he could see what they were doing, but they were out of his field of vision. Terrified that they were now pursuing him, he levelled the wings and pushed the aircraft into a shallow dive to build up as much speed and distance from them as possible.

The cries fell behind quickly. Another quick look over his shoulder revealed why. David's machine was descending in a steep spiral dive towards the jungle with a large part of the upper wing missing. He was out of control with little hope of recovery and the creatures were following him down.

'No!' Callum gasped, his heart racing as he twisted still further in the harness, trying to follow the path of the stricken machine. Before he realised it, his own aircraft was turning and nosing down into a dive.

Concentrate! he berated himself, rolling out of the turn and stabilising at a steady altitude. *There's nothing you can do for David. The best thing you can do now is to stay alive and worry about getting home in one piece.*

For the second time in as many hours, his goggles began to mist up as tears filled his eyes. Poor David! He had wanted so much to follow in the footsteps of his grandmother and become a pioneering pilot. How better to make his mark than to become the first pilot to intentionally fly between worlds? To fall victim so quickly to the perils of the air was a terrible tragedy. Worse, it was most likely a fatal one. With hindsight, Callum realised he had not planned this trip with any sort of thoroughness. If he had, he might have thought to question what other sorts of dangers might lurk ahead apart from those related to the storm they intended to brave.

Callum did not see David's machine hit the tree canopy, but when he next looked back there was no sign of him or the flying creatures. Had they followed him down? If so, David's fate might be too horrible to contemplate. He tried to focus on the sky ahead. What mattered now was staying alive. He was alone and feeling more vulnerable than he had ever felt in his life. There was a long way to go and it seemed likely that the three flying creatures were not the only hostile threats he would face. He could meet more of them at any time, or different creatures. For all he knew, there could be worse out there somewhere.

Keep your eyes open and your chin up, Callum, he

told himself firmly. *You know they're out there now. Remember what Leah said about being too scared to set foot out of the door. If she could swim in the sea with full knowledge of the monsters that lurked there, you can cross the sky. Stay alert and you should get enough warning to stay out of harm's way. Well, that's the theory anyway.*

CHAPTER TWENTY-EIGHT

Exhausted, thirsty and hungry, Callum nearly missed Brad and Leah's house, tucked away against the low bluff. If he had not seen the rooftops of several other houses of human design among the trees nearby, he might have flown straight past it.

'At last,' he breathed.

A deep sense of relief washed his body in a warm glow. There was no mistaking it – he had reached the Reserve. Several times during the past hour he had wondered if he had miscalculated the time it would take to get here and flown past it without noticing. At one point he had considered back-tracking up the coast, but had decided better of it and was pleased to see his instincts proved correct. He had been on the point of looking for a suitable place to land anyway, as the sun was sinking towards the horizon and the shadows of dusk were lengthening fast.

Circling once to determine the wind direction, he extended downwind over the tongue of rock that he and Sam had climbed and along the bay to allow enough distance to fly a sensible approach path. Turning back, he switched off the electromagnetic converters and began his final descent to land on the beach. Having followed the coast all afternoon, he knew the tide was on the way in, but it was still only half-tide and there was plenty of hard sand left to land on.

As he descended, so the light got progressively worse until it felt almost like full darkness as he neared ground level. Either night fell very quickly here or this was another flying danger that Callum had not fully considered. Could it have something to do with the curvature of the Earth and angles of sunlight? Possibly, but he could not spare the brainpower to consider it further.

All Callum could do was apply the techniques he had learned to use by day and hope they worked the same way at night. Looking well ahead, he alternated his focus between the airspeed and the horizon, trying to keep from stalling while using his peripheral vision to get a sense of how close he was to the ground. Given that by the time he touched down he could see very little, he was quite pleased with his landing. A skipping bounce and he was down, decelerating rapidly to a walking pace.

The shushing noise of the surf helped calm his racing pulse as he flicked on a single magnetic converter and used the boost of power to keep some momentum. He steered the machine round in an arc and drove it back along the beach to where he could now just make out a familiar figure emerging from the treeline. Controlling his forward speed by flicking the power on and off, Callum taxied right up to the edge of the soft sand near the path to Leah's house before turning off the power and trundling to a final stop.

Sliding the stepladder out from under the harness was a struggle, and climbing out of the machine even more so. Callum staggered as he tried to stand unaided. After being horizontal in the harness for what must have been at least ten hours, his head spun with the sudden shift to being upright and he dropped to his knees to allow the dizzy spell to pass.

'Hello?' Leah called from the deep shadow under the trees. 'Who's that and where have you come from?'

'It's me – Callum,' Callum replied, his voice sounding croaky as he forced the words from his dry throat.

'Callum? Callum! What . . . ? How . . . ?' Leah came running down the beach to meet him and helped him back to his feet. 'Oh, you poor boy! You look exhausted. We need to get you inside and get you something to eat and drink. Where are the others? Are they going to fly in as well? Is Brad all right?'

Callum was glad it was dark and that Leah was unlikely to be able to see the pained look on his face. He was not looking forward to breaking the news to her that Brad was dead.

'It's a long story,' he said. 'Leah, I'll tell you all about them, but first I need to get my flying machine above the tideline and to secure it somehow.'

'Oh Lord, yes!' Leah said, looking around. 'If the raptors saw you come down, they'll be wantin' to take it away for study. If you want to keep it, we need to hide it if we can. Where did you get it from? No. Never mind that. Let me help you. Is it heavy? Will we be able to pull it up the beach together?'

'We can try.'

Try they did, but the wheels quickly became bogged down in the soft sand and despite their best efforts, they could move it no further. Dropping to his knees again, Callum was forced to admit defeat.

'It can't stay here, Leah,' he croaked. 'I've got to

make sure it's safe. I'm not going to let the tide or the raptors take it.'

'No, of course not,' she soothed. 'Don't worry. I'll get some of the others to come and help. It should be all right here for a few minutes. The raptors are unlikely to have been watching. They don't expect much to happen outside of stormy weather. If you'd landed tomorrow evening, they'd have seen you for sure.'

'Tomorrow?' Callum asked. 'What's special about tomorrow?'

'There's a storm comin' through of course,' Leah said. 'Weren't you listenin'? They always watch the beaches and comb the shoreline durin' and after a storm.'

Callum's heart began pounding with excitement. 'A storm? You're sure?'

'As sure as I can be,' Leah replied. 'My old bones ain't been wrong in a while. Joints ache like crazy before a blow and they've been playin' up all day. I reckon it'll be a bad-un. Glad you're here. Of course it'll be even better if Brad gets back. Curlin' up next to him always makes me feel safe. I hate bein' alone when it's howlin' outside, but how we're gonna tie this thing down well enough to stop it from blowin' away, I really don't know.'

Callum didn't have the heart, or the voice, to

tell her that there was no chance of Brad coming back, nor would there be any need to secure the machine for the storm. It appeared his timing couldn't have been better. In the morning he would take off and brave the weather. He was realistic enough to know that this could be his one shot to get home. *Do or die time*, he thought, his cracked lips curling into a smile. He had always liked that phrase, though he had never thought it would apply to himself so literally.

His throat felt so dry that it was all but shut, so he didn't protest when Leah dragged him away from his machine and along the path to the house to get a drink. She asked again about Brad and Sam on the way, but Callum dodged the question again by pointing at his throat and coughing. After drinking several cups of fruit juice in quick succession and taking a few bites out of a KFC fruit, it was his turn to become insistent. He did not want to risk leaving the flying machine in the open for a moment longer than necessary. Taking the rest of the fruit with him, he returned to watch the aircraft while Leah bustled away to find some help. She did not take long.

'Here we are, Callum,' she called as she approached with two of her neighbours. 'Andy and Rhoda have kindly agreed to lend us a hand.'

After quick introductions and several complimentary

comments about his aircraft, the four of them lifted and dragged the machine the short distance to the treeline. They turned it round and backed the fan section into the trees, but the wings were too wide to fit.

'Thanks, guys,' Leah said, shaking the hands of her neighbours gratefully. 'We'll just have to leave it part-exposed for now. Callum, we'll get up early tomorrow and see what we can do to secure and cover up the rest of it.'

'Thanks, Leah,' he replied. 'But there's no need. I'm going to be flying it out of here early in the morning.'

'You are? But the storm – you could get caught up in it.'

'I know. That's the idea, Leah,' he explained. 'I'm going to fly out into the heart of it and try to get home.'

Leah's eyes went wide and her hands flew to cover her mouth.

'Oh no, Callum! I can't let you do that! It's madness! You'll get yourself killed for sure. Surely Brad didn't approve of this?'

'No, he didn't,' Callum said sadly. 'Leah, I hate to be the one to bring such terrible news, but Brad isn't coming back. He was killed on the way to the City of the Imperium. There was nothing we could do to help him. I'm so sorry.'

Leah's face froze in a mask of hopelessness that made Callum's heart feel like someone had stuck a knife through it.

'And Sam, Nipper and Grunt?' she asked, her tone heartbroken.

'Are all alive, though they're in a lot of trouble with the Imperium,' Callum told her.

'Well, that's somethin',' she said, dashing tears from her cheeks and trying to look brave. 'You mustn't go, Callum. You'll die too. I couldn't stand it.'

'I hope not,' he said calmly. 'I know it will be dangerous, but everyone I've spoken to agrees that crossings only occur over water in the eye of a storm, so that's where I'm going. Someone has to be the first to cross back to where we belong. I'm determined that person will be me.'

There were an awkward couple of minutes as Leah tried again to talk him out of it, but she quickly realised that he was not going to change his mind.

'Will it take more than one person?' Andy asked.

'Not rigged like this,' Callum replied. 'And at the risk of sounding selfish, I don't have the time or skill to re-rig it to take two. But I promise you that if I make it through to Earth, I'll try to arrange for someone to come back for you all.'

Andy nodded. 'You'll need a bit of muscle to get this thing back down to the firm sand in the morning, Callum,' he said. 'I'll come and give you a hand.'

'That would be brilliant, thanks,' Callum replied gratefully. 'Shortly after first light if you don't mind. I'd rather get airborne before the wind gets up. I've not flown much in strong winds and the tricky bits about flying are always the taking off and the landing. Once I'm in the air, I should be fine.'

'No problem. We'll see you tomorrow then. It sounds like you're going to need to be well rested, so get a good night's sleep, Callum.'

* * *

Leah looked terrible the next morning, but she insisted on coming down to the beach with Callum to see him off. Callum suspected that she had not slept at all. Her eyes were puffy and bloodshot, and her cheeks were blotchy from extended bouts of crying. She claimed that she had known Brad would not be coming back. How, she would not say, but she had thanked Callum for being brave enough to give her the bad news. The rest of his story had hardly been filled with joy: finding Sam's mother only for her to fall victim to the Imperium shortly afterward, Nipper's injuries, Sam's decision to stay and follow in his mother's footsteps and even David's crash all added to the tale of woe, though he doubted much

of it touched her. The loss of Brad was too immediate and all-consuming.

Callum felt guilty for piling all of these tragedies
on her only to fly off and potentially add to her
worries and grief. His success or failure would
produce the same result for Leah. One way or the
other, this was likely to be a final goodbye.

The breeze was already picking up and grey clouds
raced overhead as they emerged from the path on to
the beach. Andy and Rhoda were already there
waiting.

'Rather you than me,' Andy commented, looking
up at the dark sky.

'Thanks!' Callum replied sarcastically.

'I'm just being honest. Yesterday I was jealous, but
today . . . well. . .'

'I know, Andy. It's just I can't decide how many of
the butterflies in my stomach are nervous and how
many are excited. I guess that'll teach me not to eat
so many caterpillars.'

Andy and Rhoda both chuckled, but Leah's face
remained glum.

'I know I'm probably mad for trying this, but it's
something I've got to do,' Callum added, squinting
first at the sky and then out to sea. 'Somewhere out
there is a way home. I'm going to go and hammer on
the door until it gives in and lets me through.'

The shushing whisper of the sea had grown to an angry roar overnight. As far as the eye could see, the grey water was streaked with thick lines of creamy foam as roller after roller boomed and gushed towards the shore.

'How will you find the eye of the storm?' Leah asked in a hushed voice. 'Once you're over the water and the weather closes in, you won't have anything to navigate by.'

'If you stand with your back to the wind in the northern hemisphere, low pressure is always to your left,' Callum quoted. 'It's a rule I learned at my gliding club back home. The eye of a hurricane occurs at the point of lowest pressure. So long as I keep flying with the wind blowing from left to right and allow for drift, I should fly straight at the middle of the storm. Should . . . that's the theory anyway.'

'I hope you're right,' Andy said, taking a firm grip on the leading edge of the lower wing and nodding to the others to pull together. 'You're a brave lad. We'll be praying for your success. You deserve to get home.'

'Thanks. I appreciate that.'

Together they pulled, hauling the machine step by step until the surface became firm enough that the wheels began to turn freely. What the sand and salt water would do to the axles Callum did not want to

371

imagine. However, so long as they worked for long enough to get him airborne, any damage he did to them was irrelevant. They turned the machine until it was facing into the wind and as they did, it felt strangely light, as if it was keen to get into the air.

Worried that a sudden gust might flip the machine on its back, Callum pulled out the steps, gave Leah one last quick hug and scrambled into the harness. Even with his added weight, the machine rocked and flexed with every fluctuation in the wind.

'Thanks, Andy. Thanks, Rhoda,' he called, reaching forward and shaking hands with each of them in turn before pulling the steps up on to the rail under his body and easing his goggles down over his glasses. 'Goodbye, Leah. Take care. And if you see Sam, tell him to hurry up and follow me home.'

'Take care, Callum. And good luck,' she replied. 'Here, don't forget these.'

Grabbing a strut, she leaned in and tucked a leather flask of drink to the right of his chest and two whole fruits to the left.

'Thanks, Leah – for everything.'

'Good luck,' Andy and Rhoda chorused.

Waiting just long enough for them to get clear of the wing tips, Callum flicked on both electromagnetic converters and felt the hum building through the harness as they began to feed electricity into powering the fan. Excitement surged through him as the machine began to creep forward. The wind was already tugging at his hair and clothing, and he was barely moving yet.

'This is it, Callum,' he breathed. 'Do or die time.'

CHAPTER TWENTY-NINE

The aircraft leaned slightly to the left as it began to roll forwards. Although this was disconcerting, Callum knew it was due to the mismatched wheels that David had fitted after his misadventure with the raptor and the tree. The sand surface was much flatter and smoother than the ground he had taken off from the previous day, making the lopsidedness more noticeable. During yesterday's take-off, he had been bouncing around so much that he had been too preoccupied with keeping straight to notice the slight imbalance.

Today's strong breeze was already providing considerable airspeed before he began moving, so although the lean was mildly disturbing, he did not have to worry about it for long. It seemed he had barely started moving before the wheels left the sand and the beach was dropping away below him.

Although the take-off run was more comfortable than the previous day's, the same could not be said for the rest of the flight. Where yesterday the air had been smooth and warm, today the temperature was considerably lower, and from the moment Callum left the ground, he was bucked and bounced by turbulence. Close to the ground the airspeed indicator fluctuated wildly, giving him several heart-stopping moments as his airspeed dropped out of the bottom of the green zone only to race back up a split second later.

Callum shivered, already glad of Brad's old waterproof mac as he levelled off at approximately one thousand feet above the beach. Leah had insisted he have it, as she felt sure that Brad would have wanted him to go into the storm prepared for the weather. His fingers were clamped tightly round the control bar as he rode out the lumps and bumps, and he had to keep telling himself to relax as he was already aware of the tension building across his shoulders and back.

To his surprise, when he turned the aircraft out over the sea, he discovered he had barely travelled any distance over the ground. As he had climbed, so the wind strength had increased until he was barely crawling forward at all. He waggled the wings as a parting gesture to the three waving figures on the beach below and then shifted his focus to the weather ahead.

It did not take long to realise that once he was over the water, it was all but impossible to assess how accurately he was tracking towards the middle of the storm. Flying directly across the wind would mean he would be constantly blown to the right and would cover a much greater ground track to his goal. To fly the shortest ground track, he needed to offset his heading into the wind to allow for the drift. This meant he would track forwards more slowly towards his goal, but fly a much more direct route and he would always have a good idea which way to fly to make landfall if he needed to.

Unfortunately, it quickly became apparent that this safe method was not going to be an option. The wind was picking up so rapidly that even with his airspeed showing on the indicator at the top of the green sector, if he pointed directly into the wind, his aircraft would actually be blown backwards. His only option for reaching the eye was to accept the drift and keep flying with the wind blowing him left to right.

I'm like a tiny toy heading for the plughole in a bath, he thought. *I'm going to spin round the hole until I get sucked into the centre, but what direction I'll be heading when I get there is anyone's guess.*

The first grumble of thunder gave an ominous warning of what was waiting for Callum ahead. He had not seen the flash, but he knew from his experience on the boat with Sam that it would not be long now before the sky around him would light up with spectacular streaks of fire in a virtually constant display of pyrotechnics. What would happen if lightning struck his aircraft? He didn't know. He had heard of aeroplanes being struck and continuing to fly to their destination, so it couldn't be that bad . . . could it?

At the gliding club they had always avoided flying anywhere in the vicinity of thunderstorms, not because of the risk of lightning strikes, but because of the powerful up- and downdraughts associated with the storm clouds that caused extreme turbulence. The air currents around thunderstorms had been known to fluctuate so violently that they could tear aircraft apart in an instant. Gliders, with their long wingspans and lightweight construction, designed to soar on the lightest of updraughts, were particularly vulnerable. Callum looked around at the flimsy wings and lightweight struts and wires. He doubted this machine any better suited to fly into a storm than a glider. A cold knot of fear twisted inside him. Imagining bravely flying into a hurricane was one thing. The reality of it was something else.

Turning back was no longer an option. He had lost sight of land some time ago and there were no guarantees that turning the aircraft round and putting the wind on his right would take him back to land. He was committed.

'Come on, you numpty!' he urged himself as he eyed the ever-darkening sky ahead. 'Fly smart. Try to steer between the thunderstorm cells. Stay airborne and stay alive.'

His teeth chattered as he spoke, though this was as much from fear as it was the cold. A moment later, the aircraft dropped like a stone, only to be flung back skyward as it met the first of many pockets of severe turbulence. Callum gasped. He had never experienced anything like it before. This was no small burbling bump. For a moment, he had the mental image of being a football in the hands of a goalie delivering a clearing kick. First the sudden drop and then the powerful boot from underneath that sent him sailing high through the air. One of the pieces of fruit Leah had tucked by his side came loose, shooting up to hit the fabric of the upper wing before punching down through the lower wing like a bullet. It ripped through one of the repair patches, leaving a loose corner fluttering.

He swore as he tried to regain control of the machine and settle it into a semblance of steady flight. Glancing left and right at the wings, he was almost surprised to see they were still there and intact after the brutal surge. The only damage seemed to be the fruit-sized hole in the fabric below him. 'Sorry, but this is going to be a rough ride,' he said, addressing his machine as if it could hear him. 'Just hold together for me, will you? Please?'

He tucked the remaining fruit under his left hip, took a swig from the bottle and tucked that under his right. The cloud base began to drop and the first smattering of raindrops rattled across the wings and pattered against his mac and goggles.

'Here goes nothing.'

Diving down until he was no more than a couple of hundred metres above the foaming waves, he scanned ahead for any sign of a passable route. There was nothing obvious. A flashing bolt of lightning speared down at the sea from a particularly dark area to his left. Seconds later, a crackling peel of thunder reached him, setting all the hairs on the back of his neck prickling. To his relief, the wind was carrying him away from that area, but the comfort that brought proved short-lived, as moments later, a similar flash and crash split the sky to his right.

Bouncing and lurching, often with his heart pounding in his throat as the air tried repeatedly to rip the wings from his machine with vicious swirling currents, Callum fought deeper and deeper towards the heart of the howling hurricane. Despite his best efforts to steer round the darkest areas of torrential rain, there were times when he could barely see through his goggles for the pounding spears of water hurled at him from above. Then, just as he felt he must surely be getting close to the eye, disaster struck not once, not twice, but three times in quick succession.

Sizzling bolts of lightning seared out of the cloud above, striking first the left wing tip, then twice on the right in the space of as many seconds. The ear-splitting explosion that accompanied each strike left Callum's ears ringing. Every hair on his body suddenly felt as if it was a straight metal pin sticking into his skin at ninety degrees.

'AAAAARRRRgggggghhhh!'

His cry petered out as he realised first that he was still alive, and second that once again, his aircraft was still flying and in one piece. A golden after-image of the final flashing bolt filled his vision wherever he looked. After a minute or so, he began to make out scorch marks on both lower and upper wing tips, but the special flame-resistant material that David had used to cover the wings had done its job. With his heart hammering at his ribs like a mad drummer, he ran his tongue over his teeth to try to dispel the tingling he was feeling through them. Shivers ran up and down his body in uncontrollable waves and he shook himself in the harness like a dog in an effort to dispel the feeling.

Before he realised what he was doing, he began to laugh. He could barely hear himself for the deafening, ringing after-effects of the thunder, but he had no doubt that anyone hearing his maniacal cackling would have felt shivers of their own.

'Whoever said that lightning never strikes twice was a liar!' he yelled into the wind.

He was about to add another comment when he noticed the vibration through the airframe. Although he couldn't hear the wind howling louder, he could feel it battering his face with invisible fists. A glance at the airspeed indicator showed he was flying way faster than the design optimum and still accelerating.

'What the hell. . . ?'

The aeroplane wasn't diving, but it was suddenly racing faster and faster like a runaway train.

The electromagnetic limiters! They must have been fried by the lightning! What do I do? What DO I do?

There was only one thing he could do – switch the converters off and slow down. If he didn't, the fan would continue to accelerate until it self-destructed, assuming the aircraft didn't rip itself to pieces first. Would the converters start again if he switched them off? There was no way of knowing how the lightning might have damaged them.

'God, if you're out there, please let this work,' he prayed.

He flicked the first switch to the off position, but to his horror, it seemed to have little effect. Even running on one de-limited converter, the fan was still accelerating. Gritting his teeth, he switched off the second.

The effect was instantaneous. It was as if the aircraft had flown into a cloud of treacle. No longer powered, the huge fan suddenly changed from being a source of thrust to being a gigantic airbrake. Callum's harness swung forward violently and if he had not had his feet tucked into their special slots, he might have been thrown clear out of the front of the machine. The remaining fruit and the bottle of drink that he had tucked by his sides had no such restraint and he was forced to watch them shoot past him and drop away like miniature bombs into the ocean.

The harness settled, which was more than could be said for Callum's stomach. Without warning, he vomited. Three seconds later, he vomited again. For the first time since it had started, he was glad of the pounding rain. Opening his mouth, he allowed the water to collect before swishing it round and spitting it over his shoulder.

The airspeed indicator was showing in the middle of the green sector and falling. Callum lowered the nose of the aircraft into a descent to stabilise the speed and then tentatively switched on the left electromagnetic converter switch. He held his breath as he waited to feel a surge of power, but there was none. Horrified, he threw the right switch. Nothing. Panic gripped him and he flicked both switches off and on several times in quick succession. Still nothing: no hum, no power, no thrust.

The towering waves reached up towards him with foaming claws of white. He had no more than a minute of gliding time before they would catch him and draw him down.

'Damn you, God! Weren't you listening?' he cursed. 'I said "Please let this WORK!"'

He jammed the switches off and on again. To his amazement, something stirred. Power started to feed to the fan. He didn't know which converter was producing it, but he didn't dare selectively switch them off in case it wouldn't come on again.

Whether or not God had really answered his prayer was something he didn't like to think about, but he had always been brought up to be polite. Even though he found it hard to believe that his prayer had actually done anything, he could not let his change in circumstance go without acknowledgement.

'Thanks,' he muttered, feeling small and stupid. 'I owe you one.'

Raising the front of the aircraft, he settled it into a climb, controlling the speed in the green sector by varying his rate of climb. He did not have a lot of altitude to play with. The cloud base was not far above him and he did not dare enter it, as he had never been taught how to fly with reference only to instruments.

Another bolt of lightning split the sky to his right and the now familiar crash of thunder followed almost immediately. Having suffered multiple strikes and survived, the fearful sound did not scare him quite so much this time.

By all rights I should be dead several times over by now, Callum thought. *You did one heck of a job building this thing, David. If I ever get home, you'll be a legend, I promise.*

Wispy tendrils of cloud reached down from the base to stroke the flying machine and Callum was forced to level off and let the speed build again. Again, he let the aircraft accelerate until the vibration and buffeting was so bad that he felt sure it could stand no more before turning off the converter switches. This time he was ready for the sudden deceleration and effortlessly selected a suitable glide angle.

For what seemed like an eternity, he repeated this procedure, gliding down as low as he dared before flicking the converter switches back on and climbing back up to the cloud base. Turbulence bounced him; lightning struck his machine twice more – both times during a gliding descent; thunder deafened and bouts of torrential rain battered him with every gram of force they could muster, but none broke him. Somehow, he kept the machine in the air and creeping forward ever closer to the eye until suddenly he broke into clear air and his heart soared.

He had done it. Against all odds, he had reached the eye of the hurricane.

A towering wall of cloud soared behind him and he found if he followed the line of it round, he could see the full circle of the eye. It couldn't be more than about forty miles across. All that remained to do was to find a crossing point and Callum knew exactly what he was looking for.

Hitting the converter switches, he settled the aircraft into a glide towards the very centre of the eye. Excitement thrilled through him like an electric current as he scanned the water ahead for areas with unusual wave patterns. When he and Sam had crossed before, that had been the only visible, tell-tale clue to the presence of a crossing point, but would the same be true from this side? He could only hope.

Lower and lower he went, leaving it much later before switching the converters back on this time. Finally, he could leave it no longer and he flicked the switches. As soon as he did so, he noticed something different. The hum of the electromagnetic converter sounded different, rising and falling in pitch. Rather than the smooth wind-up of power that he had experienced each time he had switched them on previously, the power surged through in waves and the aircraft accelerated in a sequence of erratic lurches.

'Come on, baby!' he urged. 'Don't give up on me now. We're so close.'

No sooner had Callum uttered the words than he spotted the area of water just to the left of his track and no more than a few hundred metres ahead. It was the colour that caught his eye. The shade of blue was very slightly different and as soon as his eye latched on to it, he saw instantly that the wave pattern was conflicting with the rest of the water around it.

'Yes!' he breathed, rolling sharply to the left and levelling the wings on a direct course for what he guessed was his doorway home. His trajectory looked perfect. Everything seemed set. A grin was already spreading across his face as he pictured the look on his parents' faces. He couldn't wait to see them. They would be amazed when he told them what he had done. Unfortunately, his mental celebration was premature.

As the aircraft reached the boundary, the electro-magnetic converter that had been keeping him airborne went crazy. Suddenly screaming a high-pitched whine as it crossed the phenomenally dense magnetic field surrounding the vortex the generator shoved out a massive burst of energy. The pulse of electricity surged the fan way beyond its design parameters, sheering the driveshaft and sending it tearing through the back of the cage with a terrify-ing *DRRDRRDRRRDRR* . . . sound as it spat blades and bits of metal out in all directions round its plane of rotation. The final burst of acceleration also proved too much for the weakened airframe struc-ture, and with a rapid sequence of metallic cracks and pinging cables, the top wing separated from the bottom one and Callum's world toppled out of control.

* * *

It was early morning the day after the trip to Milton Keynes and Niamh was brushing her teeth when Aunt Aggie's uncharacteristic squeal of delight piqued her curiosity. She could not help wondering what had got Aggie so excited. The sound of low voices and the front door closing followed. Niamh put down her toothbrush, wiped her face with a towel and went to the bathroom door. The voices had stopped speaking, but she could hear footsteps downstairs. What on earth was going on?

Wrapping her dressing gown tightly round her, she crept to the top of the stairs. Whatever she had been expecting as she looked down, it was not the sight that greeted her.

'DAD!' she exclaimed, and bounded down the stairs two at a time.

He met her at the bottom step with open arms, swept her into the air and hugged her tight.

'Hey, Niamh! It's great to see you . . . again.'

She didn't miss the emphasis on the pause. He hadn't told Aunt Aggie, had he? She hoped not. She didn't want Archie getting into trouble. He'd been so brilliant about taking her to visit Dad in prison.

'How . . . ? What . . . ? I don't understand!' she gasped.

'Callum's been found,' Matt explained, a smile on his face. 'Mr Barnes spoke to my lawyer last night, and apologised for jumping to conclusions about what had happened to the boys. He's dropped all the charges.'

'That's brilliant, Dad!' Niamh said, squeezing him tighter still.

'Although Sam is still missing, the police now have no one accusing me of anything,' Matt went on. 'And the weight of evidence suddenly supports the fact that I was telling the truth and had nothing to do with their disappearance. My lawyer managed to work miracles overnight to get me out of prison so quickly. I can hardly believe things have moved so fast. The police want me to remain contactable, but they're allowing me to go back and help look for Sam. So pack your bags, Niamh, we're going back to Florida.'

'Wasn't Sam with Callum? Surely he'd at least be nearby?'

'No, there's still no sign of Sam. And Callum can't tell us,' Matt said, his voice grave. 'He's in a coma, Niamh, and I'm told his condition is critical. He's lucky to be alive.'

'What happened? How was he injured?'

'Apparently, he crashed a microlight into the sea some distance off the Florida mainland coast. He was lucky to hit the water just a few hundred metres from a fishing boat, or he might never have been found. I won't lie to you, sweetheart – he might not make it. His parents were out in Florida trying to drum up publicity for the search when they were called to the hospital to identify him. As soon as they did, they contacted the police here.'

'A microlight! Callum? What was he doing flying a microlight? Can we go and see him?'

'It's top of my list of priorities. I have a huge list of questions for that young man.'

Niamh closed her eyes and concentrated on her brother. Deep inside she could still feel the tenuous link to him, though what he was feeling, or doing, she couldn't tell. Had he simply been a long way away all along? Was the whole other world idea complete nonsense? All the progress that she thought they had made towards solving the mystery suddenly seemed ridiculous.

Come on, Sam! Give me a clue. Anything.

Darkness. He was somewhere dark. Was it night-time in America? Yes. It would still be the middle of the night. Once again, she got the impression of the same monstrous face that had shocked her once before. The scales, reptilian eyes and sharp teeth made her shiver. Was Sam asleep and dreaming? Perhaps this was a recurring nightmare. He used to suffer nightmares when he was younger. They both had. That would explain the monster and the panic. Yet she felt no intense sense of fear to go with the image. It was strange. If anything, she was sensing feelings of friendship for the beast. What did it mean?

She opened her eyes again and took a deep breath. 'So when do we leave?' she asked.

'The earliest I could get a flight was for tomorrow morning, but we're booked into the Gatwick Hilton tonight. As soon as you're ready, we'll be on our way.'

'Surely you'll stop for breakfast first, Matthew?' Aggie interrupted.

'Of course, Aggie!' he said, giving her a broad grin. 'After the food I've been eating the last few weeks, I'll be more than happy to eat one of your breakfasts.'

Niamh gave her father another hug and then turned and raced back up the stairs to pack. As she reached the top, she cannoned into Archie, who was emerging bleary-eyed from his room. To his intense surprise, she stopped, hugged him too and then kissed him on the cheek.

'Thanks for all your help, Archie,' she said in a

low, excited voice. 'Dad's here and he's taking me back to Florida. I can't believe it! And this time, believe me – one way or another, I *will* find Sam.'

* * *

Unable to sleep, Sam stared at the roof of the cave. The dim glow of a floating raptor light globe gave the place an eerie feel and despite his blankets, Sam shivered with cold. The cave had felt terribly empty since Callum and David had left. Sam had felt empty too. Where would Callum be now? Had he landed safely in the Reserve? They had seen the edge of a storm system yesterday; had Callum tried to fly into it? Sadly, Sam realised he might never know.

He rolled on to his side and looked across at Nipper's face. The raptor was resting next to him, his eyes closed and his breathing deep and strong. It would be some time before he was fully recovered from his wounds, but he insisted that none of his injuries were serious. Nipper might now be his best friend in this world, Sam realised. With Callum gone, Nipper was certainly the best friend he had here in the cave.

As he stared at Nipper's face, Sam felt sure he was being watched. Nipper's eyes opened and Sam held the raptor's gaze for a moment. Did he feel it too? What was that? For no apparent reason, Sam suddenly thought of Niamh. It was weird. Almost as if she was in the cave with him. His thoughts flashed back to other times he had felt as if she was nearby. Was she somewhere feeling the same way?

He closed his eyes for a moment and concentrated on the feeling. Was she trying to tell him something? Had Callum made it back? Was that it? If he had, then Sam felt no clear sense of it. What did surface in his mind were two words and although he didn't exactly hear them, he felt them clearly. Two simple words that filled him with both joy and worry in equal measure. . .

'We're coming. . .'